CRAZY

Also by Amir Abrams

Hollywood High (with Ni-Ni Simone)

Published by Kensington Publishing Corporation

CRAZY LOVE

AMIR ABRAMS

Dafina KTeen Books
KENSINGTON PUBLISHING CORP.
http://www.kensingtonbooks.com

DAFINA KTEEN BOOKS are published by

Kensington Publishing Corp.
119 West 40th Street
New York, NY 10018

All Kensington titles, imprints, and distributed lines are available at special quantity discounts for bulk purchases for sales promotion, premiums, fund-raising, educational, or institutional use.

Special book excerpts or customized printings can also be created to fit specific needs. For details, write or phone the office of the Kensington Special Sales Manager: Attn.: Special Sales Department. Kensington Publishing Corp., 119 West 40th Street, New York, NY 10018. Phone: 1-800-221-2647.

KTeen Reg. US Pat. & TM Off.
Sunburst logo Reg. US Pat. & TM Off.

ISBN-13: 978-0-7582-7356-7
ISBN-10: 0-7582-7356-8

First Printing: December 2012

10 9 8 7 6 5 4 3 2 1

Printed in the United States of America

This book is dedicated to my peeps,
Ni-Ni Simone,
for being one of the hottest & flyest YA authors
on the lit scene.

You're killin' 'em,
Ni-Ni boo!

Mad love,
much respect to you.

ACKNOWLEDGMENTS

First and foremost, I give thanks to the One above for being the force that guides me, and continues to bless me!

To my fam & friends, thanks for always loving me, unconditionally, no matter what!

To Sara Camilli, my agent: thank you for having faith in my ability to soar to greatness! I really appreciate you.

To Selena James and the rest of the Dafina/Kensington fam: thanks for being as excited as I am about being a part of the Kensington family. I truly appreciate the warm welcome, kind words, and mad love!

To my peeps, Ni-Ni Simone: Yo, one hot day in Harlem and a train ride home, followed by twelve pages of hotness on Ni-Ni Girlz and look at us now. *Hollywood High* is about to be a real problem, for real for real. Peeps better strap up and get ready for the ride 'cause we about to rip the lit scene to shreds!

And, last, but never least, to everyone who has picked up a copy of *Crazy Love*: thanks for taking a chance on me. I appreciate the support and for showing me love!

Peace out!

Ya boy,
Amir

PROLOGUE

"Giiiiiiiirrrrrrl, this party is fiiiiyah," Zahara shouted over the beats of a Rick Ross joint.

"I told y'all it would be," Brittani said, swaying her hips and popping her fingers. Brittani's sister, Briana, had the hookup for us because her boo-of-the-month was one of the frat boys whose fraternity was hosting the party. So she invited us to get our party on. Brittani's sister is mad cool like that. She's always getting us into all the hot spots.

"I'ma get my queen-diva on tonight!" Ameerah exclaimed excitedly as she popped her hips. We laughed at her as she flicked her tongue at this cutie who eased by eyeing her.

Anywaaayz, it was the weekend after Fourth of July and we were at an off-campus house party packed with mostly college heads. Mad cuties and thirsty chicks were everywhere, sweating it out on the dance floor. Fraternities and sororities represented, hard-rocking their colors and emblems. Hot beats were blaring through the speakers as dudes danced and grinded up on chicks who were booty-popping it all up on them.

"Ooooh, I wanna dance," Zahara said, snapping her fingers and bopping her head. She did a two-step, dropped down low, then popped it back up. She danced and twirled until she got the attention she wanted. Zahara loves attention!

Anywaaayz, Zahara, Brittani, Ameerah, and I had just finished our dance-through, where we dance in a line through a party, all sexy-like, to peep what's what and who's who before we find a spot to post up—and be cute!—when I spotted him. He was standing over in a corner with three other guys. And they were all fine, *but*... not as fine as him. I acted like I didn't see him. But the truth is, how could you *not* see him? All eyes were already on him. He was rocking a red and white Polo button-up with a pair of designer jeans and a pair of white, crispy Jordans and a red and white Yankees fitted. Tall and built, with skin the color of milk chocolate. Whew...he looked...*delicious!* Even in the dimly lit room, I knew he was fine.

And the minute I was certain he'd seen me, I stepped, making sure to throw an extra shake in my hips as we strutted off. As soon as we made it to the other side of the room, these dudes came over to where we were standing and asked each of us to dance. Zahara, Brittani, and Ameerah said yes to the dudes who asked them, and bounced their booties toward the dance floor, leaving me standing there with this tall, light-skinned guy with really big teeth and gums, grinning at me and licking his lips. He reminded me of a big yellow crayon.

"You sure you don't wanna dance?" he asked again, slowly looking me up and down, dragging his tongue across his lips. I blinked, blinked again, hoping I could erase him from my view. No luck. He was still there, staring down at me, looking like a glow-in-the-dark wand as he bobbed his head to the beats. Truth is, I did want to dance. Just not with *him*. Not that he was busted or anything. He was just too bright and his teeth were too big for me to have to look in his face. I would either have to keep my eyes shut and zone out on the music, or keep my back to him. Lucky for me, I didn't have to do either.

This brown-skinned chick with a long black weave, wearing a skintight pair of jeans and a teeny-weeny shirt, was on the dance floor near us, dancing all fast and nasty by herself. That caught his attention and he bounced on over to her. *Yuck*, I thought, shifting my eyes around the room to see where my girls were.

I glanced around the party and peeped Briana walking toward the stairs with her boo in tow. *Mmmph*, I thought, curling my lips up as she climbed the stairs. *Miss Hot-Box probably going upstairs to get her back blown out.*

I shook the thought from my head and shifted my attention toward the dance floor, watching my girls act a fool. Every so often, I glanced over in his direction and would see a buncha birds flocked around him, and he'd lean into their ears and say something to them, then they'd start smiling or giggling like real dizzy chicks before walking off. I caught him staring over in my direction a few times, trying to make eye contact with me. But I kept it fly. And, when I finally let him catch my eye, he grinned. I wanted him. Knew I had to have him. And I was going to make it my business to bag him quick, fast, and in a hurry without making myself look like a straight-up bird. Fly girls never look thirsty. They keep it cute, okay! Well, um, that's until they reel their catch-of-the-moment in. Then you can't be too proud to beg, or too scared to beat a trick down, to keep him.

As soon as Young Jeezy's "I Do" started playing, I started swaying to the beats, popping my hips just enough to prove a point. That I was the hottest chick in the room; that I could bag any of these boys up in there if I really wanted. A few seconds later, I heard him. And right then I knew my point was made.

"Wassup," I heard someone behind me say in my ear. Even over the music, the voice was mad sexy. And I knew who it was without even looking over my shoulder.

"Wassup," I coolly said back, eyeing him real slow and sexy.

"Looks like ya boy did me a favor," he said, grinning at me.

I raised my brow. "Excuse you. He did you a favor how?"

"Ole boy made it easy for me not to have to tell him to step off."

"Oh, really?"

He smirked. "Yeah, really. You know you wanna be mine."

"How you know that?"

"You been wanting me to notice you from the moment you stepped through the door with your girls."

I smiled, twirling the ends of my hair. "Obviously it worked. So you wanna dance or what?"

"No doubt."

"Then follow me and take notes," I said, taking him by the hand and leading him onto the dance floor. He laughed, letting me lead the way. We started moving to

Drake's "Miss Me." He stepped in closer to me, staring at me as he moved. I stared back, lifting my arms up over my head and matching his rhythm. Each time he stepped in closer, I stepped back. When he stepped back, I stepped in. I twirled my hips a taste. Let him see what I was working with, but didn't let him grind up on me.

I spotted Ameerah, Zahara, and Brittani dancing with the same guys, laughing and switching partners every so often. I smiled, then returned my attention back to the fine catch in front of me. We danced for three songs until some whack song came on. I grabbed his hand and led him off the floor, like he was already my man.

"Yo, so what's your name?" he yelled over the music.

"What?" I yelled back.

"What's your name?"

Just as I was about to open my mouth to tell him, this Spanish-looking chick with wavy black hair walked over to us and rudely pulled him away by the arm.

"Yo, I'll be right back," he said to me in my ear over the music. "Don't go no where. Let me get this one dance in with my homegirl real quick. I'll be right back."

"Don't keep me waiting too long," I said all sweet and sexy, eyeing him and licking my lips. But inside I was screaming, *"Oh no the hell she didn't just step up and disrupt my groove!"* But I kept it real cute as they walked off toward the dance floor 'cause that's how I do it. Still, every so often I shot her daggers on the low as she popped her booty up and down on the front of my future man's crotch. *That ho musta got the news feeds mixed up. I'm the wrong chick. I will spin her clock back.* I stared her down for a quick moment, then caught myself before I turned the party out. I wasn't about to let Mr. Fine and

Sexy see the other side of me, so I popped my hips over to where my girls were, keeping an eye on the object of my desires from afar. Oooh, he was so sexy. And I wanted him.

Zahara walked up on me, looping her arm through mine, pulling me toward the door. "Girl," she screamed over the music, "it's hot and loud in here. I need some fresh air. Let's go outside for a minute."

"Yeah, let's," I said. Brittani and Ameerah were behind her.

"Whew, I need me a cigarette," Zahara stated the minute we got out into the night air. "Did y'all see how fine my future baby fahver was? And he could dance, too!"

I laughed at her silly butt. "Girl, you don't even smoke."

"Well, not yet, I don't. But let me get a few rounds in with him and I will be."

"Mmmph...these college boys are too fine for their own good," Brittani agreed. She wiped sweat from her face with a napkin. "But what was up with that broad with the big pumpkin head on the dance floor?"

"Oh, that ho tried to play me, but I had to show her what's what."

"I know that's right," Brittani said. "I thought we were gonna hafta bring it to her face real quick."

I laughed. "Oh, trust. She didn't want it. You see she stepped."

"She better had," Ameerah stated, pulling her braids up and wiping sweat from around the back of her neck.

"Wait, what happened?" Zahara asked. "Who was tryna set it off up in there?"

"This nobody," I said. "Don't even sweat it."

"Have any of you seen my sister?" Brittani asked, pulling her hair back from her face. We all told her no. Shoot, it wasn't my place to tell her I saw her sister sneak off up the stairs with her man. Brittani rolled her eyes knowingly. "She's probably somewhere pinned up against a wall with her boo."

"Hold up, let's rewind," Ameerah said, planting a hand up on her hip. "Speaking of boos, who was the tall glass of dreamy, sweet chocolate you were dancing with? Don't think we didn't see you serving it up."

I shrugged. "Some guy who asked me to dance; that's all."

"That's *all*?!" Zahara screeched. "Girl, that chocolate-drop cutie was all that and a bag of M&M'S, okay? Melt all up in ya mouth; not in ya hands."

Ameerah and Brittani laughed. I rolled my eyes, trying to keep from laughing with them. I played it off instead. "He was all right, I guess."

"Well, you guessed wrong," Brittani said, placing a hand up on her hip. "So run along. Girl, do you need ya eyes checked? That boy is more than *all right*. Hon, he's super-duper, capital F-I-N-E. Did you at least get his name?"

I shook my head.

"*Whaaat?*" they snapped in unison, not believing me.

I shrugged. "It wasn't that serious," I stated, shifting my eyes from their stares. Truth is, it was! I needed to reel him in, and quick. "C'mon, let's go back in."

"Yeah, let's," Zahara agreed, pulling me by the arm. "If I'm lucky, I might be able to get me another dance in with that cutie, and bounce all this booty up on him again."

I laughed, shaking my head.

Once we got back inside, I glanced around the dimly lit party to see if I could spot him and that Latina hooker dancing again. But neither were anywhere in sight. I watched my girls on the dance floor, getting it in with the guys they had danced with earlier. Glow Worm found his way back over to me, grinning. "You ready to dance?"

I stared at him for a long minute, then decided he wasn't *that* bad to look at. Besides, I had finally spotted my future boo, dancing it up with some other chick. So I told Glow Worm yes, and dragged him over to where Mr. Milk Chocolate was and started dancing with him. My boo eyed me. And I eyed him back. I dropped it, popped it, locked it, then spun it around. Shaking everything my momma gave me: hair, hips, and booty. And Glow Worm had the nerve to be able to groove and keep up.

Three hours later, it was already time to go because Ameerah and I had two o'clock curfews—well, mine was really one, but I begged my dad to let me stay out an hour later. Anywaaayz, we all wanted to hit up the twenty-four-hour IHOP over in Irvington before we had to be in. I caught Briana's boo coming down the stairs, then a few minutes afterward she did, too.

We all stared at her. Her hair was all over her head and her lipstick was smeared all around her lips. She looked a hot, greasy mess!

She blinked. "What?"

"Uh, hellooo," Brittani said, rolling her eyes. "You might wanna go fix your situation 'cause you are looking real tore up right now."

"And extra funky," Ameerah added, holding her nose.

"Like a real circus clown," I stated, adding my two cents in.

We burst out laughing as Briana spun off to go to the bathroom.

Brittani huffed. "I swear I love my sister, but sometimes she acts like a real bird. And I bet she spent the whole dang night rolling around upstairs on some nasty sheets. Ugh! Let's wait for her outside."

And just as we were walking toward the door, out of nowhere Milk Chocolate appeared, stepping in front of me. "Yo, where you going, beautiful? You still owe me another dance."

I playfully rolled my eyes. "Mmmph. Oh, really? Now you want another dance *after* you dissed me for some other chick. No, thank you. I don't do sloppy seconds."

He laughed. "Nah, it wasn't even like that. That's my homegirl. I kept promising her a dance; my bad."

I smirked. "Uh-huh. It sure is. And it's your loss, too. So go on back and get the rest of the cooties."

He laughed. "Oh, damn. I don't have cooties."

"I don't know that," I teased.

"Well, come dance with me and find out."

He grinned, licking his lips. And right there, I wanted to kiss him. I stared at him, trying to act uninterested. "Not tonight, playboy. I'm leaving."

He smiled. "Playboy? Nah, that's not me."

"Mmmph, yeah right. I can't tell. All night all I saw were a buncha chicks clucking around you."

He laughed. "Yo, you real funny, for real. Wasn't none of 'em checkin' for me like that."

I waved him on. "Oh, puhleeeze. That's what your mouth says. But I know what I saw."

He laughed. "Oh, damn. It's like that? Let me find out you tryna put a claim on me."

I tilted my head, sweeping my bang over my forehead. "Maybe I am. Maybe I'm not."

He stared at me real hard, then broke into a wide smile. "You real feisty."

I smiled back. "Yup. And don't forget it."

Briana walked over with her hair pulled back in a ponytail and her lipstick wiped off from around her mouth, asking me if I was ready. She told me she'd bring the car around and pick me up out front. I waited for her to walk off, then said, "Look, it's been real. I gotta go."

"A'ight, let me walk out with you."

"Suit yourself," I said, trying to act like I wasn't pressed.

"So, what's good with you? Where you from?" I tell him I'm from South Orange. "Oh, a'iiight. That's wassup. You a freshman?"

I shook my head. "No, I'm a senior."

"A senior, daaaaamn. That's wassup. What's your major?"

"Dance."

He smiled. "A'ight, a'ight. That's wassup. I've never seen you on campus before. You go to Seton Hall?"

I shook my head again. "No, South Orange Performing Arts Academy."

He frowned, repeated what he heard. "*South Orange Performing Arts?* Wait, you're a *senior* in high school?"

"Yup."

"Damn. That's a good school. You gotta be on top of ya game to get up in there."

I shrugged. "Something like that." But he was right. South Orange Performing Arts Academy is one of the hottest schools in Jersey. Shoot…in the country! And it's one of the hardest to get into. The only way you getting in is through an examination and application process. And then you better be bringing it in the classroom, or you'll end up on probation, then tossed out if you don't step it up.

He smiled. "I'm impressed."

I smiled back. "Thanks."

"So, how old are you?"

"Seventeen...well, I will be in two months. What about you?"

"I just turned eighteen."

I smiled. "So, I guess you're too old for someone like me."

He laughed. "Nah, you good. You seem chill."

Briana pulled up, blowing the horn as if I couldn't see her. I shook my head. "Well, I gotta bounce. Nice talking to you."

"Yeah, you too. But I didn't get your name."

"That's because I didn't give it. It's Kamiyah. And yours?"

"Sincere."

I smiled. "Nice to meet you."

Briana blew her horn again. "Girl, will you hurry up already," Brittani yelled out of the passenger-side window. "We're starving."

"Yo, I'ma let you go. Can I get your number?"

I smiled, eyeing him real sexy-like. "Are you going to use it?"

He eyed me back. "No doubt. I wouldn't ask for it if I wasn't."

I motioned him with my finger to come in closer, and when he leaned his head in toward me, I whispered it, grazing my lips against his ear. He grinned.

"Yo, I'ma hit you up tomorrow, a'ight?"

"If you do, cool. If you don't, oh well. It's your loss."

He laughed, walking backward toward the house. "A'ight, hold that thought. Make sure you pick up."

I opened the car door. "You just make sure you call."

"I got you."

I slid into the backseat, then rolled the window down as Briana pulled off, and yelled out, "If you don't call me by eight o'clock tomorrow night, lose my number."

1

"**H**aaaaappy birthdaaaaaaay, baby!" Sincere sings into the phone the minute he finally picks up. He sounds like he's all hyped to hear from me, but he could be fronting, too. 'Cause I know how boys do. They stay tryna gas a chick's head. So I already know what it is. I turn my lips up. "I was just getting ready to hit you up."

Yeah, right! For some reason I roll my eyes up in my head. *Mmmph.* "For real? I was wondering why you didn't call me by now. I thought you mighta misplaced my number or forgot what day it was."

He laughs. "Never that. You know you're my baby."

I frown. No explanation. No reason as to why in the heck he didn't call me *first* thing this morning to wish *me* a happy birthday. Nothing! I mean, really. I take a deep breath. Try to keep my 'tude in check 'cause your girl can light it up if need be. My mom'll tell you I have a nasty attitude. I'm telling you, my attitude is fine unless you wanna crank it up; then it's a problem.

"Hmm, if you say so," I say, looking over my freshly painted fingernails. Girlfriend down at the shop really did me right.

"Whatchu mean by that?"

"Well, you say I'm your *baby* 'n' all, but you didn't even text or call to wish me a happy birthday. What's up with that? I shoulda woke up to a text or voice message from *you* if it was really all like that."

"Yo, c'mon, Miyah. You already know what it is with me and you. Don't do that."

"Then why didn't you call me?" I ask, whining. I know I'm bratty, but still.

Anywaaayz, he tells me he's been out all day with his mom and left his cell home. *And ya point?* Even though I'm heated with him—well, not *that* heated—I'm still happy to hear his smooth, sexy voice.

"So are you enjoying your special day?" he asks, changing the subject. I let him think I don't catch it, moving on. After all, it is all about me, and I'm not about to spend it arguing with some boy who isn't even my man. Well, he is, but I haven't served him the official memo yet.

"Of course I am! And guess what I got?"

"What?"

"A BMW!" I tell him excitedly, forgetting that quick that I was feeling some kinda way toward him. I describe my whip to him in detail, talking a mile a minute.

"Damn, baby, slow down," he says, laughing. "You mad hyped and whatnot."

"Yes, I am. OMG, you have no idea how much I love them cars. I told my dad that's what I wanted, but I didn't really think he was gonna go out and buy it. I thought he was gonna buy me a three series, which woulda been cute, too. But this right here is the truth, baby. Ohmygod, it's so fly."

"I bet it is. We gonna be riding in style now, huh? You won't have to ride up in my hand-me-down truck anymore, now that you got ya own whip."

I suck my teeth. "Oh, puhleeze. I would hardly call your Range Rover a hand-me-down. I love riding in that truck with you."

"And I love ridin' you in it."

I giggle.

"I miss you," he says, lowering his voice.

I grin, flopping back on my king-size sleigh bed. "I miss you, too. I'ma be back at my mom's Sunday night."

Even though this is my birthday weekend, it also happens to fall on the same weekend that I stay with my dad. Oh no, my parents aren't divorced. And I don't really consider them separated. They still do things together. And I know they are still getting it in between the sheets 'cause she spends nights over here, and he spends time at our house—*sleeping* in the same bed with the door closed, okay? So you tell me what it is. They're very much married. They just happen to live in separate households. Oh, and get this: they both still live in the same town! I know. Crazy, right? But to me, it's normal 'cause this is how they've been living since I was eight years old. So, basically, I have two bedrooms, two bathrooms, and two walk-in closets packed with all the hottest wears. So I'm definitely not complaining.

"Around what time?" he asks, bringing me back to the conversation.

"Like around nine, I guess. It's up to my dad. We're supposed to be going into the city to have dinner with my sister, Erika, and her fiancé, so it all depends on what time we leave to come back." Thankfully, we only live like twenty minutes or so from New York, so I won't be getting home too late.

My sister, Erika, is nine years older than me and lives in Manhattan with her extra-fine mocha-chocolate man, Winston. OMG, I like him so much better than that bum she was with before him. All they did was fight! Anywaaayz, she and Winston attend NYU's School of Law. And you should see the ice he put on her hand. Whew, it's sick!

"Oh, a'ight," he says. "I wanna see you and give you your gift."

"Oooh, you got me a gift!" I say, getting all amped, already knowing he was going to catch it something terrible if he didn't have a nice shiny trinket or something for me. "What you get me? I love gifts!"

"Slow down, baby," he says, laughing. "Of course I did. You my boo. So you know I was gonna get you something special."

And it better not be nothing cheap! "Awww, you are so sweet."

"Yeah, I know," he jokes. "And you know what'd be sweeter?"

"What?"

"You stop playin' and admit I'm your man. You ready for that?"

"Mmmph, the question really is, are *you* ready?" I smile.

"Yeah, okay. I've been ready. You the one stallin'. Stop frontin', Miyah. Are you ready to be my girl or not?"

"Maybe, maybe not…" I laugh. "I'll let you know *after* I see my gift."

"Yeah, a'ight. You already know what it is."

"Oh yeah? And what's that?"

"You're mine. So make sure you come through as soon as you get home so we can make it official."

Um, the way he says that sounds like he's *telling* me to be at his house, instead of *asking* me to. But I'ma let it go. I can tell Sincere thinks he's running things, but he has another think coming.

"What you doing tonight?" I ask, changing the subject.

"I don't know yet. Probably chill. Think about you."

I smile. "Awww, how sweet."

"You already know. I told you you're mine. So what's my baby getting ready to get into?"

I tell him I'm waiting for my mom to get here. That we're going to Medieval Times to have dinner. Then when I get back, Zahara, Ameerah, and Brittani are coming over to spend the night.

"Oh, word? And what y'all gonna get into?"

"Chill, watch movies, and probably eat all this birthday cake up; nothing major."

"Damn, save me some."

"I got you," I tell him, cheesing it up. Whew, this boy's voice makes me feel tingly all over.

"That's wassup. Let me find out you got some dudes all up over there, too; there's gonna be consequences and repercussions."

Um, hello, helloooooo . . . how in the world did we go from saving you some cake to dudes being all up in my space? That's what I hear myself saying in my head. I suck my teeth instead. "Ain't no boys gonna be over here, biscuit head." I get up off the bed when I hear a car. I peek through my curtains. My bedroom faces the front of Daddy's townhouse, so I have a perfect view of who's coming and going. It's my mom pulling up in the drive-way. Late and wrong, as usual!

He laughs. "Yeah, a'ight. I got your biscuit head all right. But you heard what I said."

"Whatever. My dad is not playing that," I tell him as I watch my mom flip down her sun visor—to freshen up her lipstick or make sure she doesn't have a hair out of place, I'm sure. It takes her five minutes and thirty-seven sec-onds—I know because I timed her—to do whatever it is she's doing before she finally steps out of her Benz, look-ing like she's preparing for a photo shoot. That's how we Nichols women do it. Always fresh, always fly, and always fine! Yes, high maintenance, you already know. She still gets on my nerves, though. But that's a whole other story. "The only boy he seems to like is you," I add, shaking my head. For some reason, Daddy's really taken a liking to Sincere. Probably 'cause he's a freshman in college, plays basketball, and is interested in pledging Daddy's beloved fraternity. So of course Daddy is gonna like him. Oh, Daddy's all about his frat. And he's dragged me and my sister to all of his alma mater's homecoming and step-show events every chance he's gotten, which is why I know so much about all the different sororities and what-not. Anywaaayz, my boo says he's gonna pledge next year.

I watch Mom as she walks up to my new car, taking it all in. Of course she knows it's mine 'cause it has a big red bow on the front of the grill. I see her shaking her head. I already know what that means. She's going to try and give Daddy the business about the car. *She's such a hater!* I step away from the window, then go into my bathroom to remove my hairpins so I can comb out my wrap.

"Oh, word." He chuckles. "That's wassup. My future frat brotha is mad chill."

"Oh, puhleeze. What. Ever."

He laughs.

"Kamiyah!" I hear my dad calling me from the bottom of the stairs, like he always does. I walk over and open my bedroom door.

"Yes?"

"C'mon, your mom's here."

"Okay. I'll be right down," I tell him, closing my door. "I gotta go."

"A'ight, have fun."

"I will. Thanks."

"And don't be havin' no boys all up in ya face, either."

"Well, don't you be havin' any chicks all up in yours," I shoot back.

He laughs.

I don't. "Oh, you can laugh if you want. But, trust. I will bring it to a bird's throat."

"No need for all that, baby. Like I said, you the only one I got eyes for."

I roll my eyes up in my head, hard. " 'Bye, Sincere. I love you." I blink, blink again; surprised to hear those three words slip from my lips. Um, I can't even front. I'm really feeling Sincere. But *love* him? Um, I don't know if I'm ready to go that far, but I just did! Okay, okay, I'll admit I think about him *all* the time—every waking moment. And I get butterflies every time he hugs and kisses me. And listening to his sexy voice sends chills up and down my spine. But it is waaay too soon for me to say I love him. But I feel like I do. No. I *know* I do. And I already let it slip outta my mouth. Shoot, after nine weeks I should be madly in love with him. Okay, okay…dang, I'm lying. Truth is, I'm crazy in love with this boy! But I wasn't ready for him to know all that yet. Not until I had him completely wrapped around my fingers.

When Erika lived at home I used to always overhear her and her girlfriends talking about boys and sex and whatnot. And the times I was ear-hustling—which was usually anytime her friends came over—I remember hearing her say, *If a guy tells you he loves you after less than a month, then he's probably a nut.* They would call little tidbits like that about guys the "Nut Alert." Well, I guess that same rule applies to chicks, too. So the last thing I wanna do is be considered a *nut.* Well, I guess the verdict is gonna be out on that one, since I know it was love at first kiss for me over a month ago; and now I've put myself out there and said it to him *first.* But *wait*! Technically, it's after the one month mark, so then I'm not a nut. Whew!

"Aaah, that's wassup, baby."

I frown. *That's wassup, baby*? Is he serious? Is that all he has to say? Didn't he just hear me tell him that I love him?

"Oh, so 'that's wassup' is all it is to you? I tell you I love you and that's the best you can do?"

"C'mon, Miyah, don't do that. You know how I feel about you."

"Um, nooooo, I don't. I wanna hear it."

"I'm real big on you, Miyah."

I hear my sister's voice saying, *If a guy can't tell you he loves you after you've told him, then maybe he doesn't. That's why you never, ever tell him you love him first. This way you don't play yourself.*

"Oh, so is that your way of nicely telling me you really don't?" I ask with an attitude. For some reason, I wanna go off on him. But it's like the words are stuck in the back of my throat somewhere, 'cause I know I have nobody but myself to blame for being the first to tell him how I feel.

"Don't do that."

"Don't do *what*, Sincere?"

"Put words in my mouth."

"I'm not tryna put words in your mouth," I say, pacing the floor. "I'm tryna understand what this 'I'm real big on you' means."

"It means I'm really digging you, Miyah. It means I want you to be my girl. It means I think you're hot. That I got you on the brain, hard."

I smile. "Oh, okay. I'm just checking."

"A'ight, cool. You know you're my baby. So stop tripping."

"I'm not tripping."

He laughs. "Yeah, okay. But you were getting ready to."

"Okay, I was. But just a little."

"You're too beautiful to be tripping. And it's your birthday." He starts singing "Happy Birthday" all off-key, and I start laughing.

"All right, all right. Don't. You're making my ears bleed."

He laughs with me. "A'ight, then. Give me a kiss."

I give him a big kiss through the phone. "Muuuuuah."

"Yeah, that's what I'm talkin' 'bout with ya sexy self. My baby's fine as hell."

I smile as I wriggle myself into a sexy pair of True Religion skinny stretch jeans, then decide to wear the matching jacket without a shirt underneath. I turn around in the mirror, admiring the way my jeans hug my curves.

"And you all mine," he says.

I keep cheesing—*hard*. "And you *better* be all mine," I warn him.

"That's what it is."

We finally say our good-byes, then hang up.

I hear my dad calling for me again. "I'll be right down," I yell out, racing around my bedroom, trying to finish getting ready before my mom starts rushing me. For some reason the lyrics to Nicki Minaj's "Moment 4 Life" pop into my head as I'm slipping on my six-inch chocolate Gucci boots that Mom bought me for my birthday.

I snap my fingers to the beat in my head as I give myself the once-over in the mirror, making sure everything's on point. Oh, wait a minute! I forgot my cherry lip gloss! Oooh, that's a no-no! I rush into the bathroom and grab it from off the counter, then glide a fresh coat over my lips. I like keeping them looking sweet, wet 'n' juicy. When I'm satisfied, I grab my shades, then turn off the lights in my bathroom and closet. I swing open my bedroom door and head down the stairs.

"The birthday diva is ready," I chime out.

2

Ohhkaaay, so we're driving back from Medieval Times—which was cute, by the way—and everything is going great until the Wicked Witch opens her mouth and out of nowhere spits haterade all over my night. She decides she wants to discuss *my* birthday gift. Not the Gucci boots, or the Tiffany tennis bracelet, or the thousand-dollar Louis bag—things *she* bought—but my whip! Not that I'm surprised, 'cause I already told you she was gonna have something to say about it. But I didn't think she was gonna try 'n' sabotage my driving it *before* I got the engine started and drove the damn thing out of the driveway.

She twists her body in her seat so she can look back at me while she speaks. "Kamiyah, I wasn't going to say anything until tomorrow because I didn't want to put a damper on your birthday..." *Well, then don't!* I scream in my head. "...but I told your father earlier that he needs to take that car back and get you one that's more economical and suitable for a girl your age."

I blink, hard. "Excuuuuse me, you did *whaaat?*" I ask with more 'tude than I mean.

She repeats herself, then goes into her reasoning why. "You're too young and inexperienced to be driving a car that fast and that expensive."

I roll my eyes, sucking my teeth. "Daaaaddy," I whine, looking at him watching me from the rearview mirror. "She can't be serious!" Now, I know better than anyone that he won't ever go against her in front me. But I know he better check her on this one, quick, before I turn it up on her.

"Kayla," he says, reaching over to my mom, touching her arm. "Not now, sweetheart."

Not now, sweetheart? What kinda ish is that? How 'bout not now, not ever!

"Erik, she's too young for that type of car, and you know it. I don't know what you were thinking going out spending that kind of money on her, without even discussing it with me."

Daddy cuts his eyes over at her. But as usual doesn't check her.

"Ummm," I say sarcastically, "*maybe* he was thinking he can trust me. That I'm responsible; that I have a four-point-oh GPA, and am in the honor society. Um, oh wait. How 'bout this one: I'm his daughter and I deserve nice things, 'cause *I* earn them and he can afford it."

"Don't go there with me," she snaps. "You get nice things, expensive things, *all* the time."

"You are such a hater."

"You better watch your mouth, young lady." She scowls. "Before I reach back and smack you in it."

"C'mon, both of you stop this bickering," Daddy says, sounding frustrated.

"Erik, are you going sit there and let her talk to me like that?" Wicked Witch huffs, shooting him a look.

He shakes his head. "Listen. For once, can't the two of you get along long enough to get through *one* whole evening?"

"It's her, Daddy," I offer, pouting. "She did the same thing to Erika, and that's why they never got along. And now she's doing it to *me*."

"Kamiyah, that's enough," Daddy warns. But I'm not hearing him.

"Girl," my mom says through clenched teeth, "I will reach back there and smack all thirty-two of them straight teeth *my* money paid for, right down your throat if you say that one more time. I'm your mother, not one of your little ghetto friends in the streets."

"I don't *have* ghetto friends, thank you very much. But it's mighty funny how you seem to forget that that's *exactly* where you came from."

Her eyes almost pop out of her sockets. "Kamiyah Mychele Nichols, have you lost your damn mind, young lady? Don't you ever, and I do mean *ever*, talk to me in that tone or fashion. You're grounded."

"*Grounded?* For what? For reminding you that you come from the guts of Newark?"

"No. For reminding me that you are too damn grown and fresh at the mouth. I think you forget who the mother is, and who the child is. So until you get your attitude in check, you're grounded. Do you understand me?"

I ignore her.

"I *said*, do you understand me?"

"Mmmph," I grunt, biting my tongue.

Daddy swerves the car over to the side of the road and abruptly stops, causing my body to jerk to the side. Mom and I both look at him, wondering what's going on.

"Both of you—stop it! I don't want to hear another damn thing from either one of you while I'm driving. So if you want to argue, do it now. Get it all out, *now*! Because once I start this car and it starts moving—again, I don't want to hear nothing else from either of you."

I think about something really, really sad, like my grandma dying, until my eyes get all teary and whatnot. I dab at my eyes with my fingers when I see Daddy looking at me in the mirror again. Tears always work with him.

"Kayla, I bought the car for Kamiyah and she's keeping it, end of discussion." I smirk, wiping a single tear that finally slides down my cheek.

Mom glares at him, then turns back around in her seat and leaves me the hell alone.

"And as for you, young lady, don't you ever let me hear you speak to your mother like that again. No matter what you feel, she is still your mother. And you are to respect her, you hear me?"

"Yes," I softly say.

"Good," he says, turning the ignition. "I love both of you, but I swear the two of you are gonna drive me to drink."

"Well, if she's keeping the car," Mom says tightly, "then we're going to need to discuss some strict ground rules."

"And we will. But *not* tonight, so let's drop it."

"And she's still going to be on punishment."

I roll my eyes up in my head.

"And she will be, but not tonight."

Mom glares at him. I'm sure she's shocked as much as I am that Daddy spoke to her that way in front of me. It's about time he checks her! Yeah—#teamdaddy all the way! He turns the stereo on. His favorite station, WBLS, is playing. I pull out my cell when I hear it buzzing in my bag. Ameerah sent me a text confirming what time to be at my house tonight. I text her back, telling her to let everyone know to be there at ten o'clock. Next I read Sincere's text: HEY, BEAUTIFUL. THNKN ABT U. CALL ME B/4 U GO 2 SLEEP.

I smile, feeling more relaxed. I text back: AWW, THANKS, BABY! I'M THNKN ABT U 2!

Sincere and I text back 'n' forth:

SINCERE: SO R U HAVN FUN?

ME: I WAS

SINCERE: WHAT HAPPND?

ME: THE WICKED WITCH

SINCERE: WHO?

ME: MY MOTHER! BUT I DON'T WANNA GET IN2 IT

SINCERE: K, COOL. I WANNA C U

ME: AWWW, ME 2. I MISS U LIKE CRAZY

SINCERE: WHAT U MISS?

ME: U SILLY

SINCERE: WHAT ELSE?

ME: LOL. NO COMMENT

SINCERE: CAN I STOP BY 2NITE 2 BRING U UR GIFT? I DON'T WANNA WAIT TIL SUN

ME: SURE

SINCERE: I'M LEAVING NOW

ME: I'M NOT HOME YET

SINCERE: I'MA WAIT 4 U BABY

ME: AWW, K. C U!

SINCERE: ☺

I slip my phone back into my bag, then lay my head back on the headrest, smiling ear to ear with thoughts of seeing Sincere, hanging out with my girls tonight, and getting behind the wheel of my BMW!

3

Like he said he would be, Sincere is sitting in his truck waiting for me when we pull into the driveway. I don't even wait for Daddy to come to a complete stop before I swing open the car door and practically jump out and race over to his truck. Sincere smiles at me and gets out of his truck. The minute I see the signature blue box from Tiffany & Co. he's holding in his hand, I know it's jewelry.

I smile wider. "Oh, wow, for me?" I ask, acting surprised.

He hands me my gift, giving me a hug and a kiss on the cheek. "Happy birthday, baby."

"Awww, thank you. You shouldn't have."

"Yeah, right," he says, laughing. He playfully tries to grab the box out of my hand. "Then let me take it back to the store."

I swat his hand away. "Uh, I don't think so; wrong answer."

"Yeah, I thought so."

I open my mouth to say something sideways but, of course, the Wicked Witch has to be all up in mine.

"Hey, Sincere," she says, acting like she's Miss Mom of the Year. I roll my eyes.

"Hi, Missus Nichols," Sincere says, giving her a wave. He's so polite and well-mannered and so dang...fine!

The minute Daddy steps out of the car, Sincere speaks to him, too. "Hey, Mister Nichols."

Daddy says hi back. Asks him how his parents are doing. He tells Daddy they're good. Daddy wants to know how he's doing in school. Of course Daddy wants to know that he's keeping up his grades so that he can pledge next semester. Sincere tells him he's doing well. Daddy goes to say something else, but I tilt my head, giving him my will-you-please-beat-it look.

"Good seeing you, Sincere," he says, taking the hint and walking toward the house.

"You, too, Mister Nichols."

"Kamiyah," the Wicked Witch says, "why don't you in-vite Sincere in until your company gets here?"

I don't answer. I turn my back on her.

"Kamiyah, did you hear me?"

I keep ignoring her.

"It's cool, Missus Nichols. I can't stay long. I only came by to bring Kamiyah her gift, and to give her a birthday hug."

"Well, that was—"

I crane my neck, glancing over my shoulder at her. "Um, hellooooo," I snap, finally turning to face her. "Do you mind? I mean, he's here to see *me*."

"Kamiyah, don't—"

"Kayla," Daddy says, coming back to the front door, cutting her off before she tries to get it popping out here. "C'mon in and let them be. I have something I want to show you upstairs." I smirk.

"Kamiyah, don't be out here too long," Daddy says to me.

"I won't, Daddy," I say, all sweet and whatnot.

The Wicked Witch stares me down. I turn my back on her again. "Good night, Sincere," she says.

"Good night, Missus Nichols."

She grits her teeth. "Kamiyah, I'll speak to *you* later."

"Whatever," I mumble under my breath as she angrily walks off, her heels stabbing the pavement with each step toward the house.

Sincere looks at me. "Why do you treat your mom like that? She seems mad cool."

"Oh, please. You don't have to live with her."

"Well, you still shouldn't treat her like that."

Well, she shouldn't be such an evil woman. And you need to mind your damn business, is what I'm thinking, but I keep my thoughts in check. "Did you come here to lecture me?" I ask, raising a brow and placing a hand on my hip.

He smiles at me. "Nah, I came to see my girl."

I smirk. "I'm not your girl." I glance down at my feet and notice there's a smudge on the toe of one of my new boots. I hand Sincere my gift so I can try to wipe it off.

"Yeah, right. You already know what it is. Now let me check out the new whip."

"C'mon." I grab his hand and practically drag him up the driveway to my car. Before I can go in to get the key,

Daddy opens the front door and disarms the alarm so I can open the door and show Sincere the inside. "Thanks, Daddy," I say, smiling. "You're the best."

"Yeah, I am, aren't I," he says, chuckling. He goes back inside and lets me and Sincere be.

"Damn, baby, this is sweet," Sincere says, sticking his head in. I tell him to get in. He does, and I walk over to the driver's side and get in. Sincere runs his hand over the dashboard and wood-grain finish, admiring all of its flyness. "Real nice."

"I know, I love it," I say, gripping the steering wheel. I am so wrapped up on the smell and the feel of my car that I almost forget Sincere has my gift in his hand.

"Here," he says, handing the box back as if he read my mind. "Open your gift so I can see that pretty smile of yours." I take it from him, grinning as I rip open the blue wrapping paper, then open the box.

I gasp. "Ohmygod, I love it," I say, reaching over and giving him a hug and kiss on the lips. He bought me an eighteen-karat white-gold heart tag charm. "It's beautiful."

"Like you," he says, smiling at me. And even though he didn't tell me he loved me today, I can tell Sincere really is big on me. But I'm not gonna be completely satisfied until I know for certain I have him wrapped around my manicured fingers.

"Aww, you're so sweet. Thanks."

"You're welcome, baby. You deserve it." He leans over and kisses me again; this time he slips his tongue in. When we finally finish our tongue dance, I'm almost dazed. Kissing him is like eating a whole bag of Reese's Pieces. And I loooove me some Reese's Pieces; whew...delicious!

"C'mon, get out so I can put on your necklace and see how fly my baby looks with it on."

He doesn't have to tell me twice. I hop out and walk over to him, turning my back to him. I pull my hair up. He kisses me on the back of the neck. His lips feel good on my skin. I want him soooo bad! But I'ma keep it fly. He fastens the clasp of the necklace around my neck. Tells me he charged it on his dad's American Express card and has to pay him back. But who cares? My necklace is beautiful. It hangs perfect! I turn to face him.

"I've never bought any girl jewelry this expensive before, but there's something real special about you and I really dig you, Miyah."

I look up, gazing into his hazel eyes, and know for certain that I *am* in love with him. "I'm never taking it off."

"It looks beautiful on you," he says, gazing back at me. His hands are on my waist, pulling me into him. They are big and strong, and feel good on my body. I'm not gonna front. I'm happy to see him, but...I'm happier to see the banging gift he bought me.

"You feel so good," he says, leaning in and trying to kiss me. I jerk my head back, pushing him back with the palm of my hand.

"Hold up. Just because you bought me a lil sumthin-sumthin'," I say, smirking, "don't be thinking you're gonna be jizzing it up on me. You got the wrong memo. I'm not that kinda girl."

He laughs. "'Jizzin' it up,' hahahaha. Yo, you mad funny. Where'd you get that from?"

I eye him real sexy-like. "Oh, so you not tryna grind up on me?"

He eyes me back. "Nah...I'm tryna hold you close and whisper something in your ear."

I playfully mush him. "Yeah, right. And what were you gonna say?"

He smiles wider, taking my hand in his, pulling me toward his truck. "Come here and let me tell you."

I glance over my shoulder to see if my nosy mother is peeking through the curtains. Surprisingly, she's not. Sincere leads me around to the driver's side, then leans up against the door, pulling me into him. He kisses me on the lips again. We kiss for what feels like forever until I break away.

"You better stop before the Wicked Witch comes out and screams on you."

He laughs. "Ya mom digs me. You see how she smiled at me when I spoke to her?"

I roll my eyes. "Boy, please. *What*ever. It's all an act, trust me. That woman is—"

He shuts me up with another kiss. It lingers longer than I'm used to. And I feel myself getting dizzy. His hands drop from my waist to the small of my back, then rest on my round behind. He squeezes.

Oh God, his hands feel so good on me. I feel myself starting to tingle inside. I pull myself away from his soft, juicy lips.

"So, um...what is it you wanted to whisper to me?"

His lips curl up into a sexy grin. He leans in and kisses me again, then kisses my neck. "You taste like candy, baby...real sweet."

I lick my lips, grinning as he pulls me closer into him. "You want this candy?" I tease.

"Yeah," he whispers into my ear in between more kisses. I feel like my whole body is on fire! *Cool it, girl.*

"Hold up...waaaaait a minute...let me get all up in it. Go get a room! Y'all two are straight nasty with it!"

Sincere and I jump. It's my girl Zahara, sneaking up on us. She's wearing a pair of black boy shorts, a cute white blouse that criss-crosses in the front and a pair of red six-inch peep-toe heels. Zahara is a pretty brown-skinned diva with big brown eyes and pouty lips. And at 5'3", she never, ever, leaves the house without a pair of heels on. She lives for a fly pair of heels. She's also the shortest one out of my clique. And she has the loudest mouth, too. But I love her dearly.

"Ohmygod, girl, will you be quiet, coming up here all loud and whatnot. You scared the crap outta me. Where the hell did you come from?"

She laughs. "My brother dropped me off on the corner. And I walked down. Heeey, Siiincere," she says, almost singing his name.

"Wassup, Zee, right?"

"And you know it. Now you gonna have to *poof*, 'cause this is an all-girls night and ain't no boys allowed up in here."

"Don't pay her nutty butt no mind," I say, shaking my head. Zahara doesn't care what she says.

He laughs, opening his door. "Nah, it's all good. I'ma let you girls have ya girls' night, but uh"—he pulls me into him—"you still didn't answer my question."

"What question was that?"

"You my girl or what?"

Well, of course I am. But I'm not going to tell him

tonight. *Always keep a guy guessing*, I hear in my head. I grin. "Maybe."

Zahara clears her throat, placing a hand on her hip. "Or maybe not. But tonight ain't the time to be tryna figure it out." She grabs me by the arm, pulling me and eyeing Sincere at the same time. "Sorry, boo-boo, but you gonna hafta get a rain check on that answer 'cause we got things to do."

He laughs, getting into his truck. "A'ight, then. I'm out."

Ameerah's dad pulls up alongside of us, letting her out. All of my girls are pretty, but Ameerah is the prettiest out of all three of them. She has this beautiful reddish-brown skin that makes her look like she's mixed with Native American. And her thick eyelashes and naturally arched eyebrows make her stand out even more. Me and Zahara wave at her dad. He waves back, then drives off. "Hey, birthday girl," Ameerah says, opening her arms to give me a hug. She stops, holding a finger up. "Uh, wait a minute. Why we got boys here? This is 'posed to be girls only, or did I miss the memo?"

I roll my eyes. "There are no *boys* here. It's only Sincere. And he's leaving."

She smacks her lips. "Oh, okay, 'cause I was sure 'bout to pull out my phone and hit up my boo, too, and tell him to come through." She waves at Sincere. "Hey, Sincere."

"Wassup, Ameerah, right?"

"All day, every day!" She turns her attention to me. "Where's Brittani?"

"Here she comes now," Zahara says, standing in the middle of the street with one hand up on her hip as Briana's black Volvo cruises down the street.

I walk back over to Sincere's truck as he starts the engine. "Thanks for my gift," I say, touching my neck. "I meant it when I said I'm never taking it off."

He smiles. "You better not. So that means I'm your man, right?"

I lean into his truck and kiss him on the lips. "I'll think about it."

He laughs. "Yeah, a'ight. Keep playin' games if you want. I already know what it is."

"Then stop asking," I say, laughing with him as he pulls off.

Brittani hops out of the car, tossing the straps of her Prada bag up over her shoulder. She looks real cute in her short faded denim wrap dress and strappy sandals. Her shoulder-length, auburn-colored weave is styled into a messy side ponytail with her bangs sweeping in the same direction as her ponytail. The hair color against her milk-chocolate skin looks good. At first glance, she looks a lot like Meagan Good. "I know that wasn't a boy I just saw," she says, eyeing us.

"It was Siiiiiinceeeere," Ameerah and Zahara sing in unison.

"And you don't even wanna know what I walked up on," Zahara adds.

"Oh, whatever," I say, laughing. "Like you don't do worse."

"Well, yeah. But I'm grown."

"So am I," I say, planting both hands up on my hips.

They start laughing when they see the Wicked Witch open the front door with a hand up on her hip.

"*Not*," Ameerah says, cracking up.

"Yeah, talk to the hand, boo," Zahara chimes in.

"Hi, Missus Nichols," they say, waving as they walk up the driveway.

"Hey, girls. Kamiyah, y'all need to come on inside."

"Let's see how grown you are now," Brittani mumbles, holding back a laugh.

"Oh, shut up," I hiss under my breath.

4

"Ooooh, I'm soooo dang jealous, boo," Ameerah says, peeking out of my curtains and looking down at my shiny new ride.

I showed them the inside of the car before we came inside, and the whole time, while they all oohed and aahed over it, the Wicked Witch was standing by the door, playing the Neighborhood Watch like I was gonna steal my own car or something. Like really, where am I gonna go with no car key? I swear, she makes me sick!

"I am so in love with your car. I wish I had a Daddy who bought me whatever I wanted."

"Yeah, you're real lucky," Brittani says. "I'll be lucky if I get a pair of Rollerblades to get around on for my birthday." Her birthday is next month.

I laugh. "And I'm sure you'll make it look mad fly, too."

Brittani shimmies her shoulders. "And you know how I do, boo. Oh, Miss Bee gonna Rollerblade it up, okay."

"Well, just make sure you don't Rollerblade your butt

into a ditch," Ameerah says, moving away from the window, "like you did when you were busy tryna be cute on that skateboard and ended up getting a mud bath. *Bam!*"

We all start laughing. Well, the truth is, she had no business up on that skateboard in the first place, tryna impress some boy; especially since she had never even been on one before. But she liked him. And when Brittani likes someone, she goes all out to let it be known. Anywho, PJ—the guy she liked—always rode his skateboard everywhere he went. So Miss Ooh-I'm-'Bout-To-Make-His-Fine-Butt-My-Man decided to tell him she loved skateboarding, too—even though she didn't own one. He invited her to go skateboarding with him and she had to beg her mom to rush out and buy her one. Then, when they finally hooked up, she skateboarded her butt right down into a ditch and broke her arm. He had to climb down and help her out of a buncha mud. Poor thing, she was a muddy mess! Then, after all that, he still wasn't her man.

"Gee, thanks for reminding me," she says, falling back on the bed. "I was never so dang embarrassed."

"And you shoulda been," Ameerah says, still laughing. "Be glad you had that helmet on; otherwise you probably would have gotten more than a broken arm. I swear, I wish I coulda seen you rolling around in that mud, looking like a pig stuck in slop."

"Ohmygod, picture that," I say, changing into a pair of pink boy-shorts. "That woulda been too funny."

"It sure woulda," Zahara agrees. "The crazy things we do for boys."

Brittani sits up, sucking her teeth. "Oh, whatever. You boogas probably woulda tweeted about it and had it posted all up on Facebook, too."

"Yup," Zahara, Ameerah, and I say, high-fiving each other and laughing.

I add, "You know we love you, boo. But you already know we woulda had ya muddy mug all over the Net till it went viral, baby."

Brittani grunts, folding her arms. "Ugh. And I didn't even get to taste his lips."

"Girl, that's all you think about," I state. "You're so boy crazy."

"Whatever, boo," Brittani says. "Ain't nothing crazy about going after what you want. And I wanted him. I woulda licked his lollipop up and down and all around."

"Ewww, yuck!" Ameerah snaps.

Brittani waves her on. "Oh, please. Don't knock it until you try it."

I put a finger up. "Wait. You're a neck bobbler?"

She bats her eyes, acting all shy and whatnot, sticking a fingernail in between her teeth. "Uh, yeah. I thought you knew, boo."

"Uh, noooo, I didn't know. But I do now."

She shrugs. "It's no biggie. Every now and then I like to hop on the mic if I think a guy's worth it."

We stare at her.

She shrugs her shoulders. "What? It's not like I'm out there having sex."

I look at her like she has the word *dumbo* stamped on her forehead. "So wait. You think oral sex isn't having sex?"

"Well, yeah."

I blink. Ameerah bucks her eyes at her. Zahara shifts her eyes.

"Girlfriend," Ameerah says, smacking her lips, "I don't

know what Sex Ed classes you've been in, boo-boo. But last I heard, doing the superhead *is* sex."

"Okay," Brittani says, twirling the end of one of her braids. "Maybe it is. But, shoot. At least you can't get pregnant. I just swallow and go. And my boo-of-the-moment stays with a smile on his face."

I am speechless.

"Alrighty, then," Zahara says, clapping her hands. "We know who failed what classes, so on to the next. Speaking of boys"—she glances over at me—"you better spill it."

"Spill what?" I ask, playing stupid.

"You know," she says, rolling over on her back. "All that goo-goo, ga-ga ish you been doing with Sincere."

I laugh, walking into my bathroom, flipping on the light. "Oh, puhleeze. Goo-goo, ga-ga nothing." I run the water, staring at my reflection as I talk to them. "Sincere and I are just talking, for now."

"Girl, shut up with your lies," Brittani chimes in. "Y'all been talking mad long. It's time to kick it up a notch. We all know you feeling him. So why don't you quit playing and get with the program?"

"I'm not in any rush," I say, flicking my wrist at her.

Zahara pops her eyes open. "It's been since July and y'all *still* not going together. Who the heck does that? Drag out a love affair? I woulda been done had him booed up."

"Yeah, Miyah," Ameerah cosigns. "Get with the program. You need to stop fronting and make it official. You know he's your boo."

"I'm not thinking about that boy," I say, lying through my pretty white teeth—compliments of Crest Whitestrips, thank you very much! Anywaaayz, truth is I can't stop thinking about Sincere! I already told you, every waking moment I have him on the brain. And I told you how bad I want him. But, like Erika and her girls used to always say, *Never let a boy think you're pressed*. But the reality is, I AM pressed!! Still, coming off like I'm some thirsty chick is not how I do mine. And I'm definitely not about to play myself like that in front of my girls, either.

"Well," Zahara says, "since you're not thinking about him, you can pass him over to me, 'cause that boy is extra-fine-dot-com. I definitely know what to do with him." She licks her lips.

Ameerah lets out a disgusted grunt. "Ewww!"

Brittani laughs.

I pop my head out of the bathroom and buck my eyes wide open, planting a hand up on my hip. "Excuse you?"

"Siiiiike," Zahara says, laughing. "You know I'm only popping junk, boo."

I raise my arched brow. "Hahahahaha, real funny."

She and Brittani keep laughing. But I don't see jack amusing. And if we weren't celebrating *my* birthday, I'd scream on her for even coming at me sideways like that. And I'd scream on Brittani for thinking that ish is funny. But I'ma keep it fly for now and turn it up just a taste to let her know I don't appreciate it.

"You can laugh all you want. But I tell you what. Go 'head and get your top rocked if you want."

"Oh, Miyah, please. We're girls, boo," Zahara says, getting serious. "You know I wouldn't do you dirty like that. Relax."

Yeah, we're girls and all, and yeah, I'm sure she was playing, but I'm not that kinda chick. And I don't get down with playing like that. And she's already done that kinda nastiness once...wait, *twice*...to her own cousin and this nondescript chick none of us liked, but still…what she did was real nasty. And if she did it to them, what should make me think she wouldn't try to do it to me, too?

"Relax, nothing," I say, eyeing her. "Girls or not, boo, I will beat the dust up off you if you ever try it with someone you know I'm dealing with."

They all stare at me. "Uhhh, hold up," Brittani says, putting a finger up in the air. "*We* thought you weren't dealing with *him*."

I frown, stepping out of the bathroom. I place a hand up on my hip, ready to bring it. "Well, I'm not. But that's beside the point. I *will* be. And, for now, I'm speaking in general."

Zahara frowns back at me. Ameerah jumps in before she can say something. "Now, hold up. Wait a minute…let me put my two cents in it." She looks at the both of us. "We *are* girls. And, hellooo, *we* have a pact. No matter how fine a boy is, we never, ever let him come between us. And, Miyah, you know Zahara's dizzy behind was only playing with you. Geesh. You must really like him."

"Yeah, Miyah," Brittani agrees. "Many times before, we've joked back and forth about passing off a guy if one of us didn't want him, and none of us have ever gotten all twisted outta shape over it before. So you must really be feeling him."

"You know what, y'all?" I stare at them, pausing. Then crack a smile. "Siiiiike. Gotcha, boo."

They start grabbing pillows off my bed and throwing them at me.

"Oooh, girl," Zahara says, laughing. "I really thought you were tryna crank it up over some boy."

I keep laughing with her, but inside I'm dead serious. I

will wrap my hands up in her weave and drag her through the streets. I'm gonna be watching her real close around Sincere. I already know. That's my girl and all, but I know how she gets down. She's kinda messy on the low. And I'm not the one. If she tries to step to my man, I promise you, I'm going to stomp her lights out. Friend or not!

"Girl, I hope you know I would never do any of you dirty like that," Zahara says after we stop laughing about it. "We too fly for that."

"You got that right," Ameerah agrees.

"Look, I don't know about you ooga-boogas," Brittani says to Ameerah and Zahara as she gets up off the bed, grabbing the remote to my stereo from off the dresser, "but I'm here to celebrate our girl's birthday. Not get into a buncha dumbness about some boy who isn't even hers yet. Sorry, boo. Borrrrrrring. So moving on." She clicks on the stereo, then presses PLAY for the CD player. She clicks through the tracks until she finds what she wants. Trey Songz's "Say Aah" starts playing. "Now *this* is who we should be beefing over. Now open wide and say aah." She starts dancing toward me, then grabs me by the arms. "It's ya birthday, boo..."

We all start laughing and dancing and just that quick I forget that only seconds ago I was ready to bring it to Zahara's face.

5

TGIF! Yes, yes, yes... I am sooo ready for last-period bell to ring so I can sling my designer bag up over my shoulder and hit the door. It's officially the second weekend of the school year and I'm ready to get it started! Sincere and I are going to the movies tonight. He wants to see that new action flick with Denzel Washington. Mmmph. Personally, I'm not interested. I mean, really. But a girl's gotta do what a girl's gotta do to compromise, especially since I had to beg him to go see a chick flick with me last month, which I absolutely loved. And even though he tried to front and say the movie was "a'ight," I could tell he enjoyed it, too. Anywaaayz, tonight's his turn to pick whatever movie he wants to see, so I'm going to sit back and make the best of it. Besides, as long as we're spending time together I really don't care what we see.

I grab the books I need for my second-period AP English class, then shut my locker. If I wasn't destined to be a dancer, I would major in Literature or something 'cause I

actually enjoy it, especially Advanced Placement English—
well, thanks to Mr. Croix. He is the first teacher—shoot,
first man—I've ever met who gets excited just talking
about literature and his love of books. He's one of the
toughest English teachers here, and his classes are de-
manding. But it's because of him that I love going to class.
He challenges us to explore the world through literature
and to discover the themes in the books we read. He ex-
poses us to poets and authors I would never have heard of
if it weren't for his class. I mean, he really takes us back
through time. Mr. Croix makes us think. And I love it.

"Yo, wassup, Miyah?"

I glance over my shoulder and see Jarrell walking up
behind me with a grin on his face. I'm not even gonna lie
and say his dimpled chin isn't real sexy, 'cause it is. But,
uh, anywaayz... I suck my teeth. "What's up, Jarrell?" I say.
I don't bother stopping.

But that doesn't discourage him from catching up. I roll
my eyes up in my head as he walk-runs up beside me. Jarrell is such a clown, I swear. And you'd never know he is
one of the smartest dudes in our school.

"Nothing much. How you?"

"I'm good. But I'll be better once I get away from you."

He laughs. "Damn, girl, that's cold."

I shrug. "Then get a blanket."

"I love it when you talk dirty," he says, laughing.

"Whatever. What do you want?"

"I wanted to walk to class with you," he says, glancing at
the book in my hand. "That's all."

Jarrell is in the same English class with me. Actually
we've both had Mr. Croix for the last two years, *together*.
For some reason, I'm starting to think it's not a coinci-

dence. But he'd deny it if I asked him, and I can't prove it. So it is what it is.

I grunt. "Mmmph. Oookay, then...walk. Don't talk. Your voice is annoying."

"Yeah, right," he says, taking the book from my hand. "Did you have a hard time reading this?"

He's talking about *Invisible Man* by Ralph Ellison. The book deals with racist stereotypes. And in today's class we have to present on what we've read. We have to discuss the emerging themes. OMG, this book is so dang deep. It was written waaay back in 1950-something. And it's about this black man, living in a racist world, trying to define himself through the expectations and values of others around him. I am so glad I didn't grow up in them days.

Jarrell flips through the pages as we walk to class.

"Nope," I tell him. "I loved it."

"It figures you would," he says, handing the book back to me. "You love anything Mister Croix gives us to read."

"Yup. Did you finish it?"

"Yeah, sort of. After reading three hundred and fifty pages of it, I stopped reading and went straight to the epilogue."

I shake my head. "Cheater."

"Yo, that book was mad thick. Mister Croix knows he needs to be smacked for having us read that big ole thing."

I laugh. "Boy, you should have just kept reading. Another eighty-nine pages and you woulda been done."

"Nah, I'm good. I got the gist of it. Dude was all effed up in the game."

"Whatever."

"Eww," Zahara says the minute she rounds the corner and sees me walking with Jarrell.

"If it isn't the little Chia Pet," he says to her.

She ignores him. "Umm, excuse me, girl," she says, throwing her hand up in his face. "Why are you walking with *that* clown?" She motions her head in his direction.

"That clown? Hahaha. You real funny. Oh, and extra ugly. But I got your clown all right."

"Whatever. Beat it," she says, cutting in between the two of us. "Sooo, wassup, boo-thang? You chilling with your girls tonight? We're going to meet up at the Red Lobster on Twenty-Two."

"I can't. I'm going to the movies with Sincere tonight."

"Okay. What are you doing tomorrow?"

"I have dance at eleven, then I'm going over to Sincere's house to spend the day with him. Let's go out to the mall next Tuesday after school. I don't have anything going on that day."

"Daaaamn, dude got it like that?" Jarrell says. "He must really be beatin' that thang up."

"Ugh," Zahara and I say at the same time.

"Mmmph, it must be nice to be sooo busy," Zahara says sarcastically. "Well, since you can't seem to fit us in tonight, then I guess next week's cool."

"Damn, Zee, you sound jealous," Jarrell says, laughing.

"Jarrell, why don't you go find a bridge to jump off of," Zahara says. "It'd really make the world a better place."

"Yo, Zee. Has anyone ever told you that you smell like spoiled clam juice?"

"Womp, womp, womp...you fail," she says, giving him the finger. "Has anyone ever told *you* that you smell like the back of a garbage truck?"

I laugh.

"Nah, they haven't. But I heard your mom's breath smells like one," he shoots back.

"OMG," I say, laughing. "That's so wrong." And I know I shouldn't be laughing, but...OMG, and I can't believe I'm gonna say this. Now, don't get me wrong. Zahara's mom is really, really nice. But, um...the truth is, her breath *is* a bit raunchy. And she stays chomping on chewing gum tryna cover it up. Ohmygod, Zahara would be so pissed if she knew I even thought this.

I can tell by Zahara's face that she feels some kinda way about Jarrell going in on her mom's breath like that. She puts a hand up on her hip, then starts neck-rolling it. "I know you don't even want it with me with your little Vienna-sausage-having self."

"Yeah, right," he says, laughing. "Stop with the lies, girl. You know ain't nothing little about my sausage."

I gasp, slapping a hand up over my mouth. *Ohmygod. Let me find out Zahara's nasty behind done tried to pop Jarrell's top on the low. Mmmph, but after that comment she made at my house, I wouldn't be one bit surprised, either.*

"That's a lie!" she snaps. Then she starts cursing him out, calling him all kinds of low-down, dirty names. Zahara's mouth is real filthy when she gets it crunked.

"Yeah, yeah, yeah," Jarrell says, still laughing. "Don't front now."

Zahara glances at me real quick to see what my reaction is. I have none.

Now, let me tell you a little something-something. You can always tell when what someone says about someone else is a lie or not by how that person responds or reacts to it. If they start getting all loud and whatnot and acting a fool, then, umm…give 'em the side eye, 'cause it must be true.

And that's exactly why I'm cutting my eye over at my girl as she starts blacking on Jarrell. Girlfriend is really making a scene. But I'm not tryna get all caught up in what's fact or fiction when I know walking up into Mr. Croix's class late is a no-no. So I toss my hand up in the air. "I'm out," I say over my shoulder as I head to class. "I'll see you at lunch, Zee. Jarrell, you might wanna get to class," I warn. But he doesn't take heed. Instead, he's still going back and forth with Zahara. And the louder she gets, the more convinced I am that Jarrell's telling the truth.

I walk into class just as the bell rings. "Ah, Miss Nichols," Mr. Croix says before I can even get in my seat. "Without opening your book, why don't you tell us why the narrator in *Invisible Man* called himself 'Jack-the-Bear' in the prologue?"

"'Cause he was in a state of hibernation," I answer, setting my bag down on the floor next to me.

"Ah, yes…"

Jarrell comes in late and wrong, tryna slip into his seat way in the back of the classroom. But even with his back to the classroom as he writes up on the chalkboard *My hole is warm and full of light*, Mr. Croix knows Jarrell's late again. And today, he's not having it.

"You're late, Mister Mills."

"Well, what happened was, I was kidnapped by this crazy girl who looks like an orangutan," Jarrell says. "She had me pinned up against a locker. Man, I think she thought I was a banana, 'cause she was tryna eat me."

The whole class starts laughing. Well, everyone except for me. I roll my eyes, shaking my head. Mr. Croix turns to face the class.

"Okay, class, settle down. Mister Mills, now that you've escaped your orangutan adventure unscathed, how about you make your way up to the front of the class and tell us why the narrator in *Invisible Man* says his hole is 'warm and full of light.'"

"Now, hold up, Mister Croix," Jarrell says. "I'm not into none of that kinky stuff. I dig the ladies, feel me? I don't know why dude's hole is warm and tight. I don't get down like that."

The whole class roars with laughter.

And I'm getting pissed because I really want to discuss the book. I jump up from my seat and turn to face the class. "Will y'all shut up!" I snap. "And, Jarrell, stop being such a jerk and answer the damn question. Geesh! And then you wonder why your dumb behind can't keep a girl."

Everyone shuts up, looking at me like I've lost my mind. But no one says anything. Not even Jarrell. Mr. Croix clears his throat. "Um, Miss Nichols, please take your seat." I sit back down. "As much as I appreciate your enthusiasm, shouting in class is not acceptable. But thank you. And, Mister Mills, your inappropriate outburst has earned you two days' detention."

Jarrell groans and tries to apologize.

"The hole," I blurt out, "was the narrator's home."

"That is correct," Mr. Croix says, sitting on the edge of his desk.

Someone in the back says, "Teacher's pet." The class

starts laughing again. But I let that dumbness go over my head.

Mr. Croix folds his arms. "If I hear another outburst from anyone in that back row, you will all get detention. Do I make myself clear?"

"Yes, sir," they say, grumbling.

"Now, let's try this again. Mister Mills, come up here"—he points to an empty chair next to me—"and take a seat."

I suck my teeth. Mr. Croix ignores me. He waits for Jarrell to shuffle himself up to the front of the class, then plop into the seat.

"Great," Mr. Croix continues. "Now I want you to tell us why the narrator says his hole is warm and...not *tight*. But *full* of *light*. And let me warn you, young man"—he narrows his eyes at Jarrell—"if you dare say anything other than what pertains to this book, I will fail you for the marking period. Do you understand?"

Jarrell nods, sitting back in his seat with his arms folded tight across his chest. "Yeah, I got you." Mr. Croix gives him another stern look. "I mean, yes."

"Good," Mr. Croix says. "Now tell me, Mister Mills. Why does the narrator introduce himself as an 'invisible man'?"

Jarrell sucks his teeth. "I thought you wanted me to tell you why his hole was warm." The class laughs again. Mr. Croix eyes him. "Okay, okay...my bad. He considers himself invisible because of the unwillingness of others to notice him as a black man."

Mr. Croix nods. "*Now*, Mister Mills, you can tell us all about the narrator's hole."

Everyone laughs, including me.

6

I wake up real early Monday, feeling refreshed and all excited to get to school because that means that I only have two more days until I go down to Motor Vehicles to get my license. But no sooner do I step into the kitchen, humming a happy tune, than the Wicked Witch comes swooping down on her broomstick.

"Okay, young lady. The party dust has settled and now it's time for us to discuss your behavior. I hope you didn't think I was just talking when I said you were going to be grounded for how you spoke to me Saturday night."

One minute I'm in the refrigerator—minding my business, trying to decide what I want to eat, and the next minute I hear her annoying voice. I don't even acknowledge her. I keep fishing around in the refrigerator, ignoring her until I find something to eat. I grab a bottled water, an apple, and a peach yogurt, then shut the fridge door.

I walk past her as if she's invisible. Wash my apple, grab

a spoon from out of the drawer, then pull out a stool and sit at the counter.

"Do you hear me talking to you?"

I glance at my watch and sigh. I have another fifteen minutes before Sincere picks me up to drop me off at school. And I gotta sit here and deal with this crap. She's standing in front of me with both hands up on her hips, shooting me daggers.

"You don't want to talk, fine. I'll do the talking. Your father might have bought you that car, but during the school week you will not be allowed to drive it."

OMG, I could effen die—right here, right now! This witch is playing real dirty. And in a few minutes it's about to go down. She knows driving my car to school is the one thing I've been looking forward to. And now she's found a way to snatch that from me. She's straight up evil!

I inhale.

Exhale.

Keep my mouth shut.

She continues, "I've had it with your mouth and blatant disrespect. And for the next week you're grounded. I really should make it two weeks. But I know you'll open your mouth to say something to give me reason to add another week. In the meantime, there'll be no hanging out after dance practices. And the days you don't have dance, you are to come straight home. Do you understand?"

I finish my yogurt, then bite down into my apple. I narrow my eyes to thin slits. Inside I am on fire!

When Erika was living at home, she and the Witch used to get into fights all the time. Difference is, Erika would actually hit her. At least I make her invisible and ignore her stank butt.

I finish up my apple, deciding I've heard enough of her monologue. I walk out of the kitchen.

"Girl, don't you walk out on me when I'm still talking to you. Get back here."

Well, too bad! I'm done listening. I keep walking. Like I *said*, I want my license. And I know if I don't keep walking, I'ma make it snap, crackle, and pop up in here today, so it's best that I keep on stepping.

"Now you just earned yourself another week onto that punishment."

Whatever! I grab my things and walk out the door toward Sincere's truck. I open the door and get in. He kisses me, then drives off. And I smile. I'm happy to see my boo. And I'm happier to be getting out of that house and away from her.

Later that night, I'm lying across my bed, skimming through an article on 50 Cent in *Vibe*. I'm not really checking for him like that so I don't give his interview much attention, and all of the words start running together. *Borrring!* I toss the magazine over onto the floor, reaching for my cell over on the other side of my bed. I scroll through my history until I find the number I'm looking for, then call.

"Hey, baby," Sincere says the minute he answers. I smile, touching the chain he bought me. Hearing his voice makes me all tingly inside.

"How you?" he asks.

"I'm good. What you up to?"

"Chillin-chillin'. Thinking about you."

Mmmhmm, you better be! "Awww, that's so sweet." I

reach over and click off my lamp, propping two pillows up against my headboard, then lean back.

"You're sweet," he says in almost a whisper. "You wanna go to a movie tomorrow night?"

I sigh. "I can't. I'm back on punishment."

"What?" he asks in disbelief. "You just got off. What happened now?"

"She's pissed that my dad bought me a BMW instead of some used Nissan. She stays pissed about something."

"Damn. I was hoping to take you to the movies tomorrow night, then get something to eat."

"Well, maybe this weekend we can do something." Usually if I'm on punishment and the Witch isn't around, Daddy will let me go out for a few hours on the weekends that I am staying at his house, so hopefully this weekend she'll be too busy flying around on her broomstick to bother coming over.

"Yeah, true. I wanna see you."

I smile, glancing over at the digital clock on my nightstand. It's almost ten o'clock. "I wanna see you, too," I say, sighing. "Maybe tomorrow we can meet after school for a bit before I have to go to dance."

"Yeah, that's cool, too. But I really wanted to see you tonight, too."

"*Tonight?*" I ask, jumping out of my bed, racing into my bathroom. I flick on the light switch and stare at my reflection in the mirror. My hair is all over my head. I have on a pair of raggedy Hampton University sweats and a ripped, bleach-spotted T-shirt with DIVAS RULE written on the front that should probably be dumped in the trash. *OMG, I look a hot mess!*

"Yeah, tonight. I've been thinking about you all day, baby."

I grin. Erika's voice pops in my head. *Mmmph. The key to getting a guy to fall for you is to get all up in his head. Once you have him constantly thinking about you, you'll have him sweating you twenty-four-seven, wanting to be with you and only you.*

"Oh yeah? And whatchu been thinking about?"

"Tasting them pretty lips."

Whew, and I wanna taste yours, too.

"But I don't want you to get in any more trouble, so I'll wait until—"

"*Not*," I say, cutting him off. "Wrong answer. I'm grown."

He laughs. "Yeah, okay. And your grown butt's back on lockdown."

"Whatever. What time you tryna come through?"

"You sure? I don't want your mom to flip."

"Oh, puhleeeze. Let me worry about that. Now answer the question."

"What question?"

I sigh. "Don't play stupid, boy. What time you coming?"

"Like right now."

"Okay," I say, racing around my room tryna find something cute to wear. "But I can't be out too long."

He laughs. "Yeah, I know. 'Cause you on punishment, but you grown." He keeps laughing.

I suck my teeth. "Whatever. Laugh all you want."

"Nah, my bad, baby. You make me laugh, that's all. I'ma see you in like twenty minutes, a'ight?"

"Okay. But don't park in the driveway. Park up in front of the bushes so the Wicked Witch can't see your truck."

He starts laughing again. "A'ight, I got you, baby."

Fifteen minutes later, I am in a sexy pair of low-rider jeans and a cute, long-sleeve black Gucci tee my sister, Erika, bought me a few months ago, getting ready to sneak outside. I grab my jean jacket and walk out of my bedroom, making sure to leave my stereo playing on low, shutting the door. I walk down the long hall to my parents'—uh, my mother's—master suite. Her bedroom door is open, but she's locked in her private sanctuary, luxuriating in her personal spa. I can hear Sade playing. I glance down at my watch. She should probably be in there for at least forty minutes. Enough time for me to chill with my man. I go downstairs, then slip out the sliding glass door.

So here I am. Standing out in my backyard with Sincere, kissing. He has his hands on my waist, kinda grinding into me. And I like how it has me feeling.

"Damn, girl, you feel good. You have a nice, tight body."

I look up at him, smiling. "It's from years of dancing," I tell him, stepping out of his grasp. I've been dancing ballet since I was two. I live and breathe it.

"Is that what you wanna be, a dancer?" he asks, reaching for my hand as we walk along the stone walkway toward the gazebo that's situated way in the back of our huge yard—out of the Wicked Witch's view.

I nod, sitting on the swing. Sincere sits beside me, draping his arm around the back of the swing. "That's all I dream about," I tell him, looking at him. *And you!* His eyes take me in. I know without a doubt that he is feeling me. *OMG, I am so dang crazy about this boy.* He strokes the side of my face, causing a wave of heat to rush through me. I take a deep breath and slowly blow it out, trying to steady my racing heartbeat. *Keep it fly, girl. Don't go gassin' his head up. Not until you have him wrapped around your finger.* I tell him of my plans to apply to The Juilliard School and the combined Bachelor of Fine Arts program between The Ailey School and Fordham University, where students can train professionally in dance while earning a degree in liberal arts. Although I have so much love for The Ailey School and have attended their summer intensive program three years in a row, I am really hoping to get into Juilliard. That's where my heart is set on going. I have everything completed except my essay and recommendation letters.

Sincere smiles at me. "Wow, that's big. Your parents must be really proud of you."

I shrug. "I guess. I mean, I know my dad is."

"What about your moms?"

I roll my eyes. "Oh, please. She thinks ballet should be a hobby. Not something I major in, or wanna pursue as a career. She'd rather see me going to med or law school, like my sister, rather than pursuing my dream." I feel myself getting pissed. She's such a damn hater!

"I feel you."

"Do you really?"

He nods. "Yeah, I do...." He pauses. I reach over and take his hand, waiting for him to finish. "Sometimes I feel like I'm living my parents' lives instead of my own. So I definitely feel you."

"Wow. I feel like that with my mother. She's always tryna shape me into a mini-her."

"Yeah, but at least you have your pops, who supports your dream to be a dancer."

I smile, knowing Daddy always has my back. "True. What about you. Do you dream about playing in the NBA?"

"Yeah, all the time, but…" His voice trails off as if he's in deep thought.

"But what?" I ask, gazing at him.

"Growing up, all I've ever heard is 'you're going to be a basketball star.'"

"And you are," I say. "You're mad talented, Sincere. I can definitely see you playing in the NBA, making lots and lots of money."

"Thanks." Although he's smiling at me, he doesn't sound happy. He squeezes my hand.

"But it's not what you want. Is it?"

He slowly shakes his head. "Nah. Not really. I mean, I dig playin' ball. It's just that I wasn't ever given a chance to do anything else. My dad put a ball in my hand when I was like three or four, and I've been on the court ever since. Don't get me wrong. If I'm able to play in the NBA, I will. I ain't no fool, feel me?"

I laugh. "You better not be. Shoot, I want me some front row seats."

He laughs. "Is that all you want?"

I only smile. He doesn't need to know the answer. Not now, anyway. I can't front. I feel sooo connected to this boy. It's like my heartbeat leaps up in my chest and gets stuck in my throat when I am with him. He's the first guy who I feel like I can actually be myself around.

"Do you love it?" I ask, changing the subject.

"Love what?"

"Basketball."

"Nah; not really. But don't tell my father that. He'll snap for real."

"Don't worry," I say, leaning over and kissing him on the cheek. "Your secret's safe with me."

"It better be," he says, laughing.

"Whatever. If you could do something other than play ball, what would it be?"

"Damn, no one's ever asked me that. Truthfully, if it were up to me, I'd run track."

I give him a surprised look. "Oh, for real?"

"Yeah. I'm big on track and field."

"Well, it's never too late. You can still do it."

"Yo, my dad ain't havin' that. He'd snap my neck for real. Besides, I have too much time invested in basketball to give up on it now."

"Then do both."

"Nah, I'm good. What about you? Do you ever think about what you'd do if you couldn't dance?"

I look at him like he's crazy. I am a gifted dancer. Doing anything other than dance is not an option for me. Oh nooo. If I have my way, Kamiyah Nichols will be touring the world, making a name for herself in the dance world. "Ballet runs deep in my veins. It's a part of me. I can't imagine my life without it." *Or you!*

"That's wassup. I bet you're mad sexy when you dance."

"Well, uh," I say, popping my imaginary collar, "what can I say. It's hard being me."

He laughs. "Ya man's gonna have to come check you out one of these days."

"Oh, you my man now?"

He wraps his arm around me, pulls me into him real tight. "Yo, stop. You already know what it is."

"Yeah, I do," I say, looking up at him. He smiles at me, then leans in and kisses me on the lips. His hand slowly moves up my thigh, over my stomach, inching its way up toward the front of my shirt to my . . . I grab it before it gets to its final destination. I'm crazy about this boy. But I'm not crazy enough to let him feel me up in my backyard. Not yet, that is. I glance over toward the house, then down at my watch. *Ohmygod, I've been outside talking to Sincere for over an hour. I gotta get back in the house.*

"Yo, I better get up outta here," Sincere says, reading my thoughts. He stands up and stretches. "I have an eight o'clock class and the professor is real strict about not being late."

"Yeah," I say, standing up as well. "I better get inside before the warden puts out an APB on me."

We kiss a few more times, then I walk him to his truck. I wait until he pulls off, then head back up the driveway toward the back of the house. I go to slide open the door, and...it's locked! *Great! Now I'm really gonna hear her mouth.*

I start to panic 'cause the last thing I wanna do is have to ring the doorbell and deal with the Witch's mouth. She'll make a big production out of it, turning it into more than what it really is, then I'll have to turn it up on her. I smile, remembering that I have one of my bedroom windows unlocked. I walk around to our glass-to-ceiling atrium, climb up the drain pipe onto the roof, then pull up my side window and slip back into my room. I take off my clothes, put on a nightshirt, then crawl into bed with sweet, sexy thoughts of Sincere.

7

When I come down into the kitchen, I am surprised to see Daddy sitting at the table eating breakfast. *He musta come through in the middle of the night or early this morning to get his groove on*, I think, wrapping my arms around the back of him, then kissing the side of his face. "Good morning, Daddy."

"Hey, baby girl."

"I'm surprised to see you," I say, easing away from him.

"Your mother invited me over for breakfast," he says, grinning.

"Oh, that's special," I say sarcastically.

The Wicked Witch eyes me with a raised brow. *Grrrreat! She's in another one of her stank moods; just what I need today.* I force a smile, glancing over at her. "Good morning," I mumble toward her, for Daddy's sake, that is.

She purses her lips, burning a hole through me with her glare. Then cuts right to the chase. "Did you sneak out of this house last night?" she asks, sneering.

I'm shocked that she's sitting here tryna play me in front of Daddy like this. I stand here, blinking at her.

"Well?"

"Did you see me sneak out?" I ask indignantly.

"Girl, don't play with me. That's not what I asked you."

I suck my teeth. Look over at Daddy. He has his elbows perched up on the table with his hands clasped and his chin resting on his thumbs, waiting, watching to see how things unfold. "Answer your mother," he calmly says.

I look from her to him. Then back at her.

I plant my hand on my hip. "No, I didn't sneak out. I walked out the back door."

"*After* I told you that you were grounded," she snaps, clenching her teeth.

"Is that true?" Daddy asks, eyeing me.

"No, it's not. She told me I couldn't go anywhere. And I didn't. I was outside, talking to Sincere."

"Outside where?" Daddy asks.

"In the backyard."

"And I told you no company," Mom states.

"No, you didn't. You said I was grounded from going out. That was it. So don't sit there and try to change it up in front of Daddy. You always do that."

She grits her teeth. "Kamiyah, I am getting really sick of you and that smart mouth of yours. I'm really trying to understand why you keep testing me."

I grit my teeth back at her. "I'm *not* testing you. I'm *checking* you; big difference. You asked me if I snuck out of the house. And I told you NO!"

"Miyah," Daddy warns, pointing at me. "What did I tell you about talking to your mother like that?"

"Erik, don't tell her nothing. Now she's grounded for another week."

"For what now?!" I scream at her.

She bangs her hand down on the table. "For being a damn brat!" she yells back, jumping up from her seat. She plants both hands on her hips. "And for being too grown. Now keep it up, and you'll be grounded for the rest of the month."

I roll my eyes, sucking my teeth. "Whatever," I snap, turning to walk out of the kitchen.

"Don't you whatever me, young lady!" she yells.

"Kamiyah, get back in here," Daddy says, raising his voice. Something he hardly ever does, especially at *me*! "Don't walk out on your mother when she's talking to you." I keep walking. "Kamiyah, do you hear me talking to you?" I stand by the bottom of the stairs, pretending like I'm already upstairs.

"I don't know what's gotten into her," I hear Daddy saying. "Kamiyah," he calls out again. I ignore him. "Let me go up and have a talk with her."

"Erik, forget it. Leave her be. But I tell you what. She can go ahead and get her license, but she's not driving that car anywhere. I don't care if I have to block it in with mine. She can catch the bus or walk to school for the rest of the month. I'm done with her nasty attitude. And she's not going to be on that computer, either. And I'm suspending her phone service."

Say *what*? No car, no phone *and* no computer! For a whole month? She can't be serious. I am going to die! I storm back into the kitchen. "You're taking my phone *and* my car? Why?"

"I've had enough of your piss-poor attitude," the Witch

states, gloating. She's clearly happy that she's finally getting what she wants. To keep me miserable like her!

"Daaaaaddy," I whine. "Will you *please* talk to her? She's being ridiculous."

He shakes his head. It's clear to me he will not go against her. He shifts his eyes from me. "You heard what your mother said. No car and *no* Internet. But you can keep your computer and your phone."

What the hell good is my computer without the Internet! I scream in my head.

"Erik..."

"You can't take everything away from her all at once, Kayla. She keeps the phone."

The Witch's jaw gets real tight. "Fine," she says, glaring at him. She's really pissed now. "I won't shut it off, this time. But the next time she sneaks up out of this house, it will be. And I don't care what you say."

"There won't be a next time," Daddy says, shooting a look at me. "Will there?"

"But I didn't sneak out of the house," I whine. "She"—I point at her—"never said I couldn't go outside."

"Oh, Kamiyah, please," she grunts. "But since I didn't make myself clear the first time, let me do so now. You are to be in this house. You are not allowed any company. And you are to come straight home from school." She's smirking. "No exceptions."

"What about dance?"

"You can still go to practice. Either your mother or I will take you and pick you up," Daddy tells me. He gets up from his seat, clearing his dishes from the table and setting them in the sink. "Now I'm going to leave the two of you to finish fighting this out. I've got to get to work.

Hopefully, the two of you won't kill each other in the process." He walks over and kisses *her* on the lips, then walks over to me. I feel like I'm gonna vomit! He gives me a hug, whispering in my ear, "Please, stop giving your mother such a hard time. Do what she says and I'll buy you something nice." He kisses me on the forehead.

As soon as the door closes behind him, I go back up to my bedroom and grab my phone off of my dresser to call Sincere to wish him good luck on his test this morning. He doesn't answer, so I leave a message.

"Oh, Kamiyah," Ms. White says, stopping me before I can walk out of her class. Ms. White teaches French and has been my teacher for the last three years. I turn to face her. "I don't want to keep you from your next class, but..."

"It's okay," I say, swinging my bag up over my shoulder. "It's only gym. And you know how much I looove gym." I roll my eyes up in my head, all dramatic and whatnot.

"Well, good," she says with a chuckle. "I'm wondering why I haven't gotten your application and permission slip back yet for the trip to France this spring. I think it'll be a wonderful experience for you; especially since we both know how badly you want to tour one day with a European dance troupe. And being that you're a senior, it'll look great on your application to Juilliard."

I smile knowingly. Every year the French club sponsors an all-expense-paid trip to France for ten days in April. Although it's mostly for members of the French club, they also have slots for seniors with the highest GPAs. She'd given me the application the first week of school, but the truth is, I misplaced it and honestly forgot about the trip.

Another truth is that I haven't even started the essay part of my application to Juilliard for next fall. And I really, really, really wanna get in. But it's so dang competitive. Juilliard only accepts twenty-four applicants a year: twelve males and twelve females. And the competition is *fierce*. The possibility of not getting in is too much to think about. I blink the thought from my head.

"When's the deadline?" I ask.

"In three weeks," she says as she writes me a pass. "We really need to have all the applications in before we go on Thanksgiving recess."

"Okay. I'll discuss it with my…dad and get him to sign the papers." She smiles, handing me my pass. I turn to leave, but quickly turn back.

"Missus White, I've been meaning to ask you. About Juilliard…"

She looks at me, wide-eyed. "Yes, what about Juilliard?"

"Would you be willing to write a letter of recommendation?"

She smiles. "I'd be honored. And I would have been very disappointed if you hadn't asked me. When's it needed by?"

"I have to have everything submitted by December first."

"Consider it done." I smile back, thanking her. *Whew… one down, one more to go*, I think, walking out of the classroom.

"Heeeeey, boo-thang," I hear in back of me as I make my way down the hall. It's Zahara. I stop and wait for her to catch up with me.

"Hey, Miss Thang-a-lang."

"Girl, where you been? We waited for you this morning."

"I was with Sincere," I tell her as we walk down to the first floor.

"Mmmhmm...so how is Mister Sexy Chocolate?"

I smile. "Good. No, actually...great. Girl, I can't get enough of him."

She throws her hand up over her mouth as if she's shocked. "*Nooooo,* not you. Since when?"

I suck my teeth. "Whatever, heifer."

"Listen, Miyah...about the other night at your house. I hope you know I was only playing when I said that stuff about Sincere. I would never disrespect you or our friendship like that."

"What stuff?" I ask, playing dumb. But, trust. I know exactly what Miss Messy is talking about. But I wanna hear her say it.

"You know that stuff I said about you passing Sincere over to me if you didn't want him."

"Oh, that? Boo, please. I forgot all about that." *Lies!*

Erika and her girls used to always say, *If one of your girls says or does something suspect, keep your eyes on her. But never, ever let her know you're watching her. You want her to think all is forgotten, so when she slips... you're right there to stomp her lights out.* Well, umm, they didn't say that last part. That's my stuff.

She loops her arm through mine. "Good. Do you have dance practice today?"

"No."

"You wanna go to the mall after school?"

I sigh. "I can't. I'm on lockdown."

She shakes her head. "Oh, gaaawd. Drama with ya

mama, again? The school year just started and you already in trouble. A mess."

"Yeah, a real hot one at that," I state, rolling my eyes.

"You two stay beefing."

"What else is new? It's her. She's a nut."

She laughs. "Uh-huh. So what'd you do or say *this time*?"

I stop in my tracks, putting my hand up on my hip. "Excuse you. I didn't do or say anything. I just checked her real quick and she caught feelings."

"Oh, okay. So basically you were being too grown."

I huff. "Whatever. I don't even wanna talk about it. That Witch is ridiculous."

She laughs. "You crack me up calling her that."

I shrug. "Well, that's what she is. Besides, it beats calling her a bit—"

"Don't you young ladies have someplace you're supposed to be?" Mr. Donaldson, one of the creative writing teachers, asks.

"Yeah," we both say. Zahara rolls her eyes up in her head, then mumbles under her breath. "He makes me sick with his ole crooked-tooth self."

I snicker.

"I heard that, young lady," he says, following behind us.

Zahara glances over her shoulder. "Well, at least I was nice enough to not say it to your face."

"Well, guess what? I'm nice enough to tell you to *yours* that you now have two days' detention."

Zahara stops in her tracks. "For what?"

"For being disrespectful," he says, looking at her like she shoulda already known the reason why. "You're a senior now, and we expect much more from our upperclass-men."

"Awww, c'mon, Mister D. You know I was only playing. Besides, I didn't even say it to you, so how can that be disrespectful?"

"Well, you said it about me and I heard it."

Zahara flips her hand up at him. "Mister D...*boom!* I'm not serving no detention for that mess. What I said is true. You *do* have an ole raggedy mouth. But I didn't say it to your face."

"Well, young lady. Now you just did—two days' detention."

"I'm entitled to my opinion. And I have freedom of speech."

"And now you have detention along with that opinion and your freedom of speech. Would you like to make it three?"

"Whatever."

He tells her to go to the principal's office, and she really goes off. I stay out of it, though. Shoot. I have my own problems to deal with. I keep walking. "Zee, I'll see you later, girl."

When I finally get to gym—which, by the way, should be banned or optional, if you ask me. I mean, really? Anywaaayz...everyone is already changed into their gym gear, on mats, stretching. I walk over and hand Mr. Bailey my hall pass. He glances at the time on the pass, then looks up at the clock. "Must have been a lot of traffic in the halls," he says, all smart-alecky and whatnot. "Hurry up and get dressed."

I walk off, rolling my eyes. He's all mad 'n' miserable 'cause his wife left him last week—well, that's what the gossip is around here. None of the students are supposed to know this. But nosy-behind Zahara overheard the secretary whispering it into the phone to someone while she was up in the principal's office last week. And now his lonely butt wants to take it out on me. *Loser!*

At the start of seventh period I find myself walking into the guidance counselors' office to see my counselor, Mrs. Saunders. She's one of the coolest counselors in the whole department. And she can dress her butt off, which is probably one of the reasons why I like her. I walk down the hallway past the bulletin board covered with information on colleges, scholarships, and work opportunities. I never stop to read what's up there because I already know where I wanna be—at Juilliard. *But what is your backup plan?* Mrs. Saunders always asks me each time she sees me. *What if by some chance you don't get into Juilliard? Then what?*

I always give her a crazy look, because for me, not getting in isn't an option. At least I hope it doesn't become one. *You need to have a backup plan, Kamiyah*, I hear her saying.

Uh, no. I need to get into Juilliard!

I lightly tap on her door. "Hi, Missus Saunders."

She looks up from her computer screen. "Oh, hello, Kamiyah," she says, smiling as she waves me in. "I was wondering when I was going to see you. C'mon in and have a seat. So how are your classes going so far?"

She clicks a few keys on the computer.

"They're going good," I say, taking a seat in front of her. "Calc might be a challenge, but other than that, everything else is a breeze."

She smiles. "Well, I'm sure you're up for the challenge,

Kamiyah. You're one of our brightest and most talented students. I am confident you'll master your calculus class with no problems, as you've done with everything else you set your mind to. So, how's dance?"

"It's going great. I was working at a dance studio over the summer, teaching a beginner's ballet class. And they've asked me to continue on, so I'll be teaching a class twice a week."

She nods approvingly. "Sounds very exciting."

"It really is. I really enjoy working with the little kids. They are so adorable. And it reminds me of when I was their age." Mrs. Saunders rests her elbows up on her desk, clasping her hands, taking in everything I say. No matter what it is, she always shows an interest in everything her students have to share.

"What age will you be teaching?"

"They're between the ages of three and five," I say, smiling.

"It'll be a great experience for you."

I nod, agreeing. "Yes, it will be."

"Have you started your application process to Juilliard yet?"

"No, not yet," I say, shifting in my seat. "I still have a few months before the deadline." I share with her the essay choices that are a part of the application process. There are three to choose from. The first choice is to describe the most challenging obstacle I've had to overcome, discuss its impact, and tell them what I've learned from it. *My biggest challenge? Hmmm, let's see…oh yeah. Living with a mother who wears a haterade pack on her back!* The second choice is about being a missionary for the arts.

I have to explain how as an artist I intend to advocate for relevancy of the arts in the twenty-first century. *Boooorrrring!* I'm definitely not going to write my essay on that one. Then the last choice is using one of the three words—*commitment*, *education*, or *dedication*—as the title of my essay, then writing about what that particular word means to me. *I'm committed to my man, and to dance!*

"Do you have any idea which one you'll choose?"

"Either the first, or the last one. I'm still undecided."

She smiles. "Meditate and pray on it. The answer will come."

I stand up before she goes into one of her long-winded sermons on faith and patience and believing our divine purposes. Blah, blah, blah...I love Mrs. Saunders to death, but I am not interested in hearing this right now. "I definitely will," I say, shifting my handbag from one arm to the other. "I'll stop back by one day next week to talk more."

She stands as well, walking around her desk. "Great. C'mon, I'll walk out with you." She shuts her door and walks me out into the hallway. Now I'm standing here tryna figure out which way she's headed so that I can go in the opposite direction. "Listen, Kamiyah," she says, touching my arm. "I've known you since your freshman year. I've watched you evolve into this beautiful young woman, talented and graceful. There are a lot of people who look up to you, who admire you, and who are expecting great things from you. Whatever you do, don't allow anything or *anyone* to distract you from your greater purpose. You understand?"

I nod. "Yes, I think I do."

"Don't think. Know." And with that said, she makes a quick right, making it easy for me to not have to ditch her. I watch as she walks down the hall, her heels clicking with each step until she disappears.

8

At exactly 2:45 P.M., I get a text from Daddy as I'm leaving my locker stating he's out front waiting for me. I could effen scream! Being picked up by your parent during your senior year is soooo not cute. Besides, I'd already texted Sincere and asked him to pick me up. And he's on his way. I quickly text Daddy back and tell him okay, then call Sincere.

"Wassup, baby? I'm on my way. I'm like ten minutes away," he says quickly.

"Well, that's why I'm calling. My dad's already out front, waiting. So you don't have to bother about tryna get here."

"Damn," he says, sounding disappointed. "I wanted to see you."

"Me too."

"You need to try to be nicer to your mom so you can hurry up and get off punishment."

I let out a disgusted sigh. "Don't hold your breath. You'd pass out first before that ever happened. That woman—"

"Hey, boo, where you off to?"

I look back over my shoulder. It's Ameerah.

"Home," I tell her, waiting for her to catch up to me. I tell Sincere to hold on. "My dad's outside waiting for me."

"Oh, that sucks."

"Tell me about it."

"I know you on the phone with your boo-thang, so tell ya man I said hey."

"Yo, Meerah, when you gonna stop fronting and let me take you out?" Jacob Langley asks, walking up on us. He's a senior, too. And track sensation. He was also one of Ameerah's Boos-of-the-Month—well, two months—last year. "It's a new school year, and I'm tryna make some new memories, ma."

"Whatever. I'm not beat. You had your chance."

"Wassup, Miyah?"

I give him a head nod and a wave, then tell Ameerah to call me later.

"I got you," she says as I walk off. The last thing I hear her say before I walk out the door is, "Jacob, sorry to bust your bubble. But you are last year's news, boo."

The door shuts before I can hear what he says. "Sorry about that," I say to Sincere, walking toward my dad's car.

"Nah, you good. I'ma hit you up later, a'ight?"

"Oh, what, you wanna go run off and do something else?"

"Nah, I'm saying. I know you getting ready to get in the whip with your dad; that's all."

I suck my teeth. "Whatever, Sincere. Go do you."

"Oh, so now you gotta attitude?"

I open the passenger-side door, getting in. "Nope," I lie. But the truth is, I do have an attitude and feel myself getting annoyed. Because once again, it sounds as if he's texting someone on his phone as he's talking to me, something he's done a few times in the past. And he knows how I hate that. It's rude! Just like I don't like it when he's all up on Facebook reading wall posts when he's supposed to be on the phone talking to me. Like really, who does that? "Look, call me later if you're not too wrapped up in *something* or *someone* else." I disconnect before he can respond. "Hi, Daddy," I say, leaning over and kissing him on the cheek.

"Hey," he says, waiting for me to put my seat belt on, then pulling off. "How's my girl doing?"

"Good."

"I spoke to your mother this morning," he says, glancing over at me. *Ohhkay, here we go!* I'm not surprised, though. She's always running off tryna rat someone out.

"She told me she's put you on punishment."

"And it's so not fair, Daddy. I mean, really. I didn't do anything to her."

He makes a right onto South Orange Avenue, sighing. "Kamiyah, all I'm going to tell you is you need to learn how to pick and choose your battles wisely."

"But, I *was* picking my battles. You said yourself that's what I should be doing. I was ignoring her so I wouldn't say anything disrespectful to her. So in actuality I *was* being respectful."

"Kamiyah, c'mon. Stop this already. You know like I do,

every time you and your mother get into a disagreement and things don't go your way, you give her the cold-shoulder treatment."

"Well, she does it to *me*."

"It still doesn't make it right."

I force myself not to roll my eyes at him. "She even does it to *you*."

"And that still doesn't make it right," he repeats, making a left onto JFK Parkway. Although I have an idea where we're headed, I decide to ask anyway.

"We're not going home?"

"No. We're stopping at the mall. Maybe an incentive will help motivate you."

I giggle. "Shopping always motivates me, Daddy."

"Yeah, well let's hope it also inspires you enough to go home and apologize to your mother."

"Fine," I say, turning my head and looking out the window. Okay, why I always gotta be the one to apologize to her is ridiculous. So what if she's the parent. It still doesn't make it right—or her right—all the time. Sometimes she's dead wrong, like now. Putting me on punishment for two weeks when I didn't really do anything. I reluctantly nod my head, looking back at him. "I'll apologize to her."

"Good. But you're not taking these things with you to your mother's house. You keep 'em in your room at mine until things smooth over between you and her. Deal?"

"Okay, deal."

"Good. Now, tell me. How was your day?"

I gladly give him the rundown, relieved to be changing the subject. "Oh, and the French club is having their annual trip to Paris during the spring break, but the permission slips have to be in soon. Do you think I'll be able to go? It's mostly for the French club, but they also extend it to honor students as well."

He takes his eyes off the road, glancing over at me. "I don't see why not. Let me talk it over with your mother first."

"Ohmygod, Daddy, do you really have to ask her?"

"Yes, I do. She's your mother. And a trip to France is a major thing. She needs to be okay with you going, too."

I sigh. "Oh well. There goes that dream," I say sarcastically. "She's gonna say no. And you know it."

He sighs, eyeing me. "Why can't you try being a little nicer and a whole lot more respectful to your mother, instead of always trying to go against her? The two of you always fighting isn't good. I can't understand it."

I poke my lips out. "Daddy, it's her," I whine. "But you don't want to believe it. Even you couldn't stand living with her."

He shoots me a look, then looks back at the road. He knows what I've said is true, even if he won't admit it. He forgets I used to hear how they would argue. Well, I don't know if you can really call it arguing, since most of the time she was the one doing all the talking.

"Listen," he says, slicing into my thoughts. "Regardless of my reasoning why I decided to move out, your mother and I still love each other very much. And we both love you. Don't ever forget that."

I cross my arms tightly over my chest. "Well, I know *you* love me." *But there is no love lost between me and the Witch. She hates me just as much as I hate her.* Of course I keep this to myself. Daddy will only side with her anyway, so what's the point. He cuts his eyes over at me, shaking his head. "Okay, well...maybe she does love me..." *But I still think she hates me more.*

Daddy merges onto Route 24 going east. We drive a few minutes with just the radio playing. The silence is probably doing us both some good. Daddy's probably over there wondering what he's going to do with me and his wife. Okay, okay, my mom...geesh!

Anywaaayz, the silence allows me to think about Sincere. I wonder if he's thinking about me. And wonder what he's doing at this very moment. And I'm wondering how many birds been clucking up in his face today. And how many feathers I'ma be plucking from the cluckers if I catch 'em.

I hear Erika and her girls in my head saying, *Boys are real stupid when it comes to girls and cheating. All you have to do is sit back, watch, and wait. If he's doing something he's not supposed to be doing, you'll catch him. And when you do, you beat down that ho he's doing it with real good, then you make him pay.*

My head starts pounding and my heart races just thinking about it. I pull out my cell and quickly text, WHAT U DOIN?

This punishment, this not being able to be with Sincere, is killing me. I hate not being able to keep track of what he's doing. This not knowing is torture. I replay in my head something else I overheard one of Erika's friends saying. *Hon, love is a double-edged sword. You gotta know how to stick 'n' move, and know which end to swing first! Or end up slicing off more than you can handle.* When I first heard that, I was like twelve years old and didn't understand what the heck she was talking about. But now I think I do. Still, I ask Daddy, to see what he's gonna say about it. These are the times I love most—when it's only the two of us.

He looks at me as if he's tryna figure out where the question is coming from. He turns into the mall entrance, then up into the parking garage. "Basically, the expression means love can either bring you joy or pain. And the ones we hold the closest to our hearts are the ones who can cause us the most pain. Now all that other stuff about sticking and moving and knowing which end of the sword to swing first is all new to me; never quite heard it put like that."

"Do you think it's possible to love *and* hate someone at the same time?" I ask, looking directly at him as he pulls into a parking space.

He puts the car in park, then stares at me. His brows furrow. "Why you ask?"

I dare not tell him that sometimes I lie awake at night thinking about Sincere and all the things I want to do with him. And all the things I'd do to him if I ever found out he was creeping on me with another chick, or if he tried to leave me. I've never felt like this before. And I don't understand where it's all coming from. But what I do know is, Kamiyah Nichols is in L-O-V-E. And I'm not about to let anyone take that away from me. So the idea of someone tryna come between us, or him even *thinking* about being with someone else, makes me want to hate him, too. I know—crazy, right? Especially since he hasn't done one thing for me to feel this way; still...I have this gut-wrenching feeling that something is gonna pop off and

I'm gonna have to turn it up. I swear I don't wanna take it to anyone's head. But I promise you I will, if anyone tries to get in between me and my man.

I shrug. "I was just wondering. That's all."

"I don't like the word *hate*. It takes a lot of energy to hate someone. And that kind of energy can destroy you. But there's definitely a thin line between the two. You can love someone yet hate some of their ways. But I don't believe you can equally hate and love someone. You either love the core of who someone is, or you hate them. These are both very intense emotions that can cloud judgment and have us doing and saying things we never would have if we were thinking clearly."

"Have you ever *hated* Mom?" I ask, watching his body language.

He doesn't flinch, blink, or shift. He looks me straight in the eye. "Never."

"Hmm," I say thoughtfully, remembering an argument I overheard them having once, but I don't wanna get into it. "But you don't like her, do you?"

He opens his car door, ignoring the question. "C'mon, let's go in."

I laugh, getting out of the car. "Fine. You don't have to answer that...." *'Cause I don't like her, either.* "But it's still not fair."

He sets the alarm, then walks over and wraps his arm around me. "What's not fair?"

"First you moved out, then Erika moved out. And now I'm stuck there with her, alone. I wish I could move in with you. My life would be so much better."

He kisses me on the side of the head. "You're right where you're supposed to be."

"Well, right now I sure am—with *you* at the mall."

He laughs. "Yeah, good answer. Let's go spend my money. And remember. When I drop you off home tonight, you're to apologize to your mother, understand?"

I roll my eyes up in my head on the sly, smiling sweetly. "Yes, Daddy."

9

"I'm sorry," I say, leaning up against the frame of her bathroom door. It's taken me three hours and forty-seven minutes from the time Daddy dropped me off to finally get around to making nice with her. Well, trying to, that is. The idea of apologizing to her is torturous. But my motivation to hop up on the Witch's broom is for four reasons: One, I wanna drive my new car to school. Two, I wanna get out of this hellhole. Three, I need to see my boo. And four, Brittani sent me a text telling me her sister's boo-thang's frat is having a Halloween party next month and she invited us to go. And you know I am not tryna miss a party. Although I still have six weeks to go before the party pops off, one, two, and three are most critical. So a girl's gotta do some damage control. Well, at least try to. Kissing up to my mother has never been one of my favorite things to do.

She's sitting at her marble vanity removing her makeup

with Neutrogena face wipes. She stops what she's doing and looks at me in the wall mirror.

"What are you sorry about?" she asks, shifting her body so that she can look at me.

I shrug. "Everything, I guess."

She raises her brow. "You guess? So basically what you're saying is, you don't really know what you're apologizing for, do you?"

"I—"

"Well, obviously not," she states, cutting me off. I hate when she does that. "'Cause if you did, you wouldn't be coming in here with this 'I guess' mess." She stares me down. "Kamiyah, your mouth and your attitude are really getting out of control. I don't know what has gotten into you. You're starting to act just like your sister did when she was living at home."

I huff. "Oh, puhleeeeze, Mom. I am nothing like how Erika was. And you know it."

"Well, you're damn near close to it," she snaps. "First I had to deal with the disrespect with Erika, and now you're trying to do the same thing. But I have news for you, young lady. I am not going to put up with it."

"Maybe if you'd try to loosen up and stop being so nit-picky all the time, we'd get along better."

She blinks. "Wait a minute. Who do you think you're talking to? See, this is what I'm talking about, Kamiyah. Here you go again, trying to give it to me. No. *We'd* get along better if you learned your place in this house, young lady. I'm the adult. You're the child. End of discussion."

I try not to roll my eyes, or suck my teeth, or put my hands up on my hips. But it's reeeeeeal hard not to. I fold my arms across my chest. "Mom, I'm not tryna be rude. But why is it if I speak my mind it's me being too grown or too disrespectful? But it's okay for you to say whatever you want? You act like you don't want me to have a mind of my own, or be able to say what I feel. I feel like you want me to be a puppet you can dangle on a string."

"Kamiyah, it's not what you say. It's how you say it. I want you to be able to express yourself. But what I want you to understand is that there are some things that are not up for debate, period. And I definitely don't want you thinking you can speak to me like I'm one of your little friends. You and I aren't girls. And you don't get to make the rules around here."

I grunt. "Well, how long are you going to keep me locked in this house?"

She takes a deep breath. "For as long as I want," she snaps, turning back toward the mirror. She starts smearing cream all over her face.

Witch!

But I don't crank it up. I spin on the balls of my feet and walk off to my room, mindful not to slam my bedroom door or throw anything. I turn on my stereo, slip in my Adele *19* CD, then flop across my bed. I log into Facebook and read the news feeds, then click onto Sincere's page. "Crazy For You" starts playing as I read his wall posts. He has a picture of me and him together as his profile pic, but his status still reads *single*. Strike one! I click on a post he was tagged on by "Sexy Latina Bombshell."

It's a picture of this Spanish-looking chick with wavy hair, blowing a kiss. *Wait, I've seen this chick somewhere before,* I think, staring at the screen real hard, trying to remember where. *Where the hell do I know her from?* I'm not gonna hate on her and say she's busted 'cause truth is, she's serving it. But the big bad heifer has no dang business tagging my man with a picture of her blowing kisses, whether they're to him or not. I click on her profile, then click on PHOTOS. Then I spend the next hour going through all two hundred and seventy-two pictures—happy chick was dumb enough to keep her photos public—until I figure out she's the same rude chick that was all up on Sincere the night I first met him. *Oh, so this is the ho who pulled him away from me.* She has about fifteen pictures of Sincere; some with her in them, and others with him alone or with other people—mostly dudes.

I'm not really too pressed, since most of the pictures were taken last year and over the summer—before *me*. Still, I want her off Sincere's page. I click back on his page and start reading some of his older posts and see all this thirstiness going on with a buncha birds sweating him.

One of these pigeons posted: HORNY.COM! SEND ME SOMETHING GOOD TO LOOK AT OR CALL ME SO WE CAN LISTEN TO EACH OTHER MOAN.

I frown.

Another post reads: HEY SEXY. WISH I HAD YOU FOR MY BOO. I'D SHOW YOU SOME NEW TRICKS I LEARNED OVER THE SUMMER. AND YES, IT'S THAT GOOD!

Thirty-seven people liked this mess, including Sincere.

Another post reads: WHO WANTS TO SEE ME SWALLOW A BANANA? HMU IF YOU WANNA CHECK MY SKILLZ. IF I LIKE WHAT I HEAR I MIGHT SWALLOW SOMETHING ELSE. LBVS.

Ewww! My first thought is to call Sincere up and scream on him, but then I remember something Erika and her girls used to say: *Never, ever let someone know you're checking up on 'em, 'cause then they'll only cover their tracks. Monitor in silence, store your facts, then give 'em enough rope to hang themselves.*

I open up another browser on my computer, then type into the search engine. When I find the site I want, I click on the link, browse their items, then add what I want to my cart and use Daddy's credit card—the one he gave me to use for emergencies *only*. Well, this *is* an emergency. I use Zahara's address as my shipping address, then make my purchase. There's no way I can have my package delivered here without my mother's nosy butt opening it up, then asking me a ton of questions. Oh no... not gonna happen.

I close out the screen, then reach for my phone and text Zahara to let her know to be on the lookout for a package for me that will be delivered in three to five days to her house.

She texts back: WHAT KINDA PACKAGE?

Me: IT'S A GIFT 4 MY DAD. Okay, that's a lie. But she doesn't need to know that!

Zee: THN Y U SENDIN IT HERE?

Me: I DON'T WANNA CHANCE HIM BEIN HERE WHEN IT COMES

Zee: K

Me: TTYL

Zee: KOOL

I close out the text screen and my phone starts ringing before I can make a call. I smile. It's Sincere. "Hello."

"Hey. Whatchu doin'?"

"Thinking about you," I say, clicking through his Facebook photos. *Mmmph, thinking about you is all I do.* "I was just getting ready to call you."

"Aaaah, that's wassup. What were you thinking about?"

Well, let's see. Who you're with when I'm not around? Why you didn't call me sooner? Who's all up in your face when I'm not around? Why the hell you got all these birds up on your wall, poking and tagging you? And the list goes on and on!

"Us," I tell him, clicking back on Ho's page. *Stay away from my man!* I log off. "Are you messing with anyone else?"

Way to go, dumbo! You never ask a boy if he's messing around on you when you know all he's gonna do is lie to you.

"Nah. It's all you, baby."

Uh, duh...you knew he was gonna say that.

"Are you sure?"

"Of course I am. Why would you ask something like that?"

I shrug as if he can see me through the phone. "Just making sure."

"Are *you* messing with someone else?" he asks.

I suck my teeth. "Ugh! *Illll*, no. That's nasty."

He laughs. "A'ight, that's what I wanna hear."

"Sincere..." I pause. Listen to the way he lightly breathes into the phone.

"Wassup?"

"Are you happy with me?"

"Hell yeah, baby. I'm not interested in anyone else."

"You better not be," I say, smiling.

"I got you, baby. Yo, who's that singing in the background?"

"Adele."

"Oh, word? She's dope. What song is that?"

" 'Make You Feel My Love,' " I tell him.

"Oh, a'ight. That's wassup. Is that what you're trying to do to me?"

"What?" I ask, reaching over on my nightstand and grabbing the picture of him I have in a glass picture frame. He's wearing a pair of basketball shorts and a tank top, holding a basketball. I roll over on my back and kiss his face, pretending he's here in the flesh. "Make you feel my love?"

"Yeah."

"Oh, what, you don't already feel it?"

He lowers his voice. "Yeah, I feel it."

"Sincere..."

"Yeah, baby," he says. "Wassup?"

"Don't ever leave me."

"I'm not, Miyah."

"Promise?"

"I promise you, baby. I'm not going anywhere."

And for the rest of the night, we listen to each other breathe and whisper sweet nothings into the phone until I fall asleep with the phone still pressed against my ear.

10

Daddy picks me up bright and early and takes me down to the motor vehicle department to get my license, then drops me off at school with a note. I am cheesing real hard right now. Finally, I am an official card-carrying licensed driver!

"Did you apologize to your mother like I asked you to?" he asks, pulling up in front of school.

I give him a frustrated look, shaking my head. "Daddy, I tried. But she wasn't hearing it. I think she's really gonna try to keep me a prisoner for the rest of my life. You have to talk to her for me."

"Try again," he says, eyeing me. "I don't want to be in the middle of this with you and your mother. She felt disrespected and you need to fix it."

"But, Daddy," I whine. "She disrespects me."

"She's your mother."

"I know. But still..."

"There's no *but*," he says, glancing at the digital clock in the dashboard. "Look, I have to get to the office for a meeting. We'll talk about this later. Okay?" Both of my parents are college-educated professionals. Daddy works in the city on Wall Street as a commodities broker. And the Witch is a high-powered litigation attorney for one of the most prestigious law firms in the country. Her law firm has offices in New York, Denver, and Los Angeles which is why she travels a lot.

I nod as the music in the car stops and his phone rings. We both glance at the number that flashes up. *Speaking of the Wicked Witch*, I think, opening the door. "Okay."

"Hey," he says, answering the call.

I hear her ask, "Did she get her license?" as I shut the door. I wave at him. He waves back and I watch as he drives off, shaking his head at something she's said, I'm sure.

I walk into the attendance office and sign in. Mrs. Bergen gives me a hall pass. It's already the middle of third period and I think it really makes no sense going to class, so I decide to go to the library instead, until the fourth-period bell rings. I quickly change my mind and head to my locker so I can get my AP Lit book. I open the door and glance at my reflection in the mirror. *Boo, you just too fly*, I think, digging in my bag and pulling out a comb.

"Mirror, mirror on the wall…who is the flyest chick of 'em all?" Ameerah says, walking up on me.

"Definitely not you," I say, smirking.

She laughs. "Whatever, pumpkin head. Are you just getting here?"

"Yeah."

"*Well?*" she huffs, putting a hand up on her hip.

"Well, what?"

"Uh, hellooooo...license, today."

"Oh, that." I laugh, fishing inside my bag for my wallet. "*Bam*," I say excitedly, flashing my brand-new ID.

"Heeeey, that's what I'm talking about. I can't wait to get mine. Two more months and counting."

"Uh-huh." I pull out a little pot of MAC gloss and dab some on my lips.

"Let me get some of that," she says, sticking her finger in, then gliding some on her lips as well. She smacks them together for effect. "Anywaaayz, boo. You need to hurry up and get off punishment already. This makes no sense, three whole days of cruel and unusual punishment. It's heart wrenching. We miss you, boo."

"Tell me about it."

"Well, I don't care if you have to beg, borrow, or steal. You need to get back in your mom's good graces, like yesterday. You know Brittani's birthday is on the first, which is next Saturday. Then at the end of the month is the Halloween party. And you know we are gonna get our trick and treat on, okay?! So you need to act like you know."

"I know, I know. I'm working on it. But, ohmygod, that woman is so difficult. I tried apologizing to her last night and she just straight played me to the left. I'm so over her right now."

She grunts. "Mmmph. Well, you better get over it. And make nice—*quick!*"

I start combing my hair out. "I will."

"Shoot. What you need to do is learn to keep your trap shut."

The bell rings and kids start pouring out of their classes, flooding the hallway.

"Ohmygod, my future baby fahver is too fine for his own good," Ameerah says, looking over my shoulder as she's standing at my locker waiting for me to finish combing out my wrap. I already know without looking who she's talking about. Joe-Joe. He's a senior and our indoor and outdoor state and regional track star in the 400- and 100-meter sprints. He also runs cross-country to stay conditioned. The boy is crazy fast.

"Heeeeey, Joe-Joe," Ameerah says, waving at him as he walks up to us.

I roll my eyes up in my head.

He steps into our space with his long-legged self, grinning. "Hey, Meerah. Wassup, Kamiyah?"

"Hey," I say back.

"Are you still gonna wait for me after practice?" he asks Ameerah. I try to act like I'm too wrapped up in making sure my do is good to be all up in their convo. He's cute. Okay, okay, he is fine and he has a banging body. But in my head I'm picturing her playing all up in his curly hair and popping them nasty zits with her fingernails. Ugh!

"Of course I am. You already know."

"A'ight, cool. I gotta get to class, but I'll talk to you later, a'ight?"

"I'll be waiting," she says, sounding real extra with it. He says good-bye to the both of us, then dips.

"Oh God, he's so fine."

I suck my teeth. "Girl, get a grip."

She scrunches her nose up at me. "And what is that

supposed to mean?" She places her hand up on her hip, waiting for my response.

I take out the books I need for my last three periods, then shut my locker. "Uh, it means you are sounding real thirsty right now. Okay, you dig the dude, but geesh, you don't have to be so desperate with it."

She puts her hand up in my face. "Screeech! Oh, puh-leeze, look who's talking. Miss All-up-on-Facebook-and-I-can't-stop-looking-at-my-phone-and-answering-on-the-first-ring."

Wait, who told her that? How she know I stay up on his Facebook page? I frown. "Wrong answer, boo. I'm not sweating Sincere like that. You got it confused. That's what you do, sweetie."

She rolls her eyes. "Lies. But, okay. If that's what you believe. Truth is, you're worse than me, boo. Admit it."

I laugh, flicking my hand at her. "Whatever."

"Exactly. It's time for—"

I dig in my bag when I feel my phone vibrating. She stops in midsentence when she sees me pulling it out. It's a text from Sincere. HEY BABY. WAS THINKN BOUT U ☺

She clears her throat. "So...who's looking thirsty now?"

"Whatever, trick," I say, stopping to text Sincere back. THINKN BOUT U 2.

"Um, are you gonna grace us with your presence at lunch today or spend it texting Sincere?"

"Girl, hush. I'm—"

I read Sincere's text. B GLAD WHEN U OFF PUNISHMENT

Ameerah walks off, shaking her head. "I'm out. You know where to find us."

"Hold up. I'm coming," I say, texting him back. I CAN'T
WAIT EITHER. WHAT U DOIN?

Sincere: GETTN READY TO WALK IN2 CLASS. LOVE U

Me: K. TTYL. IM GOIN 2 LUNCH NOW. LOVE U 2

Sincere: ☺

My man loves me! I toss my phone back into my bag,
slinging my book bag up on my shoulder, smiling as I
walk-run to catch up with Ameerah.

11

Ohhhkay...will someone please explain to me the purpose of homeroom? I mean, really. It's dumb.com for real. The only saving grace is that Mr. Langston—everyone calls him Mister L, though—who is also my advanced calculus teacher, is finger-licking fine and nice to look at. Other than that, homeroom is a waste of time. Well...my time, that is. I glance up at the clock as the announcements are being read over the intercom. I yawn.

Whew...talking to Sincere last night, then seeing him, really made me feel...um, mmmph, good! No, great! No, wait. Better than great! Phenomenal—yeah, that's it. Whew, my man knows he can kiss. His sweet lips and warm, strong hands were all over me last night. And I was all over him. I just hope he doesn't start tripping. Not a good look if he does. No, Sincere definitely better not even think it.

So, anywaaayz...guess what? This morning, the Wicked Witch told me that she has to travel for work for the next three days, some kinda conference, and won't be back until late Sunday night. So, guess where I'll be staying? With Daddy! And you know what that means? There is a merciful, Kamiyah-loving God after all! Oh yes...this morning I was jumping for joy. Then she said, "I'm taking you off punishment. Not because I think you've earned it. But since I know your father's not going to adhere to it, there's no sense in keeping you on it."

I ran up and almost knocked her down, giving her a big hug and a kiss. Although it was all phony and whatnot, I was too dang excited to care. I couldn't believe my change of luck!

"So does that mean I can drive my car to school, too?" I asked, holding my breath.

"For now you can. Your father's driving it over here now, then taking my car to drive me to the airport."

"Yes!" I shouted, pumping my fist in the air.

But, of course—like she always does—she had to toss something real slick in the mix 'cause she's real *special* like that. "Enjoy yourself while you can, because we both know you'll do or say something to get you right back on punishment."

I kinda gave her a blank stare. But I didn't go in on her. Shoot, I'm not even thinking about her. I finally drove my car to school today. I get to hang out with my girls. And, most importantly, spend time with my man. So all that ying-yang she was popping this morning went over my head.

Anywaaayz, I didn't sneak back into the house until almost one o'clock in the morning. Then I woke up mad late because I didn't hear my alarm. And I didn't have time to charge my phone. So now it's dead! And there's absolutely no way I'm gonna go all day without being able to text my man, or talk to him during lunch. I dig through my bag to make sure I didn't forget to bring my charger with me. I pull out my phone, then quickly drop it back in my bag when Mr. Langston shoots me a look.

"Uh, Miss Nichols, is that a cell phone I see in your hand?"

"Of course not, Mister L," I tell him, all sweet and what-not. "You know I wouldn't do you like that."

He chuckles. "I hope not. I'd hate to be the one to give you detention."

"It's probably her little rabbit you saw," a voice in the back of the class says.

"Yeah, you noticed she spends a lot of time in the bath-room," another voice says.

That gets the goofballs in the back laughing. Without looking, I know it's nobody but Jarrell and his whack side-kick Calvin, popping junk. Jarrell—with his thick waves and sexy dimples—has a thing for me, so he'll do or say al-most anything to try to get my attention, since I usually make him invisible. Thing is, I used to really, really, reeeeeally like him in my sophomore year. And I kinda still do, but...mmmph. No, thank you! We dated for like three days, then it was lights-out. The show was over. Kissing him made my stomach turn. It was like sticking my lips into a dishwasher with all that spit he had going on. Yuck! Fine or not, if you can't kiss, you get dissed.

Anywaaayz...maybe he's stepped up his lip game. After all, that was two years ago. But I won't know. I roll my eyes up in my head, deciding to not even entertain their dumbness.

"All right, Misters Mills and Russell," Mister L warns, eyeing both of them, "another outburst like that and—"

Fortunately for the two of them, the bell for first period rings, cutting Mister L off. Everyone scatters out of homeroom like a bunch of roaches. Mr. Langston calls me over to his desk as I'm gathering my things, then asks me if I'd be interested in being a math tutor.

I tilt my head. "Mister L, I thought only members of the math club were tutors."

He smiles. "They are. But being that you're one of my brightest students…"

"With one of the highest GPAs in the school, don't forget," I add, grinning.

"Right, right," he says, chuckling. "How could I forget?"

I shrug. "I'll forgive you this time since you happen to be one of my favorite teachers." *And you're so dang fine*, I think, staring into his dark brown eyes. I bet when he was in school he had all the girls.

"So what do you say?"

"Huh? What do I say about what?"

He repeats the question.

"Oh, that. Can I think about it for a few days and get back to you? Between both of my dance classes and keeping up with my studies, my schedule is really hectic."

He glances at his watch. "Okay. I understand. Well, think about it."

"I will." The bell for first period rings as he's pulling out a pad and writing out a pass for me. I take the pass and tell him I'll see him fifth period. I shoulder my bag and head for the door, deciding to cut my first period—something I've never done—to go to the library to charge my phone instead. I'm a senior and this is an emergency, so missing class isn't the end of the world.

The rest of the school day flies by. I chill with my girls in fourth period lunch—although I spend most of it texting back and forth with Sincere—and go to classes. But most of the day I keep thinking about Sincere, wondering what he's doing and who he's doing it with. I know he has mad chicks all up in his face over there on that campus. I just hope he's checking them birds, letting them know what's really good. Not being able to see what he's doing is going to drive me crazy. I pull out my phone and send him a text. U THINKIN BOUT ME?

Two minutes later, he texts back. LIKE CRAZY. U ALREADY KNO. CAN'T WAIT TO TTYL

ME 2 ☺

I slip my phone back into my bag as I approach my locker. I open it, then glance at myself in the mirror I have attached to the back of the door. I pull out my lip gloss to shine my lips. I'm meeting Ameerah and Zahara so we can watch the boys' gymnastic team practice and pop ish, like we normally do. I pull all of my books out of my book bag and place them in my locker, almost forgetting I have a French test tomorrow. Not that I won't ace it without my book, since I have all of my notes. Still, it's better to be safe than sorry. I kneel down to get the book from the bottom of my locker when I hear, "Aye, yo, why you always playin' me?"

I look up and it's Jarrell staring down at me with his arm propped up on the door of my locker. "Excuse *you*?" I say with 'tude, glancing up at him.

"Yo, you heard me. Why you be playin' me?"

At six feet, he towers over me and I feel like a dwarf, looking up at him. I stand up. At least now I don't feel so short. "Little boy, ain't nobody playing you."

"Little boy?" he asks, looking around. "Where you see a little boy at?"

I place a hand on my hip. "I'm looking at him."

He smirks, folding his arms. "Nah, you got the wrong one. I ain't that dude. Ain't *nothing* little about me, ma. Believe that. And if you stopped frontin' you'd already know that."

"You had your chance, boo. Sophomore year, or did you forget?"

"Yo, that didn't count. Give me another chance. I've grown since then."

I roll my eyes, sucking my teeth. "Whatever. That's not what I heard. So moving on."

He laughs. "Oh, you got jokes, right?"

I tilt my head. "Like you did this morning?"

"Nah, you know I was only messin' around."

"Mmmph...too bad I'm not," I say, slamming my locker shut.

He looks at me all serious and whatnot. "Yo, for real though. What's good wit' you?"

"Nothing. I'm chilling. Why?"

"I'm saying...when we gonna kick it? You know, chill."

I blink. "*We* aren't gonna do anything. But you can go kick rocks if you'd like."

"Damn, girl. Why you gotta be so hard on a brotha?"

"Because you act real silly and immature. And if you think I'm gonna waste my time with some *little* boy. Not."

"See. There you go with that little boy talk again."

I laugh. "Jarrell, boo...close ya eyes and picture this..."

"Picture what? You and me?"

"Close your eyes and I'll show you."

"What is it?"

"A surprise."

He eyes me doubtfully. I keep my gaze locked on his. "A'ight, yo, don't play me, Miyah."

I step up into his space, lower my voice as I'm looking up at him. I bat my lashes. "I'm not playing, Jarrell. You said you want me to give you another chance, right?"

He rubs the hairs on his chin, grinning. "No doubt."

"Then close your eyes."

"A'ight, yo." He closes them.

I stroke the side of his face, then run my fingertip over his soft lips. "And don't open them until I say so."

He smiles. "A'ight, yo...what you got good for me?"

"This," I say, stepping off, clicking my heels and popping my hips down the hall.

"Aye, yo," he yells in back of me. "That's real effed up, yo."

I laugh, throwing my hand up in the air at him. "Whatever!" I snap, not looking back.

Just as I'm turning the corner to head toward the gym, I see Zahara heading my way. She stops in the middle of the hall, puts a finger up. "Pause, boo!" she yells down to me. I stop. She looks around and I do the same, then we both straighten our backs, throw one hand high up on our hips, then Naomi Campbell–it toward each other. We high-step it, and spin. Catwalk it up, then start cracking up.

"Girl, you stoopid."

"Whatever," she says, flicking her hair. "Don't hate 'cause my runway strut was fiyah. And yours was...*boop-boop*...tired."

"Oh, puhleeeze. You saw how I was bringin' it." I snap my fingers and dip to the side. "*Bam!* You couldn't stand the heat."

We laugh, locking arms and walking down the hall.

Zahara says, "I'm surprised your mom is letting you hang out."

"Oh, the warden has temporarily set me free. She's out of town for the rest of the week. So I'm free, Miss Sophie."

She shakes her head. "And you suuuuuure is ugly," she says, cracking up with that line from *The Color Purple*.

"Whatever," I say, laughing with her.

"Annnywaaaay...girl, where the heck you been? Ameerah sent you a text. You were supposed to meet us ten minutes ago."

I tell her I didn't get it. That it must have come through while I was at my locker messing with Jarrell.

She stops. "Jarrell? Ohmygod, what he want now?"

We start walking again.

"What else. He came over to my locker asking me why I keep playing him. I'm like, little boy...*boom!* Ain't nobody playing your dusty butt."

She laughs. "Miyah, that boy's big on you *and* he's fine."

I laugh with her. "I know, right? But, oops...been there, done that!"

"Next," we both say, snapping our fingers.

When we get to the gym, Ameerah and Brittani are already posted up on the top bleacher, scanning the boys

and the bodies. "Heeeeeey," they call out, waving as Zahara and I climb up to where they're sitting. We sit in the
bleachers in front of them.

"Mmmph, look at all them hard-bodied boys," Zahara
says, leaning into my ear as I pull out my cell, "in them
sexy little jumpers."

"Girl, I'm not thinking about these hounds," I say, reading a text from Sincere. He wants to know what time I'm
gonna be home. I text him back and tell him I'll be home
by eight.

Y SO LATE?

I HAVE DANCE

O. I FORGOT. WAT U DOIN NOW?

CHILLIN' WIT' MY GIRLS

"Ohh, no...pause, boo," Zahara starts up. "I know you
not gonna sit up here with your girls, texting ya man. That
is so not cute, okay?"

"And it's rude," Ameerah adds, sucking her teeth.

"Okay, okay...chill. Just let me text him this one last
thing, then I'm done."

Zahara pops her lips. "Mmmhmmm. Make it quick."

I text Sincere and tell him that I'm going to call him on
my way to the dance studio, then toss my phone back into
my bag. "Happy?" I ask sarcastically.

"Very," she says, rubbing my back. "You have all night to
talk and text ya boo-thang. Right now, this is our time. So
act like you know."

I give her the finger. And for the next forty minutes we
start clowning so hard, until the coach yells at us and tells
us we gotta bounce. I hang around the school with my
girls for another thirty minutes or so, until it's time for me

to go. We all walk out together, making plans to hang out at the mall on Thursday after school.

Ameerah and Zahara catch a ride with Brittani and her sister, Briana. I watch as they all pile up in her Volvo. They wait for me to get into my car, then drive off when I pull out of my parking space. I press the phone icon on the steering wheel to call Sincere.

"Wassup, baby?" he says the minute he answers. His sexy voice fills the inside of my car and warms me.

I smile. "You."

"Oh, word? That's wassup. How was your day?"

"It was good," I say, making a right onto South Orange Avenue. "But hearing your voice has made it a whole lot better. And seeing you last night brought me good luck."

"Oh, word. How?"

"I'm off punishment."

"It's about time," he says, sounding hyped. "What changed your mom's mind?"

I laugh. "She had to go out of town on business and she knew my dad would let me do whatever I wanted while she was gone. But, trust me. I could tell she didn't want to take me off."

"Well, I'm glad she did."

I can tell he's smiling. "I wanna see you tonight."

"I wanna see you, too. What time do you have to be in the house?"

"Ten o'clock, 'cause it's a school night." I think about trying to sneak out in the middle of the night, but dismiss the idea 'cause a) it wouldn't be cool, and b) Daddy sleeps with both eyes open, so sneaking out is definitely a no-no. "He might let me stay out a half hour later if I ask."

"A'ight, so how 'bout you come through on your way home from dance? My parents are out until late tonight, so I have the whole house to myself for a few hours."

My smile widens. "I can't wait. I'll see you then."

"I'll be here waiting."

"You better be," I say, pulling into the parking lot of the dance studio. We talk a few minutes more, then disconnect.

12

Dressed in white tights and a pink leotard, I slip in my Adele *19* CD, and press track twelve. I take my position. Arms extended, wrists arched over my head. Feet in fifth position, I wait. The intro to "Hometown Glory" starts playing and I begin. Dancing *en pointe*—on my toes—has become my life for the last four years. Something most ballerinas aspire to.

Instinctively, I breathe in the music, going into full *pointe*, then *battement*—a fluttering movement of the foot—then half *pointe*. I allow myself to float along with the music. Everything in me comes alive. *Plié, plié, pirouette*, then into a double *pirouette*.

And another double turn.

And another.

I am floating. Twirling and bending, fluttering like a butterfly, feeling free. In ballet, I am not Daddy's little princess. I am not my mother's enemy. I am grown and sexy. Graceful and sophisticated. I am a ballerina. I close my eyes, whipping into another double turn. My steps are light. *Pointe*, leap, balance. There's something so beautiful in the way Adele sings this song. *Piqué* turns *en dedans, pas de bourrée*. Each leap is faster than the one before. I jump and turn, leaping into another perfect *plié* in *arabesque*—balancing on the supporting leg, extending the free leg behind. I go into full *pointe*, then half, stopping in a *penché*. My leg extended behind me. Head and neck lifted.

The music stops.

And then it is over.

Miss Johvonna claps. Her smile is wide; she's clearly pleased with my solo. She's been my ballet master since I was twelve. Classically trained, she danced professionally overseas for ten years before returning to the States and opening her own studio, then starting her own production company. She has no children and no husband because she chose to marry ballet.

"That was beautiful," she says, smiling. "You are as swift as a gazelle and as graceful as a swan. But you must remember, Kamiyah. There are no small details in ballet. If you wish to be the best, you must do the best. In your steps, in each movement, you must tell a story from your heart. You must pull from your soul. Be as cunning as a kitten and as sly as a fox. Never let them see you coming. Be swift. Be sharp. Be precise. Do you understand?"

I nod. "Yes."

"Good. You rest now."

I curtsy, then zip past the staring eyes of the others. Jealous hoes, hating on *me*. Pulling a white towel out of my oversize bag, I pat my face, the back of my neck, then the center of my chest. I sit on the mat with my back against the wall, and remove my *pointe* shoes. I am exhausted and exhilarated. My feet ache.

Miss Johvonna claps her hands twice. The rest of the dancers come to life. She instructs them to take their spots at the barre, in first position. And then she begins snapping out combinations. Making them all start from the top when everyone's form isn't to her liking. Miss Johvonna demands nothing but the best out of her students. And she demands that her students want nothing but the best from themselves. She pushes you, and expects you to push back beyond your limits.

I pull out my cell and text Sincere, smiling. CAN U MASSAGE MY FEET 4 ME?

It takes him ten minutes and thirty-two seconds to finally text me back. I know because I watched and waited to see how long it would take him.

LOL, K I GUESS...WHEN U COMIN?

NOW

K ☺

I quickly gather my things, jump in the shower, change, then quietly slip out into the night air, with thoughts of Sincere racing through my head. As I get into my car, I wonder why it took him so long to text me back.

Girl, you know how these boys do. Sneaky dogs!

But Sincere's different.

He's still a boy. And boys can't always be trusted around other girls.

My cell rings, disrupting my thoughts. It's Erika. I answer, pressing the phone icon on the steering wheel. "Hey."

"Hey, you," she says. "How's that new car riding?"

I smile, stopping at a light. "Like a dream come true. I love it."

"I heard you were on punishment for a few days. I know that must have been a bummer."

I sigh. "Ugh, don't remind me. Who told you?"

"Daddy mentioned it the other day when I was talking to him."

"Yeah, the Wick—" I catch myself from calling her by her nickname. "Mom really tried to do me in. But it didn't last long. She took me off before she could really torture me."

She laughs. "She must be out of town."

"Yup."

"I remember those days all too well. Some things never change, I see."

I sigh. "Oh, trust me. It's worse. *She's* worse. I can't wait to get away from her."

Erika keeps laughing. "Girl, Mom can't be that bad."

"Mmmph. You're no longer living with her. You have no idea. She nuts up over every little thing. She's always looking for a fight about something. I can't stand it."

"If I survived, so can you. And I was the child from hell."

I laugh. "Yeah, true. Still…"

"Listen, Mom means well."

I huff. "Yeah, right. The only thing she means to do is ruin my life every chance she gets."

She's still laughing. "Well, hey. Look on the bright side. You have one more year to go, then you'll be off to school."

"Yes! Thank you, Jesus! And I can finally be away from her, even if it is only across the river."

"Speaking of which," she says, "how's school going?"

I make a left onto South Orange Avenue. "Good. You know I'm doing well in my honor classes."

"That's because I have a very smart sister."

"And don't forget talented."

"That too."

"And fly," I add.

"And spoiled rotten."

I laugh with her. "Yeah, that too. How are things with you and Winston?"

"We're good. We've finally set a date, which is why I called you first."

"Ohmygod, for reeeal?" I say excitedly. Erika and Winston have been engaged like *forever*. "It's about time. Y'all were taking mad long."

She laughs. "It hasn't been that long. Only a year and some change."

"Well, that sounds like a long time to me."

"Yeah, I guess. Well, we both wanted to wait until we were almost done with law school before we actually set a date. But the plans have changed a bit."

"Oh, yeah? How?"

"Well...and don't you open your mouth to say anything."

"I won't."

"No. I mean it, Kamiyah. Not a word."

"Okay, okay. I said I won't say anything. I promise. Geesh. You act like I can't keep a secret."

"Oh, like you used to when I used to sneak in and out of the house?"

I laugh. "I only told on you when you stopped giving me money."

"It was blackmail."

"I was only eight," I say, making a left onto Grove Road.

"And you still had a big mouth," she says, laughing with me.

"Well, that was then. This is now. I'm older. And trust me. I *know* how to not say anything."

"I mean it, Kamiyah. Don't even tell your little girl-friends, either."

"Okay, I won't. Dang. Now will you tell me what it is, *please?*"

"I'm pregnant."

I scream. "Ohmygod! I'm gonna be an aunt. That's great! How many months are you?"

"I'm about six weeks," she says.

"Ohmygod. Congratulations."

"Thanks."

"So when's the wedding?"

"May nineteenth. And I want you to be my maid of honor."

"Oooh, I can't wait! When are you gonna tell Daddy and Mom?"

"We're going to make the announcement Thanksgiving Day. So you can't say anything."

"I already promised you I won't," I say, pulling up in front of Sincere's house. His parents' house is huge, like eight bedrooms, four bathrooms, and they have an in-ground swimming pool. "Ooooh, I know Daddy's gonna be real happy. He really likes Winston."

"I know he does," she says, sounding all proud and whatnot. Shoot, she should be. I'm proud for her. Like I told y'all before, Winston is one fine dish of hot, dark chocolate!

"What do you think Mom is gonna say?"

"Congratulations, I hope."

I laugh. "Ha! Good luck with that. You know she's probably gonna have a whole lot more than that to say. Oooh, I can't wait to see the expression on her face when you tell her you're pregnant. She's gonna pass out." *And I hope she bangs her head real hard on the way down.* "And you know she's gonna have a lot to say about you getting married, especially if she has to spend her money on it. Oh yeah, she's definitely gonna have something to say about all that."

This is great news! Hopefully she'll be too wrapped up in Erika getting pregnant instead of getting a job first, to be all up on me. She'll finally stay up off my back for a while so I can do me.

"You're probably right. Well, lucky for me, I won't have to be concerned about it. Winston and I are going to pay for our own wedding."

I frown. "Ohmygod, that's crazy. Why? After all she put you through growing up, that's the least she can do. I'm sorry. Take the money. Paying for your wedding is like retribution."

She laughs. "Kamiyah, girl. You're so damn silly. Winston and I decided to pay for our own wedding because it's our special day. And I don't want his mother or ours telling us what to do or how to do it."

"Oh, wait...that's a great idea. Shoot. What was I thinking? If Mom and Dad don't have to pay for your wedding, then that's more money for *me*."

"Oh, hold on, princess," she says, cracking up. "You're getting way ahead of yourself. I didn't say anything about not wanting to spend their money. I said I don't want them spending it on my wedding. I want that money for a down payment on a house. With the baby and all, we're going to need a bigger place."

"Oh dang," I say, sighing. "There goes my cha-ching, cha-ching. I was already pulling out the calculator in my head."

"Yeah, I bet you were."

"Well, let me put it away then."

"Yeah, you do that. And do *not* say anything to Daddy, Kamiyah. I know you won't say anything to Mom, since she's your least favorite person. But I know how you do with Daddy."

I suck my teeth. "Dang, Erika. How many times do I have to say it? I'm not gonna say anything."

"Good. Now enough about me. Are you still seeing that guy you were telling me about? What's his name, again?"

"Sincere. And *yes*. I'm still seeing him. Actually, we go together now."

"Dad says he seems like a nice guy."

"Erika, he really is. And he's so fine. Every time I'm with him he makes me feel stuff I've never felt with any other guy."

She laughs. "I know that feeling. Sounds like you're in love with him."

I confess. "Yes, I am. He's my whole world, Erika. I can't wait for you to meet him. I think you'll like him."

"I can't wait to meet him either. But your world shouldn't be all about him, Kamiyah." *Mmmph. Looks who's talking.* "You have school and dance to think about, too. He should be only a part of it."

Well, he's not! "I know, I know," I say, looking up at his bedroom window. It's dark throughout most of the house. The porch light comes on. "He's so different, Erika."

"I'm sure he is. Still…it's not healthy for anyone to get too wrapped up into another person. You don't need to make him your whole world."

Oh, like you did with Leon! Well, too late…he already is! "He's not." *Lies!* "But he is a very special part of it."

"And so he should be. Just don't allow him to become all of it. You have a promising future ahead of you, Kamiyah. I'd hate to see you throw it all away for what might feel like love."

"Erika, I'm not stupid," I say defensively.

"I'm not saying you are. All I'm saying is, be careful."

"I *am* careful. Very."

"That's all I ask. Are the two of you having sex?"

I tell her, "No. I'm still a virgin."

"Good," she says, sounding relieved. "Take it from someone who's been there, done that. When you're young, your emotions are all over the place and sex complicates things. Hell, it can get complicated for adults, too. I'm glad you're saving yourself for the right guy."

"Well, what if Sincere *is* the right guy?" I ask her, closing my eyes, remembering the way his hands felt on me, imagining what he'd look like naked.

"Then you need to *wait* for the right time."

"And when is that supposed to be?"

"When you've graduated high school, completed Juilliard, and have toured the world."

I laugh. "So basically, when I'm an old maid."

She laughs. "Well, not that long. But definitely long enough to accomplish what you want out of life."

"Why didn't you wait?" I ask, texting Sincere to let him know I am outside on the phone talking to my sister.

Although Erika is finishing up her law degree and is engaged to a really nice guy, she was fifteen when she lost her virginity, and had kept it a secret for almost a year until she thought she was pregnant. Luckily she wasn't. But Mom blacked on her and tried to keep her locked in the house, which is probably why they fought so much. Still, every chance she got she was sneaking out of the house to be with him.

"Girl, back then you couldn't tell me a thing. I thought I was grown. And I thought I was *in love*. I had already given Leon my heart. But when I didn't think that was enough to keep him, I gave him my body, too. I wanted him to have all of me. Problem is, that still wasn't enough. I thought having sex with him would prove to him how much I loved him. And I thought it would make him love me more. But all it did was make my life more difficult. It made letting him go harder. Everything about him was all wrong. And I knew it. But when I was in his arms, and whenever he touched me, he felt so good. Everything felt so right. And that's what kept me going back. Leon was everything to me."

Sincere texts back. K

Leon is the bum who used to beat up on her. She would lie to our parents about the bruises she'd have on her face. The ones on her body she could hide from them, but not from me. I saw those nasty black-and-blue marks. I would tell on her. But she would lie. Tell them she got hurt from cheerleading or from gymnastics. Erika was always making up excuses, always defending him. And my parents acted as if they believed her, up until the time he pushed her down the steps and she sprained her wrist and twisted her ankle. Then they realized—well, *Daddy* realized—that Leon was abusing her. They filed charges against him and everything. OMG, it was a mess! Erika was with him for almost three years before she was finally able to break away from him.

"Do you regret it?"

She sighs. "I don't regret what I felt for him. But I do regret not waiting. Once you give that part of you away, there's no taking it back. Once it's gone, it's gone for good. Sex sometimes clouds our judgment. I don't want you to make the same mistake I did."

Erika must really think I'm a member of dumbo.com or something. "I won't," I tell her, glancing at the time. *OMG, I can't believe we've been on the phone for almost thirty minutes. I need to hurry up and get off this phone so I can be with my man.*

"I don't want you to think I'm trying to tell you what to do, 'cause I'm not. I know you're going to do what you want, regardless. I just don't want to see you get hurt. That's all. You're still young, Kamiyah. I don't want you to ever have to go through what I went through with Leon. You know he was my whole life. I put him before anything and everything else, including myself."

"Erika, you don't have to worry. I'm not you. And Sincere is nothing like Leon."

"Let's hope not," she says as I'm getting out of my car. I set the alarm, rolling my eyes.

I walk up the stone walkway. "Erika, I gotta go."

Before I hit the first step, Sincere opens the front door, looking all sexy in a pair of blue Seton Hall basketball shorts and a blue Seton Hall Pirates T-shirt.

"Okay. Love you."

"Love you, too." I end the call before she can open her mouth to say another word.

Sincere smiles at me, stepping back to let me in. And I smile back. He quickly closes the door, then pulls me into his arms. "Damn, you feel good."

I breathe in his soapy, fresh-showered smell, getting lost in his scent, and his hug. "Mmmm...so do you."

13

I'm at my locker taking out books for my first three periods, lost in thoughts of Sincere. Missing him like crazy, even though I was with him Friday night, and had gone to the movies then out to eat with him. Afterward, I went back to his house and cuddled. Then I was with him on Saturday *and* Sunday, then again, all day yesterday. And when I got home last night, I stayed on the phone with him until almost two in the morning.

Then first thing this morning I called him 'cause I wanted to hear his sexy voice. But he didn't pick up. Some people need caffeine to jumpstart their morning. Hearing Sincere's voice is all I need to get my blood pumping. Anywaaayz, I've sent him three texts that he *still* hasn't responded to. And I know for a fact he doesn't have classes today until eleven o'clock. And I know he doesn't sleep past eight. *So what's up with him not hitting me back? He shoulda texted me back by now.*

I glance at my watch. I only have ten minutes until the

homeroom bell rings. Not enough time to drive over to his house to check to see if his car is in the driveway and be back here on time. *But if I slip out now, I'd only be a few minutes late. I could forge another note stating I had an emergency at home.*

"OMG!" Brittani shrieks, cutting into my thoughts. She's pointing at my neck. "Let me find out that's a hickey. *And* you played hooky from school.*"

Okay, so here's the scoop. Remember the night I went over to his house after dance last week? Wellll, Sincere gave me a soothing foot massage—yes, my man handled my feet! He even kissed them. And what?! Anywaaayz, at some point Sincere and I ended up in his bedroom. He lit candles and put in a CD that his father made, with old-school slow jams. I got so caught up in the moment that I felt myself fading, getting lost in his kisses. I didn't know what was going on until I felt the electricity and a flash of heat shooting through my body. I had never experienced anything like that before. And I loved it. And I wanted him to do it to me again and again and again. I'm not gonna front. That night awakened something in me I never knew existed. And it was right at that very moment that I felt something in me snap open...and there'd be no turning back.

So, *yes*, I skipped school yesterday to experience it all over again. I left my house at seven o'clock as if I were going to school, chilled with Sincere all day, then left his house around three o'clock to get to dance class. I walked back up in my house at seven o'clock in the evening as if I'd had a full day of school and dance. Well...I did— rolling around in the bed, though. Then as soon as I walked up in school this morning, I went into the atten-

dance office and handed the secretary a note signed by my
mother. Well, okay, a note signed by me. Yup, I forged her
signature—something I would never have done last year,
or any other year. Maybe it's because of this thing called
love that has me thinking and feeling differently. I've never
felt what I feel for Sincere with anyone else. He makes me
feel special and needed and wanted. Maybe it's because
I'm finally taking control over my life and not letting my
mother dictate my every move. I don't know. But what I
do know is, I can't wait to see Sincere!

I roll my eyes, sucking my teeth. "Geesh, broadcast it to
the whole school, why don't you," I state, mushing her.

"So what y'all do all day together, Miss Nasty?" she asks,
grinning.

"Nothing, really," I say, fumbling with the combination
to my locker. "We chilled, watching movies and whatnot."

She lowers her voice, shutting her locker. "Have y'all
done it yet?"

"Ewww, no," I state, twisting my lips up. What we did is
none of her business. I stare at my neck in the mirror
that's hanging on the back of my locker door. *The Wicked
Witch will flip her wig if she sees this*, I think, shutting my
locker. "Have you and Stevie?"

"Heck no! I'm making him wait. And if he can't, then on
to the next."

"So you're not worried if he cheats on you?"

She shakes her head, pulling out her phone and texting. "Nope, not at all. My mom says if a guy can't wait for
you, then he's not worth your time. And he's definitely not
worthy of you. So he can go ahead and act single if he
wanna, and act like he don't care, and it's gonna be a
wrap."

I laugh at her paraphrasing a line from Mary J's song. My phone buzzes, letting me know I have a text. I fish it out of my bag, then read the text: HEY, BABY. MISS U

I text back, smiling. MISS U 2

Just that quick, I forget that only a few minutes ago I was feeling some kinda way about not hearing from him.

U COMIN' OVA AFTR SCHL?

I text back: YES!

Zahara walks up on us, holding a box. "What y'all tramps up to? Oh, here"—she hands me the box I'd had shipped to her house—"this is for you."

"Oh, thanks," I say excitedly, stuffing it into my locker.

"Wellllll...*I* haven't been up to anything," Brittani says, smirking. "But this one here"—she flicks a finger over at me—"been doin' all kinds of nasty things. It's obvious she and Sincere been makin' all kinda oohs and aahs." She laughs.

"What a liar. We have not. You make me sick."

"Mmmph, well y'all shoulda been making something pop since you cut school to be with him. He must have you really strung, 'cause you ain't ever ditched school for anyone, especially a boy."

"*Whaaat*ever. Anywaaayz, y'all heard from Ameerah?" I ask, changing the subject.

"She texted me saying she's not coming to school until third period," Zahara says, pulling her books out of her book bag, then stuffing it into her locker. She shuts the door. "Are we still going to the mall after school?"

Oh, shoot, I forgot all about our plans to hang out after school today. "I can't. I told Sincere I was coming over to his house."

Zahara frowns, putting her hand on her hip. "Oh no..."

waaaait one minute." She turns to Brittani. "Boo, please pinch me and tell me that this heifer isn't about to diss her girls to be up under some boy, *after* we already made plans. And *after* she spent all weekend with him."

"Mmmph, sounds like it to me," Brittani says, twirling her hips around and turning her back to me. "So much for our pact to never put boys before our girls."

"Uh-uh," Zahara says, rolling her neck and talking with her hands. "This is *not* acceptable. You need to let Sincere know that you made other plans that *don't* include him. We are hanging out; all four of us. Just because you're *finally* getting a little sumthin'-sumthin', that don't mean you get to put us on the back burner, sweetie. We let you slide last week."

I huff. "I was on punishment *last* week."

"Whatever. And you were *still* sneaking out. But it wasn't to chill with your girls. So ya point?"

"The point is—"

She throws a hand up in my face. "*Beep!* Talk to the hand. Like I said, we let you slide all last week. But not this time. So get it together." She claps her hands together. "Chop, chop. Act like you know. Or get cut."

"Ohmygod, Zee, you are so damn dramatic," I state, laughing. "I'm not finally getting anything. And I'm not putting y'all on the back burner. What's so wrong with me wanting to spend time with my man, instead of sitting up in y'all birds' faces?"

"Nothing," Brittani says. "Go on ahead and diss us. It's all good. Do you. But know this. My birthday is *three* weekends away—October first, in case you don't remember—and we are all meeting up at my house. And you better be there. In the meantime, I'm sure we *birds* can manage without you. C'mon, Zahara," she says, looping her arm with Zahara's, "let's bounce."

"Ohmygod, y'all so wrong," I say, watching them walking off.

"Whatever, tramp," Zahara says over her shoulder. "Make sure you're in the parking lot after school so we can hit the mall, or there will be a situation. And the only feathers gonna be plucked are *yours*."

I sigh. "Okay, okay. Geesh. See y'all at lunch."

Zahara stops walking. She turns to face me, cocking her head to the side. "Ain't nobody say nothing about seeing ya ugly face at lunch. I *said* we better see you in the parking lot after school. School gets out at two forty. Roll call is at three o'clock. And we're pulling out at three ten. So you need to text your boo-thang and let him know he's on pause until *after* you chill with ya girls. You know. The ones you're tryna diss for him. Now *boom*!"

She spins on her heels and the both of them switch off toward their homerooms. I turn to go in the opposite direction toward mine, pulling out my phone. I send Sincere a text to let him know that I forgot I promised to hang with Zahara and them. I let him know I'll come over afterward.

A few seconds later, Sincere texts back. OH A'IGHT. HIT ME UP WHEN U COMN THRU

"Yo, Kamiyah, what's good?"

It's Jarrell. I glance up at him, dropping my phone back into my bag. He's smiling.

"Nothing much. What's up with you?"

"I'm waiting on you to come to your senses and give me another chance," he says, walking alongside me. "You know I'm big on you, girl."

"And you know I have a man. So let it go."

"Yeah, a'ight. What is it about this dude? What does he have that I don't?"

I stare at him, then blink. I tilt my head. "Me," I say, walking into homeroom just as the bell rings. Jarrell follows behind me. I glance over my shoulder, catching him staring at my butt. *Ugh!* He grins, licking his lips.

He is sexy, though. I roll my eyes.

"I'ma still wait on you," he says, taking his usual seat in the back of the room.

I laugh, waving him on. "Well, you let me know how that works out for you."

The rest of the school day flies by. At three o'clock—even though a) I'm not feeling it, b) I don't appreciate how Zahara came at me earlier, and c) I feel like she's trying to make me choose between them and my boo—I'm walking out to the parking lot with my phone pressed to my ear, talking to Sincere. And, *yes*, with an attitude.

"You miss me?"

"Yup, yup," he says. "How was your day?"

"It was good." *Yeah, 'cause I spent it thinking about you.*

"Kamiyah, girl, will you hurry the heck up," Zahara says, placing a hand up on her hip.

I put a finger up, signaling for her to give me a minute.

"Trick, c'mon. We're ready to go. You can talk to Sincere later. Dang."

"Yo, who's that?"

I suck my teeth. "Zahara. She's rushing me off the phone, like she's my mother or something."

He laughs. "Well, don't let me hold you."

Boy, I want you to hold me. "Oh, you're not holding me. They can wait. Talking to you is more important. The mall isn't going anywhere."

"Aaah, that's wassup. So y'all getting ready to hit the mall? Which one?" I tell him that we're going to Short Hills. "Oh, that's wassup."

I glance at my watch. "We'll probably get something to eat at The Cheesecake Factory while we're out there. But I'm only going to be out for a few hours, then I'm coming straight over to your house."

"Oh, damn," he says, bursting my bubble. "I kinda made plans to hang out with my boys tonight since you said you were chillin' with your girls."

"You did *what*?" I snap. "I told you I was coming over, so why would you go and do that?"

"Look, you need to take all that loudness in my ear down a notch."

I frown. "I don't have to take nothing down. You knew I wanted to see you."

"And I wanna see you, too, Miyah."

Yeah, right. I grunt. "Mmmph. Oh, really?"

"Yeah, really. Didn't you text me earlier and say you forgot you had made plans to hang with your girls after school?"

"Yeah, and I also *told* you I was coming over right afterward. So why would you make plans to hang out?"

"Because I figured I'd either see you later on tonight, or tomorrow. Relax. It's not that serious."

Maybe not to you! "Mmmph. Yeah, you're right. It really isn't. So, do you."

"Oh, so now you got a attitude?"

"Nope. Anywaaayz...what y'all gonna get into?" I ask,

shifting my oversize handbag from one arm to the other. I let it hang in the crook of my arm.

"I'm not sure yet."

"Well, what time you gonna be home?"

"I don't know."

"Mmmph."

"What's all that—"

"Stop the press," Zahara says, sneaking up on me and snatching my phone from out of my hand. She takes off with the phone pressed up to her ear, running around her car. "Listen up, boo-thang...no, it's Zee...wassup..."

"Zahara, give me my phone back!" I yell, chasing her.

Ameerah and Brittani are laughing.

"...Well, I don't mean to bust y'all's little lovefest up... oh, no problem...but we're trying to get to the mall, so do you mind if—"

"I'm not playing with you, tramp," I say, taking off my heels and charging her. I feel like beating her down. "Give me my damn phone back, Zahara. Now!"

"All right, all right," she says, handing it back to me. "Don't get your panties all knotted up. Geesh!"

"Whatever," I snap. "You lucky I don't put a knot upside ya forehead. You play too much. I'm sorry about that," I tell Sincere, trying to catch my breath.

Sincere's laughing. "It's all good. Yo, your girl's shot out, for real."

"She makes me sick. Anywaaayz, where are you and your friends going?" He tells me he's not sure where they might end up. "How you gonna hang out with your boys and have no idea where you going?"

"We'll figure it out when we all meet up."

"So where y'all meeting up at?"

"They're coming here."

"They all have girls?"

He sighs. "Listen. Wassup with the third degree all of a sudden?"

I frown. "You know what, Sincere? Forget you."

"Forget what? Nah, don't forget it. I wanna know wassup with all the questions."

Oh no, girl...he's really tryna bring it to you. You better pump his brakes right now. And make it quick. He's acting like you can't check for him.

Girl, stop tripping. He's only hanging out with his boys.

Mmmph. And he's probably gonna have a buncha chicks all up in his face.

I suck my teeth. "Well, I wanna know why you're acting all secretive, like I can't *ask* you any questions."

"I'm not being secretive. You can ask me anything you want. But I told you, I don't know what we're gonna do. And you're still coming at me with a buncha questions like I'm on some interview. If I knew where we were going, I'd tell you."

I blink, blink again. *Don't trip, girl. Let him do his thing.* "You're right, Sincere," I say all sweet and whatnot. "My bad. I was just looking forward to seeing you tonight, that's all."

"I feel you. I wanna see you, too. And if it's not too late, we can still chill."

"Yeah," I say, walking toward my car. For some reason I'm pissed. *Whatever. Go on and have your little fun.* "Don't be all up in no girls' faces, either."

He laughs. "C'mon, Miyah. Don't start that. You already know it's me and you."

I smile. "It better be."

"I'ma make it up to you, a'ight?"

"You better." He tells me he's gonna take me out to dinner tomorrow. That he'll pick me up at seven. "But I still wanna see you tonight, too," I say, turning my back on the staring eyes of my girls.

"Hooker, hurry up! You can turn your back all you want. This don't make any sense. You act like he's going off to war or something. Geesh. Stop acting like you're so pressed. Get off the phone and let's roll."

"Ohmygod, Sincere. Let me get up off this phone before I have to beat this chick down. She's out here talking real reckless."

"A'ight. Have fun."

"You too. Call or text me when you get home."

"I got you." We say our good-byes, then disconnect.

The three of them are staring me down. Zahara has her hand up on her hip. Ameerah's arms are crossed. And Brittani is leaning up against my car, shaking her head. I give all three of 'em the finger. "Let's go, tramps."

14

Monitor in silence! And that's exactly why I'm sitting across the street from Sincere's house at nine o'clock at night, ducked down low waiting for him to get home. Okay, okay...I know I have no business being out here. But I am. And he's lucky I don't want his parents thinking I'm some kinda nut; otherwise I'd be sitting up on his porch step waiting for him. *Never let 'em see you!*

I couldn't wait to ditch Zahara and them. I mean, the mall was cute and all. I even bought Brittani's birthday gift in Bloomingdale's while I was there. She wanted a pair of Lucky Brand "Hibiscus" tall flat boots—they're like motorcycle and riding boots in one—and they were on sale, so I bought them for her. OMG, they're gonna be real fly with a pair of skinny jeans. Well, she doesn't know exactly which ones I bought, since I had her try on four different types and styles of boots, then went back to get the ones she really wanted while Zahara and Ameerah dragged her over to Macy's. But still, the whole time I was there I couldn't think about anything other than Sincere. What is he doing? Where is he at? Who all is with him? I texted him a few times while we were eating, then called him, even though I knew he was leaving to go out with his friends. He picked up and spoke to me for a few minutes, then told me he'd call me later. Mmmph!

Anywaaayz, here I sit. And I'm not leaving this spot until I see what time he pulls up in his driveway. And *who* he pulls up with. Well, okay, I'm not going anywhere for at least the next two hours, 'cause I need to be in the house by eleven if I want to maintain my freedom. Besides, I'm not allowed to drive past 11:01, thanks to the new corny driving rules. And if I'm one minute over, it's a wrap. The Witch already forewarned me that if I don't have this car up in the driveway by the designated time, I won't be able to drive for a whole month. Mmmph. And I'm not tryna end up back on punishment, especially when I only have four weekends from tomorrow—which is Brittani's birthday—before the Halloween party at the end of next month. So I'm gonna try and stay on her good side until then. Mmmph. For some reason, she was nice enough to let me stay out past my ten o'clock curfew tonight—on a school night, which is rare, no less. And yup, I'm spending it scoping out Sincere's house. Even though my mom thinks I'm at the movies with Zahara and them.

I text Sincere. HEY. U HOME YET?

Of course I already know the answer, since I'm out here watching his house. But I wanna see what he says. So I wait and wait and wait for his reply. Tyga's "Far Away" is playing, and I start singing along. Four songs later there is *still* no reply from Sincere! I pull out the Sightmark Ghost Hunter night vision binoculars I bought online, then scan the area. Oooh, these things see everything in the dark. *Where are you, Sincere?* I toss the binoculars over in the passenger seat the minute my phone chimes. It's a text from Sincere, finally!

Sincere: NAH, NOT YET. WHERE U?

Me: K. I'M HOME. WHEN U GOIN HOME?

Sincere: N A FEW

Me: K. CALL ME WHEN U GET IN

Sincere: I WILL

I want so badly to ask him where he's at and who he's hanging with. But I don't. I'm just going to sit here and wait to see what 'in a few' means. I text back. LUV U!

The time on my phone reads 9:44 P.M. I get another text. *Ugh!* This time it's my mother. WHAT TIME IS THE MOVIE OVER?

Now I have to go online to check to see movie times. I suck my teeth. *She makes me sick!* I decide to ignore her text. I'll tell her I had my phone turned off.

It is now 9:56 P.M. Sincere finally texts back. LUV U 2 ☺

At 10:37 P.M., still no sign of Sincere. I guess when he said he'd be home 'in a few,' he meant like in a few hours, 'cause 'in a few' to me means like within thirty minutes or so.

At 10:39 P.M., I text him again. U STILL NOT HOME?

This time he texts right back. NAH. STILL CHLLIN. GOIN HOME IN A MIN

By ten forty-five I'm convinced Sincere's 'in a min' isn't going to be coming anytime soon, so I turn off my phone—pissed that I have to leave before I see him. I start my engine and drive off, determined to be home before my extended curfew. *The last thing I wanna do is hear her mouth!*

As soon as I walk through the door, the Witch can't wait to pounce on me.

"Didn't you get my text?" she asks, sitting on the sofa in the living room reading some kind of book, probably a romance novel.

"Oh, shoot," I say, pulling out my phone and looking at it. "I turned my phone off at the movies and forgot to turn it back on."

She eyes me. "Mmm... what movie did you all go see?" I tell her the new Disney movie that just came out. She frowns. "I thought that movie was already out. "

"It did. But it came out on the seventeenth in three-D. Remember when I was talking about it?"

"Maybe you did mention it. I don't remember, though. Who all went?"

"Me, Zahara, Ameerah, and Brittani."

"I know you didn't have them all packed in your car."

I keep from sucking my teeth. Look her in the face. "No. I know the rule. Only one other passenger allowed in the car unless there's a parent or guardian in the car with us."

She squints her eyes at me as if she's trying to decide if she wants to believe me or not.

"We drove in two separate cars," I add. "Briana dropped Brittani and Zahara off. And Ameerah rode with me. But anyway, why you down here?"

"What time was the movie over?" she asks, ignoring my question.

"I don't know. Like twenty-five minutes ago. I dropped

Ameerah off, then drove straight home." But what I really wanna ask is, *Why you all up in mine?* But I know if I do it'll start an argument, so I keep it to myself.

"Where'd y'all go eat?"

I blink, blink again. Then it hits me. She's not tryna get it crunked, she's tryna make small talk. OMG, I wanna roll my eyes up in my head. Doesn't she know all I want to do is go upstairs to my room, shut my door, and get on Facebook to check Sincere's page and go through his wall posts? Geesh!

"The Cheesecake Factory," I state, sitting in a chair across from her. I decide to play nice with her since a) I wanna stay in her good graces long enough to go to the Halloween party, b) Daddy promised me a new Louis bag as long as I keep the peace between us, and c) it's a rare occasion that she's even nice to me. So here we are. Let the games begin!

I think back, try to remember how long it's been since we've actually sat and talked without it getting messy. I watch her watching me and realize we haven't gotten along since I was twelve. Since Erika moved out.

Of course, if you ask her when things turned sour between us, she'll say once I started my period. Yup, she'll blame it all on me and my monthly cycle. Go figure. Anywaaayz...I decide, since she seems to be in a friendly mood, to tell her that Sincere wants to take me out to eat tomorrow night after dance.

"Is that okay?" I can tell she's shocked. I tilt my head, wait for her answer. I'm sure she'll have some excuse to say no, like the fact that it's a school night. I decided to add, "I'll be home way before curfew."

She just kinda stares at me. I can tell there's something on her mind other than me wanting to be out with Sincere. Just by the way she's eyeing me—no, *studying* me—I can tell that she's been sitting down here on purpose, waiting for me.

"Where's he taking you?"

I shrug. "I don't know where exactly. I just know he's going to pick me up tomorrow at six and take me out to eat somewhere."

"Well..." She pauses, glancing at her watch, then over at the door when she hears it open and shut. It's Daddy. He comes in from the foyer and looks shocked to see the two of us sitting in a room and there's no yelling and screaming.

"Hi, Daddy," I say, smiling.

"Oh, hey. What's going on in here?" he asks, looking over at me, then Mom. He leans in and kisses her on the lips.

She looks up at him all googly-eyed and whatnot. "Kamiyah and I were sitting here talking about her night out with her friends."

"Is that so?" he says, walking over and kissing me on the forehead. He winks at me and whispers, "That's my girl."

"Kamiyah was just telling me about her plans tomorrow night with Sincere."

"Oh yeah?" Daddy says, sitting down next to her, putting his arm around the back of the sofa. "What kind of plans?"

"We're gonna go out to eat. Is that okay? He's gonna pick me up around six."

He looks over at Mom. "I don't think it should be a

problem." She shakes her head, agreeing with him. "What time will you be home?" I tell him by curfew.

Mom's eyes stretch open. "If you're only going out to eat, why do you need to be out until ten?"

"We're probably going to hang out at his house afterward."

"And his parents *will* be home?" she wants to know.

I shrug. "I guess."

"Well, I'd rather you not be there unless there's a parent there. Understand?"

"Kamiyah, your mother's right. Anything can happen."

"But, Daddy, nothing can happen unless I want it to. Don't you think I can handle myself?"

"It's not about whether or not you can handle yourself. I know we've raised you to be responsible. And part of being responsible is doing what's right. And that's not being in his house, or anyone else's, unless there's a responsible adult there."

"You're right," I say, not wanting to get into a big lecture. "Well," I say, getting up. "I'm going to get ready for bed."

Okay, instead of her letting me go on my merry way, the Witch wants to keep yapping. "Kamiyah, Sincere seems like a very nice young man with a good head on his shoulders. I really hope the two of you aren't rushing into anything. You really need to stay focused on graduating and getting into Juilliard next year."

I frown, but I'm mindful not to raise my voice. "I *am* focused."

She gives me a fake smile. "And I want you to stay that way." Then she hops off her broom and swings the ax down on me. "I think you and Sincere shouldn't spend so much time together. It's not healthy."

"Oh, I get it," I say, eyeing her. "You waited until Daddy was here to bring all this up instead of saying something to me yourself. Mmmph. That's so typical."

"Excuse you, young lady?"

OMG, I am so not tryna do this right now. "Okay, fine. Can I go now?"

"No," the Witch says. "We're not done talking to you."

"Umm, you mean, *you're* not done talking to me."

"No, I'm not. And I don't like all those text messages and phone calls to Sincere. They seem obsessive to me."

"Ohmygod, are you serious? I have the second-highest GPA in a school of over two thousand students, I don't drink or use drugs, or run the streets, and you're worried about how many times I text or talk on the phone to *my* boyfriend? Maybe I should really give you something to worry about. Then maybe you'd get off—"

"Kamiyah, enough," Daddy says, taking up for his precious wife once again. "Your mother has a right to be concerned."

"Well, she's concerning herself over a buncha dumbness."

"Your mother and I have to trust you to do what's right, even when no one else is around. That's what one's integrity is based on. Still, that doesn't mean we're not going to be concerned about the things you do in your life. It may seem like a bunch of *dumbness* to you. But to your mother and me, it's not."

"Kamiyah," the Witch says, looking at me. "This wasn't meant to turn into a fight."

"You coulda fooled me. Just when I thought we might

make it a whole day without any problems, you come with this okey doke."

"*Okey doke?* Young lady, who do you think you're talking to? See, this is what keeps you in trouble—your mouth."

Daddy looks over at me, giving me a please-be-nice look. The LV logos on a new Louis bag start floating around in my head. I pull it together real quick. "Mom, I'm really not tryna be disrespectful. But you don't understand."

"Oh, trust me. I understand a whole lot more than you think, Kamiyah. I was your age once."

"Yeah, and you know how long ago that was? It's the twenty-first century, and you still act like you're in the seventies. You can't relate to the teens today. You couldn't even relate to Erika when she was here."

"Kamiyah, that's enough," Daddy warns.

"Daddy, why can't I ever express how I feel? Why do I always have to be the one to watch what I say when she doesn't? If it's about respect, you have to give it to get it. And sometimes I don't feel like she respects me."

"Um, excuse you. Don't stand there and talk around me as if I'm not in the room. *She* is sitting right here. And *she* happens to be your mother, young lady. You're right, you do very well in school. Your father and I are proud of you. And we *both* want to make sure you stay on track. I'm not saying you can't be with Sincere. All I'm saying is, don't be so wrapped up in him."

"Mom, I'm not." *Sorry lady, it's a little too late.* "Can I please be excused?"

She glances at her watch, then flicks her hand for me to go.

"Thank you," I say, walking over to Daddy and kissing him on the cheek. I say good night to the Wicked Witch.

"Um, aren't you going to kiss your mother good night?" Daddy asks, eyeing me.

"Nope," I say, walking outta the room. "I'd rather not."

"Kamiyah," Daddy calls out.

"Erik, don't," I hear her saying as I climb the stairs.

15

Sincere opens the passenger-side door for me, then shuts it once I'm all the way in. He gets in on the driver's side, puts on his seat belt, then starts the engine.

"So, where are you taking me?" I ask, looking over at him as he backs out of my driveway, then drives off toward Halsey Place. He bears around the traffic circle, staying on Montrose until he gets to South Orange Avenue, then makes a left.

He grins. "Don't worry about that, pretty lady. Ya man's got this. You just sit back and relax, a'ight?"

I smile. "Fine with me."

"How was your day?" he asks as he stops at a stop sign. I tell him it was good. That I couldn't wait for it to be over. I ask him how his was. "It was okay. I have a mandatory Journey of Transformation class that's like seventy minutes long, twice a week, and it's kind of interesting. But today, for some reason, I had a hard time staying awake in it."

I laugh. "Oh, poor thing. So what's the class about?" I ask, shifting my body in my seat so I can look at him. He tells me the class is about exploring different religions and the transformative journeys people experience. "Oh, okay. Sounds interesting."

"It is."

"Are you religious?" I ask.

He smiles. "Let's see. I went to a Catholic all-boys prep school. And now I attend a Catholic university. One would think I'd be very religious."

I laugh. "So, I'll take that to mean that you're not."

"Not really. I mean, I am to an extent. I do pray. And I believe there is a higher power. But I'm not all fanatic about it. Do you believe there's a higher power?"

I shrug. Truth is, I *believe* in love and I *believe* that Sincere and I are meant to be together—forever. I *believe* I can do anything I set my mind on. I *believe,* without a doubt, that I am going to be a professional dancer. And I *believe* my mother hates me. But other than that, as far as religion goes, I don't know what I believe in. "I guess. I mean, I never really gave it much thought."

He looks over at me thoughtfully. "Do you believe in forgiveness?"

OhmyGod, why is he asking me this craziness? You do me wrong, I'm sorry—say what you want—you gotta get got, then I can work on forgiving you for what you did to me. I decide to keep this to myself. "Yes," I tell him, smiling. "I feel like hearing some music."

He smiles at me, turning on the radio. "What do you wanna hear?"

Anything that's gonna get us off this conversation. "I don't care. Whatever."

He checks to see what beats are playing on Hot 97, then switches to Power 105.1 before pressing a button for the CD player. Drake's "Headlines" blares through the speakers. I bob my head to the beat, staring out the window as Sincere merges onto the Garden State Parkway, heading north. When J. Cole's "Lost Ones" starts playing, I lay my head back on the headrest and close my eyes.

Sincere touches my knee. "You all right over there?"

I look over at him and smile. "Yeah."

"What were you over there thinking about?"

"You."

He smiles, taking my hand in his. "About what?"

About what I'ma do if you ever try to leave me. "I'm thinking about how much you mean to me. About how much I love you, and don't ever wanna lose you."

He smiles. "You won't, baby." He gets off at the Bloomfield Avenue exit. "I ain't going anywhere. You're everything I could ever ask for in a girl."

I smile. "Awww, for real?"

"Yeah. You're not only sexy as hell, you're smart, funny, and mad talented."

And jealous! I grin. "Sincere, you're so sweet. I can't imagine my life without you in it. I'm so lucky to have you."

"Nah, I'm the lucky one, Miyah; for real. You got me wide open, baby."

I bring his hand up to my lips and kiss it. "Umm, Sincere. Where are we going? You do know I have to be home by ten, right?"

"I know," he says, turning onto Allwood. "We're almost there."

When he pulls into Joe's Crab Shack, I start smiling. OMG, I love lobster and shrimp!

Once we get out of the car, Sincere reaches for my hand and we make our way into the restaurant. The place is packed! And it's very noisy. I watch as the dancing servers do some kinda cha-cha-cha dance routine. We're told it's going to be an hour wait. Sincere gives the hostess his cell number so they can text him when our table is ready.

He grabs my hand once we get outside. We decide to walk through Clifton Commons, the outdoor mall area, and stop inside Barnes & Noble while we wait. "You wanna go somewhere else to eat?"

I shake my head. "No. Not really. But if you do, we can."

"Nah, I'm good. You good?"

As long as I'm with you. I nod, looping my arm through his. "Yup."

The hostess texts Sincere's phone the minute we walk into Barnes & Noble that our table is ready, so we turn around and head back to the restaurant. Now the place is packed beyond belief. And the noise level is ridiculous. It's bad enough I can't even hear myself think, let alone have a conversation with Sincere.

We share a bucket of shrimp. Then for our meal, Sincere orders the Lobster Daddy Feast and I order the Crab Daddy Feast. There are two birthday parties going on, so there's a lot of chanting going on. And every forty-five minutes, although it seems like every ten to fifteen minutes, the waiters come out dancing. It's kinda cute at first, but after like the second round it gets real old. But all you can do is laugh at how some of these waiters are dancing. Hot messes! Anywaaayz, we have outside seating, which is kinda cool. The heaters are on full blast, though, and I am starting to sweat a little. It's kinda chilly out, but overall, it's a nice night out. Sincere and I try to talk but we practically have to yell, so we just stare at each other, smiling and laughing at each other with these big bibs around our necks, getting all messy and whatnot from the crabs and lobsters we're eating. For dessert I share some of his chocolate cake.

After a while I glance at my watch. It's 8:35 P.M. I excuse myself to go wash my hands, and when I return to the table, Sincere goes to wash his.

"You ready to bounce up outta here? We can go for a ride or back to my house if you want," Sincere says, coming back to the table and flagging down the waiter.

"Yeah, sure," I say as he pays the ninety-dollar bill. I reach into my bag and pull out ten bucks for the tip.

"Nah, you good," Sincere says, handing me back the money. We get back into our jackets. Once outside, I reach for his hand.

"Thanks for dinner," I tell him as we walk toward the car. "Although I thought I was gonna lose my hearing up in there, I really enjoyed it."

He laughs. "Yeah, I enjoyed it, too. So what you wanna do? You wanna catch a movie while we're here, or go back to my house?"

I tell him, "I'd rather go back to your house, since I have to be home by eleven."

"Sounds good to me," he says, unlocking the truck, then opening the passenger side for me to get in.

I dig in my bag and pull out a pack of gum, offering him a stick. Sincere checks his phone for any messages, then starts texting someone. I pull out my phone and do the same thing, trying to keep myself occupied so I won't ask him WHY and WHO he has to text right at this very minute.

Maybe he's texting his mom or dad, I think as he starts backing out of the parking space. "OhmyGod, I'm so stuffed," I say.

He says he's still hungry.

I laugh. "That's because you're greedy."

He laughs. "I'm a growing man."

Funkmaster Flex from Hot 97 is on the radio. *Ugh! He is so annoying to me.* Luckily, Sincere changes the station before I can say something. He settles on KISS-FM, then heads toward the Garden State Parkway. We listen to R & B music on the ride back to his house. Every so often we steal glances at each other, smiling. I lean over and kiss him on the cheek. Tell him how much I love him. He reaches over and grabs my hand. Tells me how much I mean to him. I am smiling. And I am melting inside. It is times like this that I feel—no, know—that I will *never* let Sincere leave me.

16

"You wanna go for a walk?" Sincere asks, standing up and stretching. It's Saturday afternoon and we've been lounging downstairs in Sincere's theater/game room watching DVDs for most of the day. This is the first time we've spent any time together since Wednesday night. I mean, sure, we've seen each other for an hour or so, but that's nothing like spending the whole day, or at least most of it, together.

I shrug. "I guess. Isn't it kinda cold out, though?"

"Yeah, a little," he says, walking over to me. "But I'll keep you warm." He leans in and kisses me. I kiss him back. And it doesn't take long before his tongue and mine are twirling together. I close my eyes and lose myself in the moment. I could stay wrapped up in Sincere's love all day. He pulls away when his phone starts buzzing, causing a thump in my heart. It's a text. He glances at the screen. I try to act uninterested. Try to shift my attention back to the movie, but I am distracted with thoughts of wanting to know who the text is from. His phone buzzes again. This time he texts back. I count in my head. Ten...nine... eight...seven...six...five...four...three...

His phone buzzes *again*!

"Dang, who's that blowing up your phone like that?" I ask, trying really, really hard to keep it together. To not jump to any conclusions or say anything that might set it off up in here; especially when I know his parents are upstairs somewhere.

He tells me it's one of his boys.

"Oh..." I wanna say more. I wanna *know* more. But the little voice in my head says, *Less is more*. The less I ask, the more I'll eventually find out. *Less is more! Less is more!* I repeat it over and over in my head, watching as he texts back. He sets his phone down on the pool table, then goes into the bathroom, closing the door behind him. I stare at it. Try to count how many seconds it'll take for me to race over there to check his phone and get back to my seat before he finishes. I listen as he takes a leak. Consider my options—get caught or get away with it. But the toilet flushes. Then the water from the faucet runs. I decide getting caught isn't an option. So I sit still.

"You ready?" he asks, walking out of the bathroom, drying his hands with a paper towel.

"Yeah." I stand up. He shuts off the TV, grabs his cell and checks it, then heads toward the stairs. I follow behind him.

His mother is sitting in the living room, watering plants and removing dead leaves. Sincere opens the hall closet and grabs our coats. "Ma, Miyah and I are gonna go for a walk. You want something while we're out?"

She looks up from what she's doing. "Walk? It's kind of chilly out."

"Hi, Missus Lewis."

She smiles at me. "Hi, baby. How are your parents?"

"They're good."

"Ma, it's not too bad out," Sincere says, handing me my coat. I slip it over my shoulders and slide my arms in. She watches as he slips into his jacket. She doesn't ask where we're walking to. Unlike my mother, who feels the need to know every little detail of my life.

"We'll be back."

"Okay," she says, busying herself with the large arrangement of tropical plants she has throughout the room.

We walk hand in hand through his development. Surprisingly, it's not as cold as it was at ten thirty this morning when I drove over here instead of taking my butt to dance. Oh well. Anywaaayz...it's almost two in the afternoon and actually much warmer than usual for this time of the year.

"I really like your mom," I tell him as we make our way around the neighborhood of large houses and mini-mansions.

He smiles. "She likes you, too."

"That's good to know, since I'm going to be her daughter-in-law one day."

He lets go of my hand and wraps his arm around me. "Oh, so you wanna be my wifey?"

Wrong answer. "I'm going to be your wife. Not *wifey*. I have no interest in *playing* wife. I'm going to *be* the wife; big difference."

He laughs. "Right, right." We turn onto South Orange Avenue. "But can you cook?"

"Nope."

He stops in his tracks. "Wait. You don't know how to cook?"

I shrug. "Not really. It's not something I had to know. My mother either cooks or we order in."

"Well, uhhh...if you wanna marry me, then you're gonna have to learn how to cook." He rubs his stomach. "'Cause ya man's gotta eat."

"Yeah, whatever."

"Nah, I'm only playing."

I playfully hit him in the arm. "You better be. Shoot, you're gonna play for the NBA one day, anyway. And I'm gonna be a world-famous dancer. So we'll be able to afford a personal chef."

"Yeah, true that. Then when you start having my babies, you can stay home and learn how to cook."

Ohmygod, Sincere wants me to have his babies! We'll have some really cute kids with good hair and nice straight teeth, and hopefully with his dimples.

I smile. "Ummm, correction. That's baby, as in one. Not *babies*. I'm not tryna have my shape all jacked up. This body's gonna be my moneymaker. And for the record, we're gonna hire a nanny."

He frowns. "Nah, I don't want my son being raised by some old lady. He needs to be cared for by his moms."

I laugh. "She doesn't have to be an old lady. Besides, who says you'll have a son? It could be a girl."

"Then we'll have to keep trying until I have a son," he says, pulling me in closer to him. We stop for a minute and kiss. His warm, soft lips make me feel weak. OMG, Sincere knows he can kiss his butt off! It doesn't take long for us to start French-kissing all out in public. Now if me and my girls were walking by and saw someone else doing what Sincere and I are doing, we would be like, *Ewww*, then we'd yell out, *Go get a room, freaks*. But, since it's me and Sincere, that doesn't apply. When we finally pull apart, I feel light-headed.

I look up at him, all dreamy-eyed and whatnot. "I love you so much, Sincere," I say softly.

"I love you, too," he says, taking my hand again. We continue down South Orange Avenue until we get to Grove Park. There are a few joggers and walkers out, getting in their afternoon exercise. Sincere and I walk along the path that wraps around the park, laughing and talking and enjoying the weather.

The whole day is going good…no, great! Well, that's until Sincere decides he wants to walk down to Village Pizzeria to order a cheesesteak to take back to his house. Now, my gut tells me to say no. I don't know why. I mean, aside from the fact that I don't like the food there, I feel like something is about to happen. I can't put my finger on it. But I don't want Sincere thinking I'm acting all paranoid and whatnot, so I keep my mouth shut and keep walking.

We're one block from the pizzeria and the closer we get to it, the stronger this feeling's getting. And then before we get to the pizzeria, I see *her*—the ho who's always up on Facebook, posting and tagging and poking up on Sincere's wall, and my heart skips. No, it leaps into my throat. She's up ahead, crossing the street and walking into the pizzeria. I cut my eye over at Sincere to see if he sees her, too. If he does, I can't tell.

"Let's, um, let's go somewhere else," I say, tugging on his arm. "I don't want Italian."

"Nah, I do," he says as we cross the street. "We can stop in one of the other spots to get you what you want after I place my order, a'ight?"

I nod, holding my breath. "Okay."

As soon as we walk into the pizzeria, there she is. Standing at the counter with her back to us, wearing a pair of skinny jeans and wedge heels. She glances over her shoulder, and I know right then... it's about to be a problem.

"Heeey, sexy man," she sings out, grinning. She turns to face us. I take her all in as she acts as if I'm not standing here. She has on a cute vintage denim jacket. I can't hate on the chick; from what I can see, she has a nice body. But I don't like her. Her smile is dripping with hot, steamy nastiness. And I'm convinced she wants my man. Or she's already had him. Either way, I'm not feeling it one bit. And I'm about to check this ho real quick if Sincere doesn't.

Be still. First wait to see what pops off.

Sincere laughs it off. "Oh, hey, Lana. Wassup?"

Hold on, girl. Don't say anything yet.

"You," she says, all flirty-like. She cuts her eyes over at me, twisting her lips up. "How you been?"

"Good," he says, acting like he's forgotten that I'm here with him. And obviously forgetting he has a girl—*me!*

I clear my throat. Fold my arms across my chest.

"Oh, damn. My bad. Lana, this is Kamiyah. Kamiyah, Lana."

Mmmph...he didn't even introduce me as his girl. What's up with that?

"Hey," I say, eyeing this messy heifer. But I'm still keeping my cool.

"Mmmhmm," she says, barely looking at me. She turns

back to Sincere. "So, annnyway, why haven't I heard from you? I miss you. We really need to *stay* in touch. And not just on Facebook, boo. We need to kick it, like old times."

Okay. This skank is straight up disrespecting me. And Sincere is standing here and hasn't opened his mouth to say one damn thing to check her. I already warned him about this kinda crap.

"Ummm, listen up, *boo*. You better back the hell up. You've been standing here disrespecting me from the minute we walked through the door. And I'm not the one. I let you get that off for a minute, but be clear, *trick*. My man won't be kicking a damn thing with you. But if you keep disrespecting me, I'll be *kicking* your azz."

She laughs. "Yeah, right. Picture that. Umm, Sincere, you better tell her."

"He better tell me *what*?"

"C'mon, y'all, chill," Sincere says, shifting his eyes around the restaurant. He spots a few heads from his school. They speak as they walk by, slowing down to catch the happenings. He gives them head nods. "Lana, why you gotta always play? Damn."

She smirks. "Oh, I'm playing? Sincere, you already know what it is."

"Well, I don't, ho," I snap, placing my hand up on my hip. "So why don't *you* let me in on it."

"Sincere, you better tell this—"

Attack when they least expect it. Every muscle in my body tenses. And I don't wait for her to finish saying what-ever she was gonna say. And I don't wait for Sincere to open his mouth to say anything that he shoulda already said. I lunge at her, wrapping her hair around my hands real tight, then swing her around the restaurant. Yes, I catch her off guard and I air her scalp out. She's screaming and trying to fight me off of her.

"Get your hands off my hair and fight me!" she yells, swinging her arms wildly.

She keeps trying to fight me off. But I got a strong grip on her hair and I'm swinging her around like a merry-go-round. I can tell I'm starting to make her dizzy. "You want my man, trick?! You think you can disrespect me to my face? Well, guess what? I'm not the one."

"Aaaah...get off of me. If he's your man, I can't tell.... aaaaah...ohmygod...Sinceeeeere, get this crazy ho off of me..."

I'm not sure when Sincere jumped in. But he is trying to pry my hands out of her hair. He is yelling at me to let go. But I am holding on with all my strength. When I finish ripping hair out of this ho's scalp, they'll be calling her Patches. I swing her into tables, knocking things over. Swing her into a wall. Customers are scattering out of the way. She tries to grab for my hair, but it is pulled back in a tight bun. I'm so glad I didn't wear my hair out like this tramp. Her nails dig into my hands, then my face. But I don't care.

"Yo, Miyah, let her go," Sincere says, grabbing me from behind. "C'mon. Stop it." He grabs my wrists. Someone comes behind her and tries to pull us apart. But she isn't going anywhere until I decide to let go of her hair. I yank until she is screaming at the top of her lungs for them to get me off of her. I show her no mercy. Throwing herself at my man—I don't think so!

Sincere's trying to peel my fingers back, but he isn't able to. I have her long hair twirled around my hand like a jump rope. There is so much commotion going on in here that it hypes me up even more. I keep swinging and yanking and pulling her head and hair. She keeps screaming and swinging her fists. But she can't get a good hit in. I knee her in the stomach. Finally it takes six people to break us up.

"This ain't over," she yells as two guys drag her out of the restaurant. Her lip is bloody. "I promise you, I got something for you!" They get her outside and she's still popping off. "She snuck me. Can you believe it? She snuck me. Ohmygod, and pulled my hair out!"

"Whatever, trick! Bring it!" I yell back. "That trick don't want it with me." Sincere and three other guys are still holding me back. I have a clump of dark, thick hair in my hands. "And come get your hair, ho. Better yet, I'll save it for the next whooping!"

I throw it toward the door.

"C'mon, Miyah, calm down," Sincere says. He's trying to catch his breath. "Why'd you attack her like that? She was—"

"Disrespecting me," I snap, cutting him off. "That's what she was. And you thought that was cute."

"I wasn't thinking about that girl," he tries to explain. But I'm not tryna hear it. I'm pissed.

"You stood there and let that ho disrespect me! I wouldn't have had to go off if you woulda opened your mouth and checked her from the jump! But, noooo. You let her come at me all sideways."

He looks at me. "Miyah, will you stop? You got all these people out here looking at us." I see a mixture of embarrassment and hurt and disgust in his eyes when he says this. But I don't care.

"No, *you* have these people looking at us. All you had to do was check her and it woulda been all good. But since you wanted to let her play me, I handled her."

The manager tells us we gotta get out of his restaurant. Tells us we're not allowed to ever set foot inside his establishment again. Like I give a damn! I can tell Sincere wants to blink his eyes and disappear. That he wants to leave, but is afraid what might happen when we walk out this door. He sees that ho still outside. She's on her cell, yelling and screaming and walking in circles.

I hear sirens. One, two, three... *three* police cars are now out front.

I see kids holding up cell phones and red lights blinking and people whispering. Then it hits me. This whole mess has been videoed.

17

"Have you lost your damn mind, Kamiyah? What in the hell is wrong with you, girl? Out here fighting like some wild hood rat," my mom screams the minute she slams her car door shut and is out of earshot of the police. My parents have just picked me up from the police station, and she is beyond pissed. She shifts her body around to look at me. "You have two seconds to tell me what the hell is going on with you, or I'm going to be swinging you around next. And where the hell is your car?"

"It's at Sincere's house."

"And where is *he*?" she wants to know.

"His mom came and picked him up."

"Great. So you were out there fighting some girl over a boy? Is that what you're telling me?"

I shake my head. "No."

"*No*? Then what the hell were you fighting for?"

Daddy is quiet. But I wish he would say something...

anything. He glances at me every so often through the rearview mirror as he drives toward Sincere's house to get my car.

"She disrespected me," I say softly, shifting my eyes from the look of disappointment I see in his stare.

My mother huffs. "What? Speak up!"

"I said she disrespected me."

"She *disrespected* you? How, Kamiyah? What did that girl do for you to attack her like that? You know your father and I didn't raise you to be out here in the streets, fighting like some gutter trash." She shoots a look over at Daddy. "Erik, aren't you going to say something to her?"

"I will, as soon as we get home. I'm just as upset about this as you are. Yelling and screaming at her now isn't going to solve what already happened."

She huffs. "Well, obviously she needs to be yelled and screamed at, since she wants to be all out in the streets making a scene. Now explain to me how she disrespected you."

Right at this minute, I know I am in soooo much trouble when I get home. I wish I could crawl into my own hole and become invisible, become nonexistent, like the dude in that Ralph Ellison book I read in my AP English class. I think, try to make up a story that will lessen whatever punishment I have coming to me. But I know there is nothing that I can say—even though that tramp instigated the whole thing. And Sincere did nothing to prevent it.

"She was acting all stank, flirting with Sincere and playing me like I wasn't even there. I tried—"

"She was acting all *stank*? What in the hell does acting all *stank* look like?"

"She was—"

"You know what? Don't open your mouth to say another word. I don't even want to hear it. You will apologize to Sincere's parents and you will not be allowed to go over there again. Do you understand?"

I feel like she's just snatched the air from my lungs. She's trying to cut my lifeline. And now I am scrambling to find the right words to save myself. "Why? Sincere had nothing to do with this. Why are you trying to hurt me like this?"

"Well, too bad. I'm not trying to hurt you, Kamiyah. You're doing a good job of that all by yourself. I'm trying to keep your butt from making some very serious mistakes."

I start crying. "You can't do this to me. Mom, pleeeease ...Daddy, talk to her, *please*. You know how much Sincere means to me."

"Then *maybe* that's part of the problem," she says, narrowing her eyes at me. Her brown eyes have turned dark, almost black. "He means a little too much to you. Sincere really seems like a nice young man, but..."

"He *is* a nice guy. You can't stop me from being with him. He had nothing to do with what happened. It's my fault. I know. And if you have to punish me, then fine. But don't try and stop me from seeing Sincere, *please*. Besides Daddy, he's the only one who really cares about me."

"Girl, nonsense. I'm your mother. I care about you."

Whatever, Witch! "No, you don't. You hate me. And you know it!"

"C'mon, you two, let's talk about this when we get home." Daddy finally speaks up. *Why can't he ever speak up when I need him to? Why does he always have to sit back and let* her *run everything? I'm so sick of him being so passive with her.* "Kamiyah, your mother and I both care about you. We love you. And we don't want to see you get hurt."

Then stop trying to ruin my life! Worry about your own relationship and stay the hell out of mine! I blink my thoughts away. I am already in enough trouble. And I am smart enough to know to keep my true feelings to my-self—for now.

"Oh, we can talk about it all right," the Witch says, cut-ting her eyes over at Daddy. As always, she disregards him. "She is not allowed over at his house." She turns back to me. "Do you understand me?"

I stare her down. I am crumbling inside at the thought. I sit on my hands to fight the urge to wrap my hands in her hair, too.

"I *said.* Do. You. Understand?"

I swallow back my attitude. Swallow back my hate to-ward her. Take a deep breath. "Yes," I say through clenched teeth.

Daddy pulls around Sincere's parents' circular drive-way and stops the car in back of mine. "C'mon, let's go," he says, not looking at me. I open the door and get out. My mother waits for me to get away from the car before she gets out. And I can tell she wants to go off, but she won't because we're out in public.

Daddy walks up to the door and rings the bell. I am shaking. And I am ready to pass out when Sincere answers the door. I can tell he's pissed, too. But I can handle that. It's the punishment, the not being able to see him, that is going to kill me.

"Hello, Sincere," Daddy says, sticking his hand out. "Are your parents home?"

Sincere shakes his hand. "Hi, Mister Nichols. My dad's outta town. But my mom's here. Come in." He steps back and lets us in. And just when I think my day can't get any worse, my mother comes walking up the steps. I could drop dead on the spot. And she is determined to put the nails into my coffin. Sincere opens the door for her. They exchange hellos.

Sincere calls out to his mother; tells her that my parents and I are here. A few minutes later, Mrs. Lewis walks into the room, smiling. "Hello," she says, shaking their hands. "Please sit." This is the first time they have been inside Sincere's parents' home.

"You have a lovely home," my mother says, smiling wide and bright as if she wasn't just going off in the car.

"Oh, thank you." Mrs. Lewis looks over at me. "Kamiyah, I'm glad to see you're all right. Sincere told me what happened. I don't know what in the world is wrong with these young girls today. They're so wild and reckless."

I shift my eyes. *Ohmygod, what did he tell her? That I jumped on that ho and ripped her hair out? He probably has her thinking that I'm some wild, out-of-control girl.*

"Thank you," I say, glancing over at Sincere. He shifts his eyes from mine.

My mother arches her brow. "Speaking of which, this whole incident is shocking to her father and me. And we're here because Kamiyah has something she wants to say."

Everyone's eyes are now on me.

I nod, looking into Mrs. Lewis's eyes. "I apologize for you having to go down to the police station to pick up Sincere. I didn't mean for him to get dragged into it."

She waves me on. "Oh, please. No need to apologize

for that. I would have been more upset if he would have let you go down there by yourself. I know how much my son cares about you. Mister and Missus Nichols, you have a lovely daughter."

I glance over at Sincere, but he's too busy giving his mother a look to tell her to shut up to notice.

"Thank you," they both say.

"And please," my mother says, "call me Kayla. And this is Erik."

"And I'm Linda. It's nice to finally meet the both of you."

"Likewise," they both say.

The Witch continues, "I wanted to let you know that we don't condone what happened today. We didn't raise Kamiyah to be out in the streets fighting and getting arrested."

"Oh, I can tell she comes from a good home. Kamiyah is always well-mannered when she's here. My husband and I really like her."

My mother cuts her eye at me, then turns back to Mrs. Lewis, smiling. "And we feel the same about Sincere."

Mrs. Lewis looks over at Sincere. I can tell she hears the 'but' in my mother's tone. "Sincere, why don't you and Kamiyah go downstairs in the family room so we can talk for a minute?"

There's a part of me that wants to hang around to hear what they have to say that needs to be said without me and Sincere in the room. The other part of me is relieved to be away from their prying eyes. And out of earshot, so that I can speak to Sincere alone.

"Okay," he says, glancing at me. His face is expressionless.

"Don't get too comfortable, Kamiyah," the evil Witch says. "We'll only be a minute."

I don't answer. I follow Sincere down the stairs, back to where we started off earlier. Smiling, laughing, and enjoying each other's company. Oh, how I wish I could turn back the time and start this day over.

I don't wait for him to say anything. I start apologizing. Although I don't think, or feel, I should have to. I still believe if he woulda checked that ho, I wouldn't be in this mess. I feel like slapping his face. He stares at me, long and hard, then reaches out and takes my hand, walking me over to the sofa. We sit.

"You were right," he says softly. "I should have checked her."

Yeah, you really shoulda!

"But still...you didn't have to jump on her like that."

"She was asking for it," I state. "And I warned you from the beginning to not ever let another chick disrespect me."

"Kamiyah, you have to let some things go over your head. She wanted to get to you, and you let her."

"Well, *you* made it easy for her to do that. Why didn't you introduce me to her as *your* girlfriend? You made it seem like I was just some random chick you were with. Then you stood there and let her practically throw herself at you. You acted like it was cool."

"It wasn't cool. And I was dead wrong for that. I promise, it won't happen again. I'm not gonna let anyone else ever disrespect you like that. But you have to know that if we're gonna be together, then you can't be getting all jealous and acting all crazy like that. You have to trust me. I'm not doing anything with anyone else."

Sincere might be different. Maybe you can trust him.

You still need to keep your eye on him. "Well, did you do anything with *her?*"

He shifts his eyes to the floor, then back at me. "We talked for a few weeks over the summer."

"Did you and her do it?" He tells me *yes.* Tells me she let him *hit it* a few times. "So why'd y'all break up?"

"We were never together. She was a chick I chilled with. It wasn't anything serious."

I stare at him. "But you were having *sex* with her. Sex *is* something serious, at least for me."

"Sex is only serious when it's with someone you really care about. I didn't care about her, Miyah. So it wasn't that serious to me. I wanted sex. She was willing to give it up. So I took it." *And now that trick-ho wants another round.* "But it's different with us. I care about you, Miyah." He leans in and kisses me on the cheek. He takes a finger and lifts my chin, turning my face toward him. He looks into my eyes. *"You* are my girl." He kisses me softly on the lips and my heart leaps in my chest. "And I love you. But you gotta trust me." He closes in for another kiss. I open my mouth, welcome him in. This time we French-kiss. And I quickly forget how pissed off I am at him.

"Your lips taste so sweet," I say to him in between kisses. "I can get lost in your kisses."

He smiles at me. "You really got me going through it, Miyah. I've never felt this way about anyone the way I feel about you."

And you never will. I replay a conversation I overheard Erika having with one of her friends. *Seduce him mentally, hook him emotionally, and he'll never leave you.*

"I'm all yours, Sincere."

"All of you?"

I can't lose him!
"Yes."

We move from one kiss to the next, each kiss becoming more intense; each kiss causing more heat between us. We are...well, I know I am, swimming in thoughts of desire. And I can tell by the way he is kissing me that he is, too.

I won't lose him!

I pull back from him. "I want that girl off your Facebook page, and I want her blocked."

He looks at me. He doesn't blink. "A'ight, you got that."

I stare him down. "Do it now."

He gets up, trying to hide his excitement from all the kissing we've been doing. I smile, knowing he is turned on as much as I am. I watch as he walks over and grabs his phone from off the bar, then comes back over and sits next to me. I keep my eyes on him, and the screen, as he scrolls through his phone, then clicks on the Facebook app. He clicks on her page, then unfriends her.

One click, and...*poof!* That ho is deleted!

I lean into him and kiss him softly on the lips, parting my mouth, welcoming him back in. We continue our tongue dance until we hear his mother at the top of the stairs calling down to us.

"Sincere? Kamiyah?"

"Yeah, Mom?"

"C'mon up. Kamiyah's parents are ready to leave."

"We'll be right up."

We pull ourselves together. I grab my bag that I had left behind when we went walking. Sincere kisses me one last time.

"I forgot to ask you what you told your mom," I whisper as we make our way up the stairs.

"I told her that Lana started it. That she kept provoking you."

"Oh..." I say, feeling relieved and surprised. I am smiling.

"Ohmygod...ohmygod! Girl, you are all up on Face-book *and* YouTube!" Ameerah states excitedly the minute I answer my cell. I am looking in the mirror in my bed-room at Dad's house, staring at the scratches on my neck and across my face. Ameerah has me on speakerphone with Zahara and Brittani.

"Say *whaaat*?!"

"Girl, you heard her," Brittani chimes in. "It's all up on Facebook *and* Youtube."

"Ohmygod, are you serious?" I say, shocked. Well...I mean, not really, since I saw heads with their phones out. But still, I didn't think Zahara and them would hear about it; not like that.

"Honeeeey, it's all over the Net," Zahara says, as if she read my thoughts. "Someone posted the video of you fighting some chick in the pizzeria and it's getting mad hits. Now, spill it. Who is this broad you stomped? When did this beatdown go down? And what did she do for you to do her like that? 'Cause honeeeey...from that video, you were airing her out."

"How did y'all find out about it? It happened like five hours ago."

"One of Briana's Facebook friend's friend linked it on another friend's page, and that friend's friend shared it with someone else and somehow Briana saw it. She texted me and told me to go onto her page and see it for myself."

I cut off the bathroom light. Then walk over and plop

down on my bed. I'm sore and tired. This whole day has been one big tragedy. *It's all Sincere's fault. All he had to do was check that ho!*

"And how do you know it's on YouTube?"

Zahara says, "Girlfriend, all you gotta do is type in *beatdown in South Orange pizzeria* and *whooop*...there it is. Now enough with all this back-and-forth; we want details."

I type *beatdown in South Orange pizzeria* in the search engine. And sure enough, there it is. I am tearing the place up. I feel sick to my stomach! It's bad enough I have to pay for damages to the property. And it's even worse that I have charges pressed against me by that chick. Now this! If my parents see this, especially my mother, I'm dead for sure. I watch the video, telling them what popped off between me and that chick.

"Oh, she deserved that, then," Zahara says. "That stunt she pulled was a definite no-no. She better be glad we weren't there with you. You know we would have tag-teamed that ho."

"Yeah, girl," Brittani agrees. "She was definitely outta pocket."

"But, damn, Miyah," Ameerah says. "It looks like you were trying to rip her scalp out. You could have really hurt that girl."

I sigh. "Yeah, I know. Well, she shoulda stayed in her lane. I bet you she'll think twice before she pulls that little stunt again."

"Do your parents know?" Zahara asks.

"Yeah, they know. They had to come down to the police station to get me."

"The *police*?" they say in unison.

"Oh no. Poor ting-ting," Zahara says. "I know your mom

musta been flipping her lid on you. What did she say or
do? How long are you on punishment for?"

"Oh no, girl, wait. You better not be on punishment for
my birthday," Brittani adds.

I sigh. "I know, right. So far she hasn't said anything to
me. I mean she screamed on me in the car, but after that
she hasn't said one word. I think she's extra pissed over
the whole thing."

Zahara grunts. "Mmmph, and I can't understand why
your man was standing there looking all dumb and whatnot."

What in the hell? I frown. "Hold up. He wasn't looking
all dumb," I say defensively. "He tried to check her," I lie.
But so what! I can talk about Sincere, but I'm not about to
sit here and let her, or anyone else, pop junk about him—
even if he was dead wrong. "That broad was straight bel-
ligerent with it. She wasn't tryna hear it. She just kept
going."

"Still," Zahara continues, smacking her lips together,
"he couldn't even handle the situation. He shoulda squashed
that before it got messy. He's a real bum for that one, boo.
I know that's your man and all. But I'm saying."

"You saying *what*, boo?" I snap, hopping up from my
bed. I am pacing the floor now, trying to calm myself before I go off on her. "Don't be calling my man no bum.
Yeah, maybe he coulda handled it differently. But he didn't.
And it doesn't matter 'cause I handled it for him, for the
both of us. So watch what you say."

"Or what?" Zahara challenges. "I'll say what the hell I
want. I said he was a bum for that. And that's what I
meant."

Or you'll end up getting what that ho in the pizzeria got. "You know what. You're the damn *bum* with that raggedy weave all up on your bald-headed scalp. Don't be going in on my man. Find a man of your own first."

"I don't need a man," she snaps back.

I laugh sarcastically. "I guess not, when you're too busy tryna scheme on everyone else's."

I hear a few *Ohmygod*s in the background. Probably from Ameerah and Brittani.

"Oh, wait one damn minute. What is that supposed to mean?"

"C'mon, y'all," Brittani says, tryna play peacekeeper. "Y'all can't be beefing over no boys. That's not how we get down, and y'all know it."

"Mmmmph," Zahara grunts. "Tell that to her. She's the one always getting defensive anytime someone says something she doesn't like about her so-called man."

"I do not."

"Whatever, ho. You do, too. Ever since you got with him you been acting all funny-style. I'm done with it. Ameerah and Brit, I'll get up with y'all. Call me when you're finished talking to her."

"Whatever," I say. "The only ho is you. Slurping all up on Jarrell and anyone else you can drop down on your knees to."

She curses me out, calling me all kinds of names, then disconnects from the line.

"Ohmygod," Ameerah and Brittani say.

"What in the heck was that all about?" Brittani wants to know. "And what do you mean, she's slurping down Jarrell? They're messing around? Since when?"

I sigh. "Just drop it." I sit back on my bed.

"Dang, Miyah," Ameerah says. "Why you do her like that? You know Zee wasn't tryna go in on your man."

"I know. But still. Sometimes she goes a little too overboard. Look. I'm tired, y'all. I'll call y'all tomorrow." We talk for a few minutes more, then disconnect. *Zahara is a damn hater!*

18

It's early Sunday morning—a little *too* early for me. It's 7:38 to be exact—when I hear what sounds like a heated discussion between my parents. I open my door. They are downstairs in the living room. I tiptoe—why, I have no idea, since our floors are carpeted—toward the top of the stairs and listen.

"I'm not saying she can't see him, Erik," I overhear. The Wicked Witch is arguing. And Daddy is doing what he normally does—letting her go on and on and on. He has told her that she is being unreasonable by forbidding me to go over to Sincere's house anymore. "All I'm saying is, it needs to be monitored more closely. Kamiyah is too young to be getting so serious with him; with anyone, for that matter. First it's with the constant phone calls and excessive texts. And after this mess with her fighting some girl over him, I'm convinced it isn't healthy."

"Kayla, I agree. She is too young. But we've already been down this road with Erika. And you know how that turned out. It was disastrous. The two of you fought constantly. And in the end, she was still with that boy, what's-his-name."

"Don't remind me. Still, Kamiyah is getting too wrapped up in her relationship with Sincere. And I don't like it."

"Look, I hear you. But I'm not going through what we went through with Erika again. And I don't want the cops being called again because my wife and daughter can't get along with each other. Every other week the cops were being called. I won't have it. Kamiyah can still see him. As long as Sincere's parents are home, she's allowed over there. And that's that. His mother doesn't have a problem with it and neither do I. When she's here with you, if you don't want her there, then fine. But when she's with me, she's allowed to go as long as someone is home."

"Are you serious, Erik? I mean, really. That's part of the problem. I say one thing, and you turn around and let her do the exact opposite. I can't understand why you undermine everything I do and say when it comes to that girl."

"*That girl* is our daughter."

"And *I* am your *wife*."

"I don't need you to remind me of that," Daddy says. "I know who I'm married to."

"Then act like it! And stop undermining everything I do. Stop letting our daughter run you."

"Oh, so that's what you think she's doing? Running me? Like you've been doing?"

"Excuse you? I've *never* tried to run you, Erik. And I resent you for saying that."

"Look. I don't want to turn this into an argument. I apologize if you feel that way. It's not my intention to undermine you. I simply don't always agree with your approach, which hasn't been too successful, thus far."

Uh-oh, I think, leaning up against the wall. *This is about to get real ugly.*

"Excuse *you*?! What exactly is that supposed to mean?"

I hear Daddy sigh. "Look, forget it."

"Oh no. I don't think so. We're not about to forget nothing. If you have something to say, then say it. First you accuse me of trying to run you. Now you're questioning my parenting."

"Kayla, listen."

"No, Erik. You listen. Before you start throwing darts at me, take a look at your own crap. I am the *only* one who has ever been consistent with our children. So don't go pointing fingers at me without pointing them at yourself first."

"I shouldn't have said that."

"Well, you did."

"I know you love our daughters as much as I do. I have always tried to stay out of how you parented them because they're girls, and you are their mother. But you were too hard on Erika. And that only pushed her farther away. Then when she moved out, you started doing it to Kamiyah."

"*Doing it?* What is *it* I'm doing, Erik?"

"Controlling everything she does. Suffocating her."

Oh, wow…you go, Daddy! I'll have to be sure to use that one.

"So, you're saying *I'm* the problem here? Is that what you're getting at?"

"No. I'm saying keeping Kamiyah chained in the house isn't the right approach. Not allowing her the freedom to make mistakes and hopefully learn from them isn't helping her. In the end, it will only hurt her more."

"So you're saying it's okay for her to be out in the streets fighting and getting arrested. Is that what I'm hearing?"

"C'mon, Kayla, be for real here. You know that's *not* all right."

"Mmmph, sounds like it is to me."

"We didn't raise her to go looking for trouble. But we did raise her to defend herself."

"*Defend* herself? Did you not read the police report? Kamiyah wasn't defending herself. It sounds more like she was trying to defend her position in her relationship with Sincere—who is the common denominator in this mess. Kamiyah attacked that girl. It's no different from when she attacked that other girl two years ago—*again*, over some boy."

OMG, she doesn't even know what she's talking about. I didn't attack anyone. When I fought that girl, Jessica what's-her-face, it was because she deserved it. She was tryna ho herself out to James, who she *knew* was my boyfriend at the time. She and I weren't the best of friends, but we were still cool. And the fact that she would smile up in my face, knowing she was scheming behind my back on how she could get with my man, was just cause for me to drag her out of her house and beat her down. Okay, so I broke her nose and my parents had to pay for her medical bills and I was put on punishment for a whole month afterward—still, she deserved it. And it was well worth it. She was a skank. And, I quickly learned, so was he.

"The only difference this time," she continues, "is that she got arrested and charged for it."

"Kayla, you heard what Sincere's mother said. That girl was provoking Kamiyah."

"Mmmph…that's the story Sincere told her. If you want to buy it, too, then you go right ahead."

"That boy has no reason to lie to his mother about what happened."

"And I bet you he has one good reason to: Kamiyah."

"You know what, Kayla. Do whatever you want. You seem to always have the answers. But I'm telling you, trying to stop her from seeing Sincere is only going to backfire on us. You know it as much as I do."

I hear her huff. "Fine. But she's going to to be on a very, very short leash."

"And you think trying to control her is going to make things better? That it's going to stop whatever you think is going to happen?"

"I'm not trying to *control* her. I'm trying—"

"Kayla, stop it. Everything is always about control for you, even down to this marriage."

I am shocked to hear Daddy tell her this. I know, I know. I shouldn't be ear-hustling on their conversation, but it's the only way I know what's really going on with them. And besides, you never know what might be heard that I can use against her—or at the very least, throw back up in her face.

"Erik, how dare you? That is not so."

"It is. And the sooner you recognize it, the better."

"Kamiyah is changing. I can't put my finger on it. But I am telling you, it isn't for the good."

"Our little girl's growing up, Kayla. And she wants to make her own decisions. That's all. And we as her parents have to be able to allow her the room to do so, within reason. That is the only way she will learn."

"You know what, Erik. Do whatever you want. I'm done. But know this. When the shit hits the fan, do not say I didn't warn you." And with that said, I hear the door open, then shut.

I tiptoe back to my room and peek out of my window. I watch as the Wicked Witch hops on her broomstick, then speeds off—pissed! *Whatever!*

Later on in the evening, I am downstairs in the basement working on a contemporary ballet piece. Daddy had a room built down here specifically for me to practice dance in when he first moved here. There are mirrors—which happen to be a dancer's best friend—all over. There's a beautiful wood floor and I have an adjustable barre. The only furniture is a white leather sofa.

I've gone through Daddy's extensive music collection and have found the perfect song. An instrumental piece called "Moments in Love" by Art of Noise—this white group from waaaay back in the day. It's a rare version he has. OMG, it's sexy. And it's absolutely beautiful. It's the song I wanna use for my Juilliard audition.

I have the stereo on blast. I close my eyes and let the music lift me. Deep breath; shoulders back. I am so caught up in the moment, lost in the music—in its instrumentation—that I don't even realize I am crying or that I am being watched until the music stops and I hear clapping.

Startled, I look over and it's Sincere, standing in the doorway. "That was beautiful," he says, smiling.

"Thank you," I say, walking over to him, wiping my eyes with the back of my hands. I am so happy to see him.

"Damn, you a'ight? Why you crying?"

I shake my head. "I'm not crying."

He eyes me. "Looks like it to me. But a'ight; if you say so."

I smile. "Trust me. I have nothing to cry about." I know it's a lie, but the truth is, I don't know why I was crying. "How long were you standing there?"

"Long enough to see how talented you are."

I smile. "My dad let you in?"

He shakes his head. "No, your mom did. She told me you were down here practicing."

I am shocked. "Wow," is all I can say. I lift up on my tippy-toes and kiss him.

"You're real sexy in them tights."

I laugh. "It's a leotard."

"Yeah, you're real sexy in that, too."

I smile.

"So, what was the name of that song you were dancing to? It was sounding a'ight."

" 'Moments in Love,' " I tell him, grabbing a towel and dabbing the sweat from around my neck. Sincere walks over to the sofa and takes a seat. "I wanna use it for my Juilliard audition." I toss the towel over on the barre.

He leans back, legs wide, staring at me intently. "Real sexy," he says, licking his lips.

"What's real sexy?"

"You. That little thing with all them sexy spins you were doing. The music. All of it."

I realize that that was the first time Sincere has seen me dance. "Thanks. I'm glad you liked it."

"Nah, I loved it. Damn, Miyah, you got real skills, baby.

I didn't know you were *that* good. You're about to be the Beyoncé of ballet."

I laugh, walking over to him. "Whatever." I sit on the sofa next to him, lifting his arm up, then draping it over my shoulder. I lean back on him. "Well, I'm good at a lot of things."

"Oh yeah? Like what?"

I look up at him. "Like this," I say, kissing him on the lips.

"Yeah, okay. What else?"

I grin. "I'm not saying. You'll have to find out."

He laughs. "Oh, word? It's like that?"

"Yup."

He kisses me again, gazing in my eyes. "Dance for me."

"Now?"

"Yeah. Do something just for me."

I smile, getting up. "And I have just the song," I tell him, walking over to the stereo. I shuffle through a stack of CDs until I find the one I want, slip it in, then skip through the tracks. Jill Scott's "He Loves Me" starts playing. And for the next five minutes and forty seconds, I give Sincere a dance he'll never forget. I give him my heart and my soul. I give him everything that I am. And everything he is to me.

19

Okay, so I'm not on punishment. Well, I am. But I can see Sincere, and I'm going to Brittani's birthday party this Saturday. Still, I'm not allowed to drive my car for the next two weeks. Mmmph, I don't even know the point of having it, since it's been parked more than it's been on the road. Anywaaayz, I have to go straight home after school on the days I don't have dance. So I'm not allowed out of the house. Whatever. I can still have company over, only for an hour, though—supervised, of course. Blah, blah, blah. Still, I'm not complaining.

I am at my locker when I spot Zahara and Ameerah coming around the corner. Zahara and I haven't spoken in two days, since last Saturday night when I was on speaker with her.

Ameerah smiles at me. Zahara cuts her eyes and keeps on walking.

Sometimes you have to admit when you're wrong,

even when you're not. I sigh. "Zahara, wait up, girl," I say, walking over to her.

She stops. Places a hand up on her hip, giving me attitude I guess I deserve.

"What is it? I'm gonna be late for class."

"Since when you care about being late for class?" I ask.

"Since my so-called best friend started coming at me all sideways," she says sarcastically.

"I'm sorry, Zee. I shouldn't have said that."

She rolls her eyes. "Oh no, sweetie. Don't apologize. You said exactly what you felt. But be clear. I don't care what you think of me. I'm still fly, boo. You gotta man, I'm happy for you. But ever since you got with him, you've been changing up. And it ain't cute."

"I haven't changed," I say defensively. "I just have a lot going on with school and dance."

"*And* Sincere," she adds, twisting her lips up.

"Okay, yes. With Sincere, too. But we're still girls."

"Mmmph. I thought we were, but I guess I was wrong." She glances at her watch. "Look, I gotta go. The homeroom bell is going to ring in two minutes and I'm not tryna be late for some chick who doesn't know how to treat her friends." She walks off, leaving me standing in the middle of the hall, feeling like a fool. But I know Zahara. She'll stay pissed at me for a few days, then get over it. We'll be back laughing it up in no time. I walk up into my Advanced Calculus class just as the bell rings. I take my seat.

"Okay, class," Mr. Langston says, grabbing a stack of papers from off his desk. *Oh, great!* "Please take out a pencil and put away everything else. This is your first test of the marking period. You may use your notes from previous class discussions only. If I see you glancing over at some-one else's desk, I'm going to take that as you're cheating. And you will automatically be given an F. If you ask to use the bathroom, you must turn in your exam first. And it will not be given back when you return." The whole class groans. I glance over my shoulder and catch Jarrell staring at me. He winks at me. I roll my eyes, turning back to face the front of the class. "Does anyone have any questions?"

Someone in the back wants to know, "What if we fail it?"

"Then you will have to try harder on the next exam. But there'll be extra credit you can take to help with your end of the marking period average. Are there any other questions?"

"Yeah, Mister L," Jarrell says. "You real foul for dumping this on us like this without any warning. Wassup with that?"

"And *you're* real foul for not paying attention, Mister Mills. Now wassup with that?" Everyone laughs. "Settle down. You were all told the first week of school that this is an advanced math class, that besides weekly homework assignments and quizzes there would be at least two surprise exams and one final. And so, surprise, surprise. Here's your first exam. Anything else before we get started?"

"Can I make a quick cheat sheet?" someone else asks. *What a loser!*

"Sure you can, if you want to fail." Mr. Langston hands me my exam. "Okay, let's get started."

Someone says, "Dang. This is a lot of formulas and concepts."

"No talking," Mr. Langston warns.

I sigh. There are eight problems and three concepts to answer. The first question wants us to explain how to solve for the equation of a tangent line. That one's easy. The second problem wants us to define an equivalence relation on X. Then we have to justify our answers. *Okay, another easy one.* The problems get progressively more difficult. And now I am wishing I would have been paying closer attention to the notes on the board instead of doodling Sincere's name and writing him love letters all in my notebook. I inhale, then exhale. This is going to be one long period.

"Looka here," Brittani says, dragging Zahara by the arm over toward my locker. It's the end of the day. And the only thing on my mind right now is seeing Sincere. He's picking me up from school, then driving me home. "The two of you need to peace this dumbness up right here and now, so we can get on with being girls. My birthday is in five days—that's this Saturday, okay? And the two of you need to air it out, then get the hell over it 'cause both of my besties are gonna be there, and I don't want either one of you acting all stank, ruining my damn day."

"I tried to apologize to her earlier," I say, shutting my locker, "but she wasn't tryna hear it."

Zahara rolls her eyes up in her head, all dramatic and whatnot. "Oh, puhleeeze. Is that what that mess was earlier? Give me a break. Honey, that was an epic fail!"

"Whatever. I said I was sorry."

"And we *both* know you didn't mean it."

"I did mean it. I was wrong for coming at you like that."

"Mmmph. Then you try to play me with Jarrell. I'm not even thinking about that boy."

"Well, that's not what he said," I say, eyeing her.

"Well, I don't care what *he* said. That's not what it is."

Mmmph, then why you getting all defensive? "Look, I don't care one way or the other if it is or isn't. I'm not messing with him, so it's whatever. I'm sorry if I offended you. If you wanna stay mad at me, then stay mad. I still love you, boo," I say, pulling out my phone. Sincere has sent me a text letting me know he's outside.

"Well, this isn't about Jarrell," she states, frowning. "This is about you coming out of your face talking about I stay scheming on other chicks' dudes, like I'm some sheisty chick. Then you pop ish about my weaves and thangs, calling me knotty-headed and whatnot, like I'm some real live ooga booga or something."

"Well, half the time your weaves *are* a mess."

Ameerah and Brittani give me a look.

I shrug.

"Whatever," Zahara huffs. "It's my hair. I paid for it and I'll wear it however I want."

"Do you, sweetie," I say, getting annoyed.

Ameerah huffs. "Look, will y'all two stop all this ying-yang back-and-forth and make up? Damn! I don't have all day to be standing here listening to this retardedness. I wanna get to my boo's practice."

"Well, I said I was sorry, but she still wants to act all funny about it, so whatever."

"Yeah, I'm acting funny about it the same way you've been acting funny since you got with Sincere."

"Ohmygod..." Sincere sends me another text. I text him back, telling him I'll be right out. "Look, I gotta go. Can we talk about this later? Sincere's outside waiting for me."

Zahara turns her lips up. "Mmmph. What else is new? Sincere, Sincere, Sincere. Instead of tryna peace things up with your girl you'd rather run off to ya man. Go do you, 'cause I'm done." She walks off.

Brittani and Ameerah shake their heads.

"I'm sorry, but you was dead wrong, Miyah. You didn't have to go in on our girl's weaves like that," Ameerah says.

"But wait," Brittani says. "Forget the weaves. I wanna hear more about her and Jarrell. Did she...?"

I shrug, shaking my head. "I don't know if she did or didn't. I only know what I heard."

They both shake their heads again. We go back and forth a few minutes more, then bounce. I race out the door and hop in Sincere's truck. I lean over and give him a kiss the minute I shut the door.

"Damn, you smell good," he says, smiling.

"So do you," I say. Sincere has one hand on the steering wheel and his other hand on my thigh. I have on a short skirt and leggings today. He licks his lips. "What time is your mom gonna be home?"

I shrug. "Like around six or seven."

He grins, moving his eyebrows up and down. "So you think we can get it in real quick?" He inches his hand higher up my thigh. My legs part slightly. I know I'm not supposed to have company, especially a boy, in the house when no one's home. But it's Sincere. And his hand feels good on me. And I wanna feel them both all over my body.

"Yessss," I whisper. "Let's hurry up and get there."

20

Okay, so it's Brittani's birthday, whoopty-do. Right now I'd rather be somewhere, anywhere other than here listening to them sing "Happy Birthday." Like chilling with my man.

I am staring around the room as everyone sings. We're all at Brittani's, celebrating her birthday with her parents, Mr. and Mrs. Wynn, her sister, Briana, and three of her female cousins—KreeAsia, Tiffany, and Shawna—from Newark. I don't really know them all that well. I mean, I've been around them before, but never really made any effort to get to know them. And, truth be told, I still won't. They're not the kinda chicks I wanna hang with on the regular. Tiffany and Shawna aren't so bad. But KreeAsia—with her multicolored bob weave and skintight leopard jeans—is a loud, obnoxious mess.

Anywaaayz, as a gift, Briana's parents bought her the iPad 2 and a cute pink cover to go with it. I got her the boots, which she loves—of course! Zahara got her some

Bath & Body Works products, and Ameerah bought her a charm for her Juicy bracelet.

And for the grand finale, Brittani was told she's going to be getting Briana's Volvo because her sister's getting a new car. Brittani's extra-hyped now. And I don't blame her.

"Wait, wait," Zahara says, holding her hands up, all dramatic and whatnot. "Ameerah and I have another verse to sing." She glances over at Ameerah, then me—as an afterthought, I'm sure. She's nice enough to include me. Zahara starts off. "Happy birthday to..."

Then Ameerah chimes in.

Then I start singing my verse—even though I don't really wanna be a part of it

Brittani is cracking up 'cause it's the birthday song sung by the lion, giraffe, and hippo in the movie *Madagascar*. Although it came out when we were mad young, it's still one of our favorite movies.

"Now make a wish with your big bubblehead," Briana says, laughing.

"Forget you, with your nappy-headed self," Brittani says, laughing. She closes her eyes for a few seconds, then blows out the candles. Everyone claps.

"What'd you wish for?" Zahara asks.

Brittani scrunches her nose up. "That your breath didn't smell like hot skunk piss."

We start laughing.

"Oooh, boo. Don't do it," Zahara warns, wagging a finger at her. "Or you'll be wishing for a new set of teeth. You know you don't want it with me."

"No, boo. You don't want it with this fist," Brittani snaps, making a fist, then moving it back and forth in front of her face, across her eyes. "One right hook and *pow* . . . have your sockets knocked out."

While the two of them are going back and forth, clowning each other, I glance down at my wrist, checking the time—7:18 P.M. *I wonder what Sincere's doing.* I slide my hand down into my bag on the low and pull out my phone. I check for any messages or texts. There are none.

Brittani stops clowning Zahara, looking over at me. Zahara rolls her eyes. Brittani shoots daggers. "Oh, I know you not about to stand here and start textin' ya man, Miss Thang-a-lang," she snaps, putting a hand up on her hip and neck rolling it up, "while we celebrating my birthday. This is supposed to be about me. *Not* Sincere. So all eyes on *me*, not ya cell phone, boo."

Zahara smirks, rolling her eyes.

I suck my teeth, more so at Zahara than Brittani. I drop my phone back down in my bag. And give her my undivided attention.

"Girl, hush," her mom says, handing her a cake knife. "You worry about cutting this cake, so me and your father can go upstairs and let you young folks have the rest of the night to yourselves."

"You tell her, Missus Wynn," I say, laughing.

After Brittani finishes cutting the cake, she places two large pieces on plates and hands them to her mother. Her father walks over and gives her a kiss on the forehead. Tells her how much he loves her, wishes her a happy birthday again, then says good night to the rest of us.

"Good night, Mister Wynn," Ameerah, Zahara, and I say. We watch as he walks out, then climbs the stairs.

"Whew, I'm soooo glad Auntie and Unc done finally

dipped," KreeAsia says, slipping her iPod into the station dock. "Now we can really get the party started. Just wish we had some boys here."

I roll my eyes. Walking off to the bathroom, I shut the door and call Sincere. When he doesn't pick up, I leave a message, then grab a few napkins and wet them. I text Daddy to come pick me up, then press the damp towels to my lips, walking back out to where everyone is loud-talking and dancing, and tell them I'm not feeling well. I clutch my stomach for emphasis.

Brittani walks over to me. "Thanks for the boots, boo." She gives me a hug. "I love 'em." I frown as if I'm in severe pain. Well, I am in pain. I'm pained that I can't get in touch with Sincere. And this not knowing what he's doing or who he's with right now is hurting me. "Miyah, girl, are you all right?"

I shake my head. "No. I think I'm coming down with something."

"Oh no," she says, sounding concerned. "You want me to get Brittani to take you home?"

"No, that's okay. I texted my dad to come get me." My phone buzzes and I quickly pull it out of my bag, hoping that it's Sincere. It's Daddy. "This is him now," I tell her. "He's on his way."

Ten minutes later, I am walking out the door with everyone telling me they hope I feel better. Well, everyone except Zahara. She's eyeing me with one brow raised. I act like I don't see it and wave good night.

"How come you didn't text me back earlier?" I ask, the minute I am finally able to get in touch with Sincere. It's nine thirty at night.

"I met up with a few of my boys and we got it in at the gym," he tells me. "Then we went to get something to eat."

I twist my lips up. "Oh, for real? Around what time was that?"

"Like around six, seven. Why?"

" 'Cause I called you. Then sent you a text."

"You sent me three texts."

"And...you didn't respond to any of 'em."

"I didn't have my phone."

"Oh, really?"

"Yeah, really. I left it at home."

"Let me guess," I say sarcastically. "On the charger? How convenient."

He lets out a sigh. "Yo, why you tryna pick a fight?"

"I'm not tryna pick anything. I'm simply tryna understand why all of a sudden you're forgetting your phone all the time."

"It's not all the time. I've forgotten my phone *twice* since we've been together."

I huff. "Whatever, Sincere. It's starting to look like a pattern."

He laughs. "*A pattern?* Girl, you buggin', for real. The only thing that's starting to look like a pattern is you nagging me, for real. Seems like every other day you coming at my neck with something. I really care about you, Miyah. But on some real, I'm not beat to keep going through this with you."

I feel a sharp pain shooting through my heart as he says this. *Girlfriend, you better fall back with all the extras before he dismisses you.* The thought of Sincere trying to break up with me over something this silly is…unthink-able!

"So what are you saying, Sincere?" I ask, holding my breath for his response.

He lets out another sigh. "You need to chill, for real."

"I know," I say, relieved I don't have to turn on the tears tonight.

"Why you always bugging?"

I'm staring at the picture that's up on my dresser of the two of us. We took it over the summer at the Lincoln Park music festival in Newark. It was like the end of July. OMG, it was so hot out that day! And the park was packed with heads—young and old—from all over, jamming to all types of house and club music. I had on a cute denim mini, a white tank top with the words *Divas Rule* written on the front in silver, and a pair of white strappy heels. My hair was pulled up in ponytail. Sincere wore a wifebeater and a pair of jeans with some crispy white sneaks. And his white fitted was cocked to the side, making him look extra sexy. I reach for the frame and pick it up. We had only been talking for like a good week when we took it. I smile, setting it back up on the dresser.

"Sometimes I get scared," I say.

His tone softens. "*Scared?* Of what?"

"Of this…" I pause. "You…us. You're my dream come true, Sincere. And sometimes I feel like it's all gonna come crumbling down around me. That one day I'm going to wake up and it's all going to be one big, nasty nightmare. There'll be no you in my life. And that scares me. I'd kill myself if we ever broke up."

It gets silent on the other end of the phone. Trust me. I've never thought about killing myself, and I still don't.

But if Sincere and I ever break up, I know worrying about who he's with and what he's doing would definitely kill me. And it'd be a slow, torturous death, I'm sure.

"Sincere?"

"Yeah, I'm here."

"Oh, okay. You got real quiet on me."

"You effed my head up with that 'I'd kill myself' comment. Don't talk like that. It isn't cool."

"I know. And I didn't really mean it like that. I just don't wanna lose you to anything or anyone, that's all."

"I'm yours, baby. I'm not going anywhere. But you have to stop buggin' over nothing. You hear?"

I nod as if he can see me. "Yes."

"So wassup with you?"

"Nothing."

"Oh, a'ight. Then why you always acting like you don't believe me when I tell you things?"

'Cause I don't! "I didn't hear from you all day," I whine.

"I'm sorry about that, baby. This morning I was with my mom, visiting my grandfather at the nursing home, then I got up with the boys and went to the gym, then ended up hanging out afterward. Like I said, I left my cell phone on the charger, so I didn't have any way of calling you until now."

"I wanted to hear your voice. That's all."

"I know. But it wasn't that serious. Getting all nutty on me ain't it, Miyah. You know I was gonna call you."

"I know," I say, rolling my eyes up in my head. *It shouldn't take you all dang day to get back to me when I hit you up, either.* "I didn't hear from my man all day and got worried."

"C'mon, Miyah, damn. I went to the gym, came home,

showered, then went out with my friends. You act like you don't want me to have friends."

"That's not true," I say defensively. "You can have all the friends you want. I just don't want you up in no chick's face, that's all."

"I'm not all up in no chicks' faces. And they're not all up in mine."

"Oh, okay. So answer me this. You have over three thousand Facebook friends, and most of 'em are chicks. Why?"

"I don't know. They request me, and I accept."

"Mmmph. Do you even know most of 'em?"

"Nah, not really."

"Then why do you accept them then?"

"C'mon, Miyah, they're just girls who requested me as a friend. That ain't about nothing."

"Then delete 'em."

"Why should I?"

"The question is, why won't you?"

"I'm not deleting them because I don't think it's a big deal."

I huff. "Well, it's a big deal to me."

"Because you're making it out to be. I'm not interested in any of them girls. Most of 'em live outta state anyway."

"Oh, so if they were in Jersey, you'd be tryna get with 'em?"

He sucks his teeth. "Kamiyah, you trippin', for real. I'm with who I wanna be with. You need to relax, for real."

"I am relaxed."

"Then stop tryna make it more than what it is. You my girl—not anyone else."

"Then why don't you have it up on your status that *I'm* your girl?"

He sighs. "It says I'm in a relationship. Will it make you feel better if I put who I'm in a relationship with?"

"Yes."

"Then I'ma do it right now."

"Good." I glance at the clock. It's almost one o'clock in the morning. "Can you come see me?"

"*Now?*"

"Yes, now. I wanna see you, Sincere."

"I wanna see you, too, but my parents will flip a lid if they hear me leaving up outta here this time of night, especially my dad. I'm eighteen, but he ain't playing that coming in and out whenever you want. Once I'm in, they expect me to be in."

I sigh. "Then I can come to you. Can you sneak me in?"

He laughs. "Miyah, you're crazy, girl."

"I'm crazy for you," I say real low and sexy. "I just wanna taste your lips."

"I'll be right there."

21

Monday morning, during fourth period, I'm sitting in the cafeteria with Ameerah and Brittani at our usual table—the one that's on the far right by the windows so we can see the comings and goings, 'cause we nosy like that. We rotate who's down here first, to make sure no one else tries to house our table. Today happens to be my turn.

"Ohmygod," Brittani says, dropping her book bag onto the floor, then pulling out a chair. She practically flops down in it. "I am soooo over this school year. I ain't even gonna front. I swear I'm counting down till winter break."

She's sitting across from me, pulling her hair up into a ponytail. I stare at her, wondering why she insists on wearing so much weave. I don't know whose weaves are worse, hers or Zahara's. Uh, on second thought, I do know. Zahara's! I mean, weaves are *cute*, I guess—not that I have one, or ever needed one—but when it's hanging down to your lower back and you don't have an ounce of Indian in your blood, then you are being too extra with it.

"I know, right," Ameerah says, pulling out a bag of Cool Ranch Doritos. She offers us some. We don't want any. "Good, more for me. Anyway, I can't believe how fast the weeks are flying by."

"Mmmph, not fast enough, if you ask me," Brittani responds, letting her hair fall back down over her shoulders. "Between chemistry and Latin, these classes have been killing me."

"Don't remind me." Ameerah sighs. "I am so over all of this and it's only October. Y'all wanna hang out at my house this weekend? My parents are going to be away."

I shake my head. "I can't. I'm going into the city to chill with Erika this weekend. Hopefully she'll take me shopping and I'll come back with some bangin' stuff."

"I wish I had a sister like yours," Ameerah says. "You're so dang lucky. She spoils you. I'm lucky if I can get ten cents outta mine."

"I guess," I say, all nonchalant like it's really no biggie. "Y'all wanna go to the winter formal this year and turn it out?" The winter formal is a holiday party that South Orange Prep has every year before the Christmas break.

"Girl, I can't even think that far ahead," Ameerah states, shaking her head. "I mean, I guess it could be a lot of fun."

"Shoot, I don't even know if I wanna go," Brittani says, twisting her lips up. "I can see my mom now, acting all stank, telling me what kinda dress she's *not* gonna pay for."

Ameerah laughs, shaking her head. "So what you're saying is, you'll be wrapped from head to toe in a mummy suit if it's up to her."

She rolls her eyes, sucking her teeth. "Basically. She

gets on my nerves, always tryna clock 'n' block my moves. I'm like, damn, can I breathe? Let me do me."

Brittani's mom doesn't allow her to rock cute, clingy outfits, or wear anything that is too short or too low. Mmmph... *borrrring!* Whew, I'm glad that's not my headache. My mom may be a meddling witch when it comes to everything else, but she never, ever tries to dress me. I wear what I want. Well, okay, okay... within reason. Anywaaayz, Brittani's mom be acting like making her wear them old lady wears is gonna keep her from getting a rep for being fast. She can't even wear thongs. *Thongs!* Can you believe that?

I laugh. "Why you care? It's not like you listen to her anyway. If she knew you had a stash of hootch wear in your locker, she'd lose her mind."

She laughs. "And you know it."

"Where's Zahara?" I ask, glancing at my watch. She's not pissed at me anymore, so we've picked up right where we left off as girls. Of course, I had to apologize like fifty more times this morning before she finally let it go.

Brittani sweeps her bangs across her forehead. "You already know," she says, taking a seat across from me. "She got issues today."

"Issues" is how we refer to our periods; or when one of us is PMSing real bad. I twist my lips. "Mmmph. Well, she needs to hurry up and get down here," I say, texting her. "I have to meet Sincere at twelve thirty."

As soon as I press SEND, I see her coming through the doors rocking one of our FFFF T-shirts (FFFF stands for Fly Fine Friends Forever), the black one with the gold lettering. She has on a pair of black stretch jeans and a sexy gold-coin belt around her waist. And her hair is pulled back into a spiked ponytail; her bangs are swept to the side. "Never mind, I see her now," I say, setting my phone down on the table. Brittani cranes her neck to look over her shoulder.

My cell dings. It's a text from Sincere. HEY BABY, JUST THINKN ABT U. C U AT 12:30. I smile, texting him back. C U THEN.

When I look up, Ameerah and Brittani are all up in my grill. "What?" I ask, trying to play it off.

"You real strung out on him, aren't you?" Ameerah asks.

I suck my teeth, smirking. "Whatever. No, I'm not strung out on him."

Ameerah and Brittani look at each other, then over at me, twisting their lips up. "Mmmhmm," they both say. "If you say so." They laugh.

I roll my eyes, flicking my hand at 'em. "Y'all think what you want."

"What y'all over here laughin' at?" Zahara asks as she comes around the table, droppin' her black D & G book bag into an empty seat. She pulls out the chair next to me and sits down.

"Kamiyah all up on her cell with you-know-who, who she claims she's not strung out on."

Zahara twists her lips up. "No comment. We just started back talking and soooo, moving on...nice weather today, isn't it?"

I laugh. "Whatever. All y'all heifers can kiss the back of my Juicys."

"So, let's cut out all the okey-doke. You finally let him hit it yet?" Zahara asks, leaning in toward me like she's waiting for me to give her some juicy, top secret information. " 'Cause you really starting to act like he's giving it to you real good."

I frown. "Hell no, I haven't started letting him hit anything. I ain't no ho, boo." *Like you!*

"I'm not saying you are. I'm just saying, though. The way you be acting...never mind, forget I asked."

What Sincere and I are already doing is about as far as I'm ready or willing to take it. I just turned seventeen. The last thing I'm beat for is to be stressing about sex—well, going all the way, that is. I can look around this lunchroom and point out every single girl who's having sex, or had it, and they've either been pregnant, caught an STD, or they're running around acting like real fiends 'cause they can't get enough of it. No, thank you. I'll take staying a virgin for two hundred, please!

"Girl, I hear you," Brittani says. "Ain't no need to rush it. Like some people we know." She cuts her eyes over at Zahara.

Zahara rolls her eyes. "Whatever, trick!" she spits, looking over at me. She puckers her lips up. "Shuga, if you know like I know you'll pull back them sheets and let 'im climb up on top of you," she says, grinding and winding in her seat while doing a Monique impersonation.

I laugh 'cause she's silly as heck.

"Whatever, Miss Panty Droppa," Brittani says, smacking her lips. "Anywayz, when Stevie was tryna push up on me, I did a Beyoncé on his butt. I looked 'im in his face and told 'im if he wanted to see me naked, he better put a ring on it. Then I dropped down low and coochie popped it out the door."

We start laughing, imagining her no-rhythm-having-self

dropping down and sweeping the floor with it, trying to be like our girl Beyoncé, dancing her way out the door. That mess is hilarious 'cause we all know she's as stiff as steel wool.

Brittani rolls her eyes.

"Any of you hookers have an extra tampon in your locker?" Zahara asks, fishing through her book bag. She pulls out a bag of sunflower seeds. "I used my last one a few minutes ago, and I'm going to need another one for later."

"Ugh, TMI," Ameerah says, twisting her lips up. "I don't know why you use them things anyway."

Brittani laughs. "Girl, you know why. She likes things being stuck up in her."

Ameerah chokes on her drink, laughing. "Oooh, you so wrong for that."

Zahara gives them the finger. "Lick me!"

"Ewww," Ameerah says, slapping her hand up over her mouth. "You almost made me throw up in the back of my mouth. Yuck."

"Ugh, thanks for ruining my lunch," Brittani says, tossing her bag of Doritos on the table.

"Oh, before I forget," I say, changing the subject. "Y'all know we have to go check out that new movie with Antonio Banderas in it when it hits the screen next Friday, so don't ya'll make any plans."

Zahara sighs. "Ugh, is this another *Shrek* movie?"

I laugh, knowing how she hated being dragged to the movies to see all four *Shrek* movies with me when they first came out. "Noooo, it's not. Thank you very much. And it's gonna be good."

She rolls her eyes.

"You know I'm in," Ameerah says.

Zahara grunts. "Well, be clear. We'll see your little movie thingy, but y'all will go see whatever I wanna see the next time we go to the movies."

Brittani and I groan.

She laughs. "Oh well. If I gotta suffer through a movie of a talking cat in high-heel boots, then y'all can handle a vampire love story."

Out of nowhere, Ameerah breaks out and starts singing the lyrics to Beyoncé's "Irreplaceable," which happens to be one of her favorite songs.

"Girl, I am so over that song," Zahara states, rolling her eyes. "You need to let it go, boo."

Ameerah gives her the hand, getting all amped. "Not. You *know* I love me some Beyoncé, okay. And 'Irreplaceable' is my song right there." She goes back into song, then Brittani and I go into the chorus, throwing our right hands up in the air, gesturing to the left.

"Oh God, speaking of to the left, to the left," Zahara says, cutting us off, "here comes Stix and his sidekick, Bones. And I am *not* in the mood for Bones's retarded butt. Not today. I'm cramping too bad."

I look over in their direction. They both got their nicknames 'cause they're tall and thin. Stix is like six-three, and Bones is six-four. And, yeah…they both play varsity ball. And, umm, I'm not gonna front. They're both cute, too. Not as fine as Sincere, though. Anyways, they stay rocking the fly gear. And both of 'em have these spinnin' waves that can make a blind chick dizzy. I swear, you'd think they were brothers if you didn't know they were cousins. The only problem with Bones is, he's effen annoying. And none of us can stand him 'cause he's always saying something slick out of his mouth—well, not ever to *me*, but to my girls he does. Then we all gotta jump on him 'cause if you disrespect one of us, you disrespect all of us. That's how we roll. Oh...and he has big lips that are always chapped and sometimes cracked 'cause he's always licking them, which doesn't do any good. It's like if he kissed you, he'd cut up your face and lips. Mmmph. Nasty!

As soon as they get to our table, Zahara pulls out her *Teen Voices* magazine and tries to act like she's reading it. I laugh 'cause we all know she's big on Stix. And he digs her, too, so I don't know why they don't quit with the BS and make it happen. Geesh!

"Yo, what's good, y'all?" Stix asks us, looking over at Zahara. We all speak to him, but the minute Bones opens his mouth, we ig him. Zahara keeps flipping through the pages of her magazine. And I do what I do best, tossing my hair to the side and turning my head in the other direction.

Bones smirks. "Oh, y'all birds can't speak?" He knows calling us out of our names is usually gonna get one of us started. And that's all he wants. I swear. He's so desperate and pathetic for attention from us, even if it's negative.

Brittani looks at me, shaking her head.

"Oh, word? It's like that? Y'all gonna sit here and act like you don't hear me speak? I saaaaid, wassup?"

"Yo, man," Stix says, lightly tapping him on the arm with the back of his hand. "Let's roll."

"Hol' up, yo," Bones says, looking over at Zahara. "Yo, Zee, what does FFFF stand for?" She glares at him. He laughs. "Never mind, I got it. Fake, funky, fart faces."

We all shoot him a look. "Womp, womp, womp," I say. "You fail!"

"Ohmygod, what a *loser*," Brittani adds, shaking her head.

"Girl, I know you ain't talkin' with ya peanut head," he snaps.

She jumps up from her seat and starts rolling her neck and pointing her finger all up in his face. "Boy, we're over here minding our business and you coming up over here disrupting our flow like you have nothing else better to do. How 'bout you go throw ya'self over a bridge."

"How 'bout you suck my—"

Before he can get the rest of his words out, Brittani mushes him dead in his face.

"Don't even try disrespecting me like that, little boy. How 'bout you go drink bleach," she says, mushing him again. "Ya breath smells hot, with ya busted, ashy-lipped self."

We all start laughing. Even Stix chuckles. And this only pisses Bones off more. But he started it. So it's about to be on.

"Yo, man, let's go," Stix snaps, yanking him by the arm. "I don't know why you can't chill. You always gotta start with them."

"Yo, man, eff them birds."

"And eff you, too," Zahara says, shutting her magazine. "That's why you got flies around your funky mouth, 'cause you smell like doo-doo." Then, as if on cue, we jump up from our seats and start singing that ole-school joint, "Doo-Doo Brown." We start dropping and popping it, which draws a crowd. We get it real crunked and everybody around us starts singing and chanting and dancing, too. I look around and see others are on the cafeteria floor cracking the hell up. Bones is too through! His face is *cracked*! And the only thing he can do is bounce his cornball butt on his merry way. *Poof!* Like I said: mess with one, mess with us all!

"Oh, shoot," I snap, grabbing my things. "I gotta meet Sincere." I tell 'em I'm out, popping my hips out the lunchroom.

22

I'm fifteen minutes late meeting Sincere. I have two missed calls and three texts from him wildin' out. Well, okay, I'm exaggerating. He wasn't wildin'. But it felt like it in my head. He only wanted to know what was taking me so long. And for some reason that got on my damn nerves—questioning me like he's my father or something. I hear another nut alert in my head: *If he starts questioning you like he owns you, check him real quick, then proceed with caution. If he tries to make you choose him over your friends, make it clear they were there before him and they're gonna be there way after him, so he can either accept it, or step.*

As soon as he sees me, he starts walking toward me all fast and whatnot, mean-mugging me. I can see his jaws tightening. In the three months we've been dating, I've never seen him like this. *Girl, make sure you check him if he comes off crazy.* I shoot him the evil eye, ready for him.

"Aye, yo . . . what took you so long?" He is so close up on

me that if I were as tall as him, our noses would be touching. "I thought we agreed to meet at twelve thirty."

"Umm, we did," I say nonchalantly. "But something came up."

He frowns. "Like?"

Like none of your damn business. "I got sidetracked in the cafeteria."

He huffs. "*Sidetracked?* Doing what?"

I feel my top about to pop. "Look, first of all, don't question me. But since you asked, I got caught up buggin' out with Brittani 'n' them."

He blinks. "Wow. So you can question me anytime you want, but I can't. Oh, a'ight. I see how you doin' it."

"You see how I'm doin' what?"

"You got me out here looking like a fool, waiting on you while you all up in the cafeteria with ya girls, dancin' and prancin' like a buncha hoes all up in them dudes' faces." I give him a shocked look. "Yeah, my peoples hit me up and already let me know what it is. I don't appreciate your silly-behind tryna play me like I'm some duck."

Ohhhkay, now I'm extra pissed that he's called me silly. Then he has the nerve to have his boys hawking my moves. Shoot, all this time I didn't even know he knew anyone that went here.

"You knew you were running late. All you had to do was hit me up real quick and tell me so. Not have me standing out here looking all crazy, yo. You real stupid for that."

Oh hell, naw! I put my hand on my hip, take a deep breath. See, in a split second, I'm about to—as my favorite cousin, Brandon, would say—read him for *filth*! "First of all, don't get it twisted. You don't own me."

"I never said I—"

I put up my hand, cutting him off. "I'm still speaking. Second of all, don't call me stupid. That's one thing I'm not. Third of all, don't ever disrespect me or my girls. They're not hoes and neither am I!"

"Hol' up. I never said y'all were. I said—"

"I know what you said, *punk*. I don't need you to remind me."

"Yo, hold up. You have a problem with me calling you names, so don't do it to me."

"I'll call you whatever I want."

He frowns at me."Yo, how you figure? You sound real crazy right now."

"Don't be calling me crazy, boy. You know what? I'm soooo done with you and this conversation. I'm out! Now go back and tell that to your little watchdogs." I hit him with the deuces, then bounce.

As soon as I get about ten steps away from him, he runs up on me and grabs me by the arm, swinging me around. Okay, I'm exaggerating. He didn't really swing me around. But still I don't like the fact that he's grabbed me. "Aye, yo, don't walk off on me when I'm still talking to you. What the hell is your problem?"

I snatch my arm away from him. Then, before I give it much thought, I spaz out and slap him. "Don't you ever put your hands on me! Have you lost your mind, grabbing me like that? I don't know what type of chick you *think* I am, but I ain't *that* one. And if you put your hands on me like that again, I'ma show you."

He catches himself real quick, holding the side of his face. "Yo, you'd really put ya hands on me?" he asks, lowering his voice, rubbing where I slapped him. I can tell he's shocked, and hurt.

Oh well. He shouldn't have come at me like that. The last boy who called himself tryna man-handle me got his face and neck clawed up and I flattened his tires. "Ohmygod, Sincere," I say, reaching for him.

He steps back. "Yo, I can't believe you just slapped me."

And I'll do it again if you press me. "I'm so sorry. I don't know what came over me."

He stares at me for a minute, then spins away from me. "Sincere, wait," I call out to him. "Where are you going?"

"I'm out," he snaps, walking back toward his truck.

Everything has backfired on me. I'm supposed to be spinning off on him, not the other way around. I follow behind him. "Sincere, wait. Please let me explain."

He stops and turns to face me. I can tell he's heated. Still, he had no business grabbing me.

Girl, you gotta let these boys know from the gate what it is, or they'll be snatching you up every chance they get. "I didn't mean to slap you like that. It's just that when you told me someone told you what I was doing in the cafeteria, that pissed me off. Then you grabbed my arm like that. And I lost it."

"Yo, I was wrong for grabbing you. But if you gotta problem with something I say or do, tell me. Don't put your hands on me, 'cause I'm not gonna put my hands on you."

"Well, don't have anyone checking up on me like I'm some child."

"That's not what I was doing. I kept calling your cell

and you weren't picking up, then you didn't answer my texts, so I called my boy's brother, who goes to your school."

I frown. "Who is he?"

He raises a brow. "You don't need to know all that."

"Motherf…" I catch myself before I flip into curse mode and blast his behind. OMG, he's about to see the other side of me if I don't roll out, now! "Whatever, Sincere," I snap, flipping the script, playing it like he's the cause of what just popped off. "I have to get to class. And I'm already late, thanks to you."

"Thanks to *me*?"

"Yeah, you."

"A'ight, whatever, yo."

"Yeah, whatever. Talk to the hand 'cause I don't give a damn." I say over my shoulder, flicking my hand up in the air.

"Say what?"

I turn back around. "You heard me. Talk to the hand. Translation: Don't call me. I'll call you." I walk off, leaving him standing in the middle of the school parking lot, looking like the damn fool he is for thinking he can try to keep tabs on me and put his hands on me, and it's gonna be all good. Not!

Needless to say, the rest of the day drags 'cause all I can do is think about Sincere. I'm still pissed that he has someone at this school who can keep tabs on me. But I'm more pissed at myself for telling him I was done with him. But there's no way I'm gonna call him and tell him otherwise. Nope, not gonna happen. Erika and her girls used to say, *Once you say it's over, then let it be over. And if you don't*

mean it, then act like you do till he begs you back. So
that's exactly what he's gonna have to do. So here I am,
sitting in my calculus class, staring at equations that become one crazy blur. We have to solve each one, but I
can't. I'm sitting here too wrapped up in tryna figure out
how to solve my man problems.

At the end of the school day, I'm at my locker waiting
for Ameerah to meet me so we can dip. Zahara has some
student council meeting and Brittani is riding home with
her boo, Stevie. So it's me and Ameerah rolling out. While
I'm waiting for her slow behind, I pull out my iPhone,
looking at the screen. There are no missed calls! There are
a few new e-mails and texts. I scroll through them. But
none of them are from Sincere's biscuit head! Forget him!
I feel sick!

What if he wants to break up with me?

Girl, stop trippin'. You won't let him!

I roll my eyes when I finally spot Ameerah strolling
down the hall toward me. She's all grins and giggles as
she's walking and talking to Joe-Joe. He's a'ight-looking.
But he could be better-looking if he didn't have all them
nasty-azz pimples all up on his forehead and whatnot.
They're all red from him popping and picking at them.
But he has thick, curly hair and a nice chiseled body that
make up for it.

He smiles when he sees me. "Hey, Kamiyah, wassup?"

"Nothing much. What's up with you?"

"Chillin'."

"I hear you," I say, looking over his shoulder at this
dude who's walking toward us. He peeps me staring at
him, and nods. My gut tells me he's one of Sincere's little

Seeing Eye dogs. I feel like walking up on him and punching him dead-up in his chest. I roll my eyes and give him
the finger. He laughs. *Punk!*

"Look, ma," Joe-Joe says, gazing at Ameerah, "I gotta get
to detention. I'ma hit you up later, a'ight?"

She grins. "Cool."

He leans in and kisses her on the cheek. "I'ma be
thinkin' 'bout you."

She blushes. "Me too."

I let out a disgusted sigh. "Okaaaay, let's break up this
love train. I got things to do."

"Whatever," she says, waving me on.

"A'ight, I'm out," Joe-Joe says, squeezing her waist.
"Later, Kamiyah."

I give him a nod and a fake smile.

"Ohmygod," Ameerah says as he walks off. "I swear. If I
didn't love you, I'd hate you. You can be such a snotty brat
sometimes."

"Yup, that's me," I say, laughing. "So, get over it. And
let's go."

She sucks her teeth, walking off. I pull my phone out of
my bag and check it one more time for any messages,
knowing darn well nothing's come through since the last
time I checked fifteen minutes ago. My heart sinks. I feel
like crying. I am missing Sincere so much. I just wanna
hear his voice. *If he doesn't call me by the time I get home
from dance class, I'm going to die! I have to get my man
back, and quick!*

23

I'm at Daddy's—why? Because my mother had to leave for Denver tonight for some kind of meeting she has in the morning. Whatever! Why I can't stay at the house by myself is beyond crazy. She's only going to be gone until tomorrow night, for Christ's sake! They act like I'm still a little kid or something.

Anywaaayz...I'm sitting at my computer, browsing the Internet while listening to music. I am so pissed! It's almost nine thirty and Sincere *still* hasn't called me! And I'm starting to feel desperate. Erika's voice plays in my head. *If he really cares about you, he'll keep calling you even when you tell him not to.* The nerve of him! I told him not to call me, and the fool listens. How stupid is that? Obviously, he *doesn't* care!

Jazmine Sullivan's "Lions, Tigers & Bears" is playing. Even though I don't want to, I start humming along. Bored, I change the track, logging onto Facebook. Nicki Minaj's "Your Love" starts playing. As soon as my page comes up, who do I see, Facebooking it up like crazy? Sincere!

I twist my lips. "Mmmph, so this is how he's doin' it," I say, clicking on his page. I see he has a buncha new posts on his wall from chicks and a few of his boys. And he's added new friends—*females*. And a few of them birds have been poking and tagging him up and whatnot. Mmmph. This boy's doing all this, instead of dialing my digits. "Oh, it's on and popping," I say as I type on my wall: IT'S OFFICIAL Y'ALL . . . DA FLY, FABULOUS DIVA IS BACK ON THE BLOCK CHECKIN' FOR THEM REAL-TYPE CATS! NOT LITTLE BOYZ PUTTING THEIR HANDS ON GIRLZ. OR PLAYIN' HEAD GAMES. SO IF YOU REAL WITH IT, THEN HOLLA AT YA GIRL!

I bet this'll get his attention, I think, smirking. *Let's see if he calls now.* I stare at the screen for a few minutes, then reply to a few messages, click on a few profiles, add four new friends, then click back on Sincere's page. I click on his photos. He has about ten flicks of me and him together, twenty of himself—some with his boys, others with his family—and another fifteen of me by myself. I talk myself outta posting on his wall. Instead I remove him from my friends list, then log off.

Five minutes later, my cell rings. I know by the ring tone that it's Brittani. And *yes* I'm disappointed that it's her instead of Sincere.

I answer on the third ring, flopping down on my bed. "Wassup, girl?"

"Chillin'. I saw you come through Facebook. What's up with that post on ya wall?"

I sigh. "Just what it is."

"Mmmhmm. So what happened between you and Sincere?"

I hear Erika's voice in my head again. *Never tell your girls what's really going on with you and your man unless you are absolutely, one hundred percent sure you want it to be over. Otherwise they're gonna be looking at you real crazy if and when you take him back.*

"Nothing, really," I reply, glancing down at my feet. *OMG, I need a pedicure, fast!*

"Did that mofo put his hands on you? 'Cause you know we don't play that."

"Hell, no. You already know what it is. He'd catch it upside his head real quick if he did some mess like that."

"I know that's right. So then why you post that craziness 'bout not checking for boys who put their hands on girls?"

I let out a nervous chuckle. "Oh, that. Girl, I was tripping offa something I read online about a girl getting boxed up by her boyfriend; that's all." Of course it's a small lie. Well, a big lie 'cause I didn't read anything. I only posted that up on my wall to see if Sincere is gonna call me. But I can't tell her that I only wrote that on my wall to get Sincere's attention. She'd think I was nuts.

"Mmmm," she says, pausing. I'm sure trying to decide if she's gonna believe me or not. "Okaaay, if you say so. Earlier today you was all boo'd up. Now all of a sudden you on Facebook, posting you back on the block. Y'all must be beefing or something."

"Not really. I'm just not feeling him like that anymore, so it is what it is."

"I feel you, girrrl. On to the next!"

"Yup."

"Well, I gotta do this whack homework before it gets too late. Mister Rios be wildin' with all these assignments."

"*Pobrecita*," I say in Spanish. "*Nadie dijo que tome español con él.*"

"Poor baby, nothing," she repeats back in English, laughing. "I took Spanish with him 'cause he's cute. But had I known he works his class to death, I would have passed. I didn't sign up for all of this dang homework, not in my last year. Senior year is supposed to be a breeze, boo. So, *bese mi culo*, show off!"

I laugh with her. "Right back at ya, trick!" We talk a few minutes more before hanging up. I get up and walk over to my computer, deciding to log off and read a book. I grab *Shortie Like Mine* by Ni-Ni Simone from off my bookshelf, then lie across the bed on my stomach.

When Rihanna's "Hate That I Love You" starts playing, I grab the remote to my stereo and change the disc. When Styles P's "Harsh" comes on, I suck my teeth, changing it. Tyga's "Coconut Juice" comes on and I turn up the volume, bopping to the music while reading the first chapter of my book.

Ten minutes and two songs later, I am still on the first page of this book. I can't effen think straight. I don't want it to be over between Sincere and me. Shoot, he's everything to me.

My cell rings again. Still, no Sincere. Its ring tone alerts me that this time it's Ameerah. As soon as I answer, she starts speed yapping. "Brittani told me you and Sincere are over. Girl, tell me he didn't put his hands on you. You know we will set it off on his monkey-behind if he even thinks it. And why you post that on your wall, anyway? What's good with that?"

"Ohmygod, if you'd slow down and come up for air maybe I can get a word in edgewise. No, Sincere did not hit me." Well, that's not a lie. But she doesn't need to know I slapped him up. "And I never said he did. That post on my wall had nothing to do with him."

She blows air into the phone. "Oh, 'cause I was about to say, let's go stomp the yard on his head."

I smile, happy to know I have friends like her to always have my back. "No need, but thanks."

"So what's this about you being back on the block? Are you still his wifey or what?"

"Girl, I was popping mad junk; that's all. Besides, Sincere's not my husband. So how am I gonna be wifed up? Duh!"

"Tramp," she snaps, "you know what I meant. Are y'all still going out or not?"

"I, um..." There's a knock on my bedroom door. "Hold on," I tell her, getting up to answer it. My mouth drops open. It's Sincere. He's standing in the doorway, looking like a lost puppy. I smile inside. "Ameerah, let me call you back."

"Ohhh—"

I hang up on her before she can get the rest of her words out.

"How'd you get up here?"

"Your dad," he says, stuffing his hands in his pockets. I roll my eyes, annoyed that my dad let him in. Well, okay, okay...I'm lying. I'm happy to see him, but he doesn't need to know all that.

"I effed up, Miyah," he says, looking real sad. "I shoulda never grabbed your arm like that."

Never give in too easy. "You're right. So what do you want?" I ask, folding my arms across my chest.

"Can we talk?"

I glance over my shoulder, checking for the time. It's almost ten thirty. "Talk," I state, trying to act all nonchalant, but inside I'm struggling to hide my smile that he's standing here in a blue Seton Hall T-shirt and a pair of sweats. "You have five minutes to say what you need to say. Then bounce."

He shifts his weight from one leg to the other. "You're not gonna let me in?"

I shake my head. "Nope. You can stand right there and say what you need to say."

He stares at me.

I tilt my head. "Well, talk...your time's ticking."

"I'm sorry, ba—"

"I'm not your baby, so don't call me that," I snap, cutting him off.

"My bad, Miyah."

"It's Kamiyah, to you. And you're wasting my time."

"Damn, c'mon. Don't do that. Nothing's changed with us. You still my girl. And I'm still your man."

I am smiling inside. *Always flip the script and make it be all his fault.* "Yeah, whatever."

"C'mon, Miyah. You know I'm sorry, for real. I'm all effed up over what went down earlier. I don't even know what happened. I was pissed. You were pissed. And we both said some things I don't think we meant. At least I know I didn't. The last eight hours have been hell for me. I miss you, baby." He reaches for me, but I back away from him. Not that I don't want to be in his arms, but I need to teach him who's in charge in this relationship.

"Mmmph. Yeah, right. But you were all up on Facebook, poking and tagging and posting it up with them birds." For some reason, mentioning him Facebookin' it

up, I feel the urge to slap his face again. I will my hands to
stay still, planting them on my hips. "If you missed me so
much, why were you all up on them hoes' pages, posting
up on their walls?"

"That wasn't about nothing. I was only passing time.
But I saw what you posted. So, you back on the block? Is
that how you doing it?"

I smile inside, pleased to know my stunt to get him
over here worked. I keep my hands on my hips. "Maybe."

Alicia Keys's "Try Sleeping with a Broken Heart" starts
playin'. *Oh, wow...how fitting*, I think, trying to block the
lyrics out of my head.

"C'mon, Kamiyah. I'm sorry, baby. Don't let this one
thing mess us up. I can forgive you for slapping me if you
can forgive me for grabbing you by the arm. Can we just
sit and talk for a few minutes, please?"

I sigh. "You got five minutes," I say, stepping back and
opening the door to let him in. He steps in. I close the
door behind him. I brush past him. His six-foot frame
looms over me. There are tears in his eyes. And I feel myself becoming unglued. *Me!*

"I never wanna hurt you, Miyah. I care a lot about you."

"Well, you have a fine way of showing it," I say, finally
sitting down on my bed.

He takes a seat next to me. His leg brushes against
mine.

"Let me make it up to you."

I look him in the eyes. "How?"

"I can show you better than I can tell you," he says,
touching the side of my face with the back of his hand. I
don't stop him. "You're so beautiful, Miyah."

I feel myself getting hot from his touch. Oh, he is soooo

dang sexy! The idea of him being with someone else...uh-uh, I'm not even going there. I shrug, forcing myself to think up something really, really sad to make me cry. Learning how to turn my tears off and on at the drop of a dime has taken me years to perfect. But I finally have it mastered, as you've already seen.

"I'm scared, Sincere," I say, blinking my wet lashes.

"What you scared of, baby?"

"You have my heart, Sincere. Every single piece of it. I ain't beat to be getting all caught up in you and then you play me. I don't wanna get hurt."

He swipes at my tears with his fingers. Promises me he would never do that. That I'm all he ever thinks about. That I'm all he needs and wants. Tells me I'm his world.

I better be, I think, giving him a half smile. "For real?"

"No doubt," he says, smiling back at me.

I decide to ask him what he wants from me.

"To be your man," he answers. He leans in, pressing his forehead up against mine. "I know you don't believe this, but I never felt like this—the way I feel about you—toward any other girl."

I rest my hand on the back of his neck. Pull his face closer to mine till our lips meet.

"Can I be your man again, baby?"

I shake my head.

He snakes his arm around me. "Go 'head with that, Miyah. You know you don't want me to go nowhere. You know I don't wanna go anywhere. So stop playing." He lightly kisses me, staring into my wet eyes. And I stare back into his. "Miyah, I'm crazy 'bout you, girl. Don't do this to us. Don't keep me from you, baby. I promise I'll never hurt you."

I keep myself from smiling. *You have him hooked, boo! Now it's time to reel him in.*

He kisses me again. And this time, without thinking, I part my lips and allow his tongue to touch mine. It tastes like a watermelon Jolly Rancher. And when we finally come up for air, I've forgiven him for taking all night to finally come to his senses.

"Am I still your man, baby?"

This time I nod, whispering, "Yes."

And just like that, with one simple kiss, this is how it all begins and ends. With Sincere being right back where he belongs—with me. And there will be no breaking up unless *I* want there to be.

24

Three days later, Sincere and I are chilling up in his bedroom, cuddling and watching the movie *Takers* on DVD. Of course I'm supposed to be in school today, but I'm not. I'm here with my man, laid up in his bed, being all grown and whatnot. His parents are away for the week, leaving him the house to himself. He's lounging in his Polo boxers and a wifebeater. And I have on one of his button-up shirts that fits more like a minidress on me. Although we've been spending a lot of time together, we still haven't officially had "sex." We do a lot of making out and other things that leave us both very satisfied. Sincere never pushes the issue to go further than what we already do. And I love him for that. Anyway, Sincere says if I don't want to go all the way, then he'll wait for me.

Of course, leave it to Zahara to say he's getting *it* in somewhere else with one of them hot-box hoochie-coochies on campus. "Girl, please. If he ain't gettin' it from you, he's definitely gettin' it somewhere else, 'cause he sure ain't playin' with himself. *And* he's in college. Oh yeah, them college hoes are tossin' him them panties left and right." That's what she keeps saying.

Then there's Erika's voice in my head, nagging me about cheating guys. *Under the right conditions, if he thinks he can get away with it, all guys will cheat. They can't help themselves. It's in their nature to be doggish, which is why you have to always keep 'em on a very short leash and yank it every so often to let 'em know who's in charge.*

I've asked Sincere many times if he's ever cheated on me, and he tells me no. He says he would never cheat on me. He tells me I mean too much to him for him to do something like that. And I believe him. Well, um, I try to believe him. I mean, I really *want* to believe him. But something in my head tells me I better keep my eye on him.

Last night when I was on the phone talking to Erika about what Zahara said and about those things Erika used to say about guys, she said to me, "Now that I'm older, I don't think all guys cheat, but I still believe that most will."

"Has Winston ever cheated on you?" I asked her.

"Not that I know of, but I'm not worried about him cheating on me."

"Why not?" I asked, curious. She sounded so confident.

"Well, one, he's never done anything to give me a reason to worry. I trust him. But, trust and believe, don't think for one minute that I don't keep my eyes and ears open; just in case."

"Well, how will I know if Sincere is cheating on me?" I asked her.

"Your gut will tell you," she answered. "Trust me. You will know it and *feel* it in your bones."

I was so relieved that *that* wasn't something I was feeling in my bones when it comes to Sincere.

She asked, "Has he given you any reason to think he's cheating on you?"

"No, not really," I told her.

"Good. And hopefully he never does. Still, keep your eyes open; watch him closely. Trust me, if he is doing something he shouldn't be, he'll slip up and show you everything you need to know." We talked a few minutes more then hung up.

Unfortunately, talking to her didn't really make me feel any better about what Zahara keeps saying about him sleeping with some trick. I know me. And I know *if* he is cheating on me—or if I even *think* he is, there is going to be hell to pay.

Sincere nudges me, snapping me out of my thoughts. "What you thinkin' about?"

I look up at him, shaking my head. "Nothing."

"You sure?"

I shift my body to face him. I stare into his eyes. "Does it bother you that we aren't having sex? I mean, I want to, but…"

"Nah, not at all," he says, rubbing my hair. "I told you, it's cool. When you're ready to go all the way, then I'm ready." He lightly kisses me on the lips. "Until then, what we already do is good enough for me."

I smile at him. "Are you sure?"

He smiles back, pressing his body into mine. "No doubt, baby." I lower my hand, reach for him, and feel how excited he is. I squeeze. He groans.

"You like that?"

"Yeah, baby," he says, pulling in his bottom lip, then biting down on it. I kiss his lips. *If I ever catch him with another chick,* I think, slipping my tongue in his mouth, *I'ma set it off!*

Thirty minutes later, Sincere is downstairs fixing us something to eat. I glance at the clock on his nightstand—1:38 P.M. I get up and sit on the edge of the bed and decide to text my girls to let 'em know where I'm at. As I'm texting back 'n' forth with Zahara and Ameerah, Sincere's BlackBerry starts buzzing. I glance over at it sitting up on his dresser. The buzzing stops. Two minutes later, it starts buzzing again. Now, I know I should mind my business and leave it alone. But I don't. I can't. And I won't. The temptation is too great. And against my better judgment, instead of ignoring the constant buzzing, I get up and press the space bar. His screen comes to life. I scroll over to his messages, then press the thumb ball. He has two new text messages and twelve new e-mails; mostly from Facebook. *Kamiyah, don't do it. What if he went through your phone? You know you wouldn't like it.* I try to talk myself out of it, but the voice in my head tells me this is what I'm *supposed* to do. *Keep your eyes open!*

The texts are from a Miranda. I click open the first text message. I read it. Then reread it, blinking. HEY SEXY… WHEN AM I GONNA C U? I MISS U

I click open the next text: CALL ME WHEN U GET THIS. I WANNA HEAR UR VOICE.

"I don't think so," I mumble, deleting both texts. Oh, but not until I memorize the number. *I'ma check this ho real quick!* I put his phone back where it was, then sit back on the bed, fuming.

My hands shake as I punch in the number. I wait. Four rings later, a chick answers. "Hello?"

"Listen," I say, "I don't know you and you don't know me, but do me a favor, sweetie. Don't text my man again."

"*Excuse you?*" she says with attitude. "Who is this?"

"Don't worry about who I am. All you *need* to worry about is not texting my man."

"And who's your man?"

"Sincere," I snap. "And like I *said*, don't text him again."

She laughs. "Oh, you must be that little girl he calls himself messing with."

"*Little girl?* Trick, puhleeze. This little girl will beat the snot outta you, okay? So try it on my time if you want. Don't send him any more texts."

She laughs. "I heard how you attacked that other girl a few weeks back. I wanna see you try it with me, *sweetie*. I'll text your so-called *man* all I want. And for the record, my name is Miranda."

"I don't care what the hell your name is. Don't call or text my man."

She laughs again. And this only pisses me off more. "Little girl, the only thing you are to Sincere is a little plaything. Trust me. When he gets tired of messing with you, he'll come back where he belongs—with a real woman. Now get the hell up off my phone, little girl." *Click!*

"Oh, no the hell she didn't!" I snap, calling her back. She picks up and before I know it, this chick and I are arguing back and forth, threatening each other. I'm yelling at the top of my lungs. And she's yelling back. I don't even hear it when Sincere barges into the bedroom to see what all the commotion is about.

"Yo, why you screaming? Who you on the phone cursing at like that?"

"Some trick named Miranda," I snap, throwing my phone at him.

He tries to duck, but the phone catches him upside the head. "Owww! Yo, what the eff?! Why you do that?"

My nose is flaring. I'm punching my fist in my hand, pacing the room like a wild animal. "Who the hell is Miranda?!"

He frowns. "Who?"

"Don't play stupid with me! You heard me the first time. Now, who is she?!"

He doesn't answer me. He rubs the side of his head. His jaw tightens. "What the hell you doing going through my phone?"

"What is that bird texting you for?" I ask, not answering him.

"How am I s'posed to know? I haven't talked to her in weeks." He walks over to his dresser, snatching his phone up. He starts going through it. "Well, where are the texts at?"

"I deleted them," I state, placing a hand on my hip.

"You did *whaaat*?"

I repeat myself.

"You buggin' now, for real, yo."

"No, *you* buggin'," I shoot back, glaring at him.

He mumbles something under his breath. And when I ask him to repeat it, he brushes me off. The next thing I know, I slap him in the back of his head.

"Yo, Miyah, go 'head with that puttin' ya hands up on me. I'm not with that."

I mush him in the back of the head again.

"Yo, I'm warning you, like for real. Keep your hands to yourself. You didn't like it when I snatched you up by the arm, and I told you I wouldn't do it again. Now I'm telling you to not put your hands on me."

"Excuse you?! That broad straight disrespected me, and you're gonna stand here and try to act like I'm outta pocket. I don't think so."

He gives me a confused look. "You *are* outta pocket. But, tell me. What did Miranda do that was so disrespectful?"

"She texted you, that's what she did. Then she started popping off at the mouth when I told her to not text you anymore."

"Well, you had no business calling her. And you're probably the one who came at her all sideways."

"I called her to tell her to beat it. And she started talking all reckless."

He laughs.

And that only pisses me off more. "Oh, you think that's funny?"

He frowns. "You're joking, right?"

"Does it look like I'm joking?"

He shakes head. "You got some issues, yo. You called her. She didn't even know you were here, number one. And number two, if you hadn't gone through my phone, you wouldn't have known she texted me. So the only person who's been disrespected here is *me*. The only person who should be pissed off is *me*. You had no business going through my phone."

Before I realize what's happening, I run over to him and punch him in the back.

Sincere quickly turns around. "Yo, what the hell is your problem, Miyah?"

"You're my problem!" I yell, glaring at him. "I wanna know why she's texting you, talking like the two of you got something going on."

His nose flares. "Yo, how the hell am I supposed to know? I already told you I haven't spoken to her in weeks. But I'm telling you, yo. Don't put ya hands on me like that again. I let you get that off three times already. I don't hit you, so keep ya damn hands to yourself. I think you should leave."

I slam my hands up on my hips. "Excuse you? I'm not going anywhere."

He starts picking up my clothes off the chair and tossing them over to me. "No, for real, Miyah. You need to leave."

"Oh, so you can call that trick up?"

"Her name is Miranda," he says, pacing the floor.

I can tell he's heated. But that chick had no business coming at my man like that. "Oh, so now you wanna take up for her. Whatever."

"Yeah, you right. It is whatever. Now bounce."

For some reason, I feel like I've been slapped. I blink. Then it's on and popping like hot grease! I lunge at him, digging my nails into his neck, yelling and screaming and cursing. He grabs my wrists, trying to get my hands from around his neck. I keep screaming and cursing at him. He throws me onto the bed, pinning me down.

I try to wrestle and wiggle my way from under him, but he is too heavy.

"Sincere, get the hell off of me!"

"No, not until you calm down!" he says, out of breath.

I try to kick him off of me. But he has his legs wrapped around mine. He is strong as hell. "I didn't put my hands on you. I don't hit chicks, but you're really pushing it."

"Hit me then. I dare you, *punk*." I keep trying to break free, but he has me pinned down tight. "Get off of me!"

"Not until you calm down."

"Oh nooo, calm down, hell! Get off of me."

He's squeezing my wrists and holding my hands up over my head. "You shouldn't have put ya hands on me. I asked you not to, and you did it anyway."

He has all of his weight on me, practically crushing me. I keep screaming and yelling at him to get off of me.

He refuses. "I'm not letting you go until you calm down."

Since he won't let me go, I do the next best thing. I spit in his face. My spit clings to his skin. His eyes widen in shock.

"Oh, you wanna do the spitting game, huh?"

"Get off of me, Sincere!" I yell, still struggling to break free.

Sincere is yelling back at me in my face. "Let me show you how to spit!" He hawks up a bunch of snot and spits it dead in my face. It's thick and nasty. He does it again. And I am through!

25

I am on Facebook, creating a new page. Sincere has left me no other choice, since he has blocked me from his Facebook page and I can't see what he's up to. I'm using a picture of one of my favorite cousins, Shalonda, as my profile picture. First I had to make sure she wasn't in any of the pictures in my Facebook album. Thankfully she wasn't. Anywaaayz...she has these real sexy eyes with long dark eyelashes and shiny black hair. She looks Hawaiian, almost. But she's half Asian and half black. Her father is my dad's brother, and they live over in Germany. He's in the army and that's where he's been stationed for the last three years. Shalonda's dad won't let her have a Facebook page, so I won't have to worry about her finding out about this page being up with her photo. I hope. *Well, it'll only be up for a few days. I just need it to spy on Sincere. I need to see what he is up to.*

I pick up my phone to check to see if I've missed any calls or texts or e-mails from him. There are none. I feel the tears welling up in my eyes. He's changed his Face-book status to *It's complicated*. OMG, what's so compli-cated about it?! Either he loves me or he doesn't.

I can't lose you, Sincere. I grab my phone beside me, then scroll through my pictures. I go through every one of them: pictures of me and my girls, pictures of Sincere— mostly of Sincere. I have tons of pictures of him, from our first date back up to three weeks ago. Before that trick texted him, before he spit in my damn face! Pictures of him sleeping, pictures of him driving, pictures of him eating.

I turn up my stereo. Let Rihanna's "Breakin' Dishes" play. I don't wanna fight Sincere. I don't. I wanna love him. And him to love me. But he keeps letting these hoes disrespect our relationship and I gotta check him. If he acted right, if he knew how to keep them hoes in check, I wouldn't have to go off on him. I wouldn't have to resort to creating fake Facebook pages, or sneaking out of my house and walk-running six blocks just to see if his car is home, or leaving notes on his windshield. If he just stopped doing things to make me go off, we'd be good.

I reread my profile. It says that I am seventeen, from Brooklyn; that I attend Medgar Evers College in Brooklyn. I send Sincere a message from my new profile: YOU'RE HOT! Then I send him a friend request. And wait. I request a few other people. And wait.

My cell rings. I glance at the screen, hoping it's Sincere. It's Erika. I really don't wanna talk to her. I ignore her call. Two minutes later, I hear the house phone ringing and know it's her.

"Kamiyah, it's your sister," I hear Daddy saying as he knocks on my door. I want to ignore him, too. Want to tell him to get away from my door; that I'm in the middle of tracking my man. I don't. I get up and open the door. He hands me the phone. I try to close the door before he can see me. But he catches a glimpse of my swollen, red eyes.

"You okay?"

I wanna slam the door in his face. "No," I tell him, turning away from him before he sees me fall apart. "I'm not feeling well."

He reaches for me as I try to walk away, pulling me into his arms. "I love you," he says, kissing me on top of my head. "Talk to your sister. I'll be up to check on you later." He walks out, closing the door behind him. *I love you.* I wanna hear those words from Sincere. Why can't he just effen call me!

"Hello? Hello?"

I have forgotten Erika's on the other end. "Yeah," I say, sitting at the foot of my bed.

"I called you on your cell. Why didn't you pick up?"

"I didn't hear it," I lie.

"Mmmm. Daddy says you've been moping around for the last two days. What's going on?"

Hmmm, let's see. My man is cheating on me. He spit in my face. And now he's not speaking to me. Oh, and by the way...I'm spying on him. I wipe my tears, sniffling.

"Nothing."

"Daddy seems to think it has something to do with... uh, what's his name?"

"Sincere," I say. My heart aches saying his name. "His name is Sincere."

"Yeah, Sincere. I don't know why I can't ever remember his name. I hope to meet him when I'm there for Thanksgiving. Anyway, what's going on with you two?"

"Nothing."

"Well, it doesn't sound like it. You wanna talk about it?"

"There's nothing to talk about," I say, reaching for my laptop.

"Well, sounds like there's something going on, even if you say there isn't. What is it?"

"I said it's nothing. I'm not feeling well, that's all."

"Okay, fine. I'll drop it. Are you coming down with a cold or something?"

"I guess." I glance at the clock on my nightstand. Fifteen minutes have gone by and Sincere still hasn't accepted my friend request or responded to my in-box message.

"What's up with the attitude?"

"I *told* you I'm not feeling well."

"You know what? I'm gonna let you go, then. But know this. If you need, or want, to talk, you know you can always call me, right?"

I nod as if she can see me. "Thanks."

"I love you."

"I love you, too," I say, hurriedly disconnecting the minute I see that there's a message in my in-box from Sincere. I click it open. WASSUP? DO I KNOW U?

Finally, I have contact with my man! I type, NO. NOT YET. BUT I'M HOPING THAT CAN CHANGE SOON. I SAW YOUR PROFILE AND THOUGHT U WERE REAL SEXY.

He responds back. ☺ THANKS! U KINDA HOT 2.

I frown. *So who the hell else you up here saying looks hot?* I type: DO U HAVE A GIRL?

I wait for him to respond.

SUMTHIN LIKE THAT

O, WAT DOES THAT MEAN? Y'ALL FIGHTIN?

YEAH

My heart aches. U WANNA TALK ABOUT IT?

NAH, I DON'T KNOW U.

O, TRUE. MAYBE WE CAN GET TO KNOW EACH OTHER. CAN WE BE FB FRIENDS?

YEAH

A few minutes later, I have an e-mail notification from my other Yahoo! e-mail account—the one I made up this morning—that Sincere Lewis has accepted my friend request. I don't waste any time clicking on his page to read his updates. I scroll through his friends list to see if I see that Lana chick. I don't. I look for that chick Miranda's name. When I see it, I click on her page. *If I ever catch you, you'll be next to get swung down.* I click on her page. *Ohmygod, what an attention whore*, I think as I read all her status updates. I want to send her a message, telling her to watch her face. But I won't, not yet. I need to sit back and watch what's going on. I wanna catch her somewhere out and about when she least expects it.

I grab my cell and scroll through my call log until I come across her number, then grab the cordless phone and dial her number. I decide to call her from the home phone since our number comes up *private* on caller ID.

"Hello?"

"Stay away from my man," I say, deepening my voice. "Or I'ma beat you."

"*Whaaat?* I don't know who this is, but, ho, you don't really want it!"

"Don't—"

There's a knock on my door. It's Daddy. I quickly disconnect the call and shut my laptop, telling him to come in. "You want something to eat?" he asks, leaning up against the doorframe. I made some barbecued salmon and garlic mashed potatoes."

I shake my head, shifting back on my bed. "I'm not hungry."

"You've been up here all day, Miyah. You have to eat something."

I can't. I don't want food. I want Sincere! I want to hear his voice! And lie in his arms! "I can't eat anything right now."

He stares at me for a few seconds, then walks in and sits on the edge of my bed. I scoot over.

"What's bothering you? You and Sincere have a fight?"

I nod.

"You wanna talk about it?"

I shake my head. "No, not really."

"C'mere," he says, opening his arms. "Give your old man a hug."

I go to him and he hugs me tight. I hug him back, wishing it was Sincere.

"It'll work itself out."

"I hope so, Daddy."

He kisses me on the forehead. "It will. Trust me. Now come downstairs and eat something for me."

"I will. I promise. As soon as I finish this homework assignment I'm working on."

He gives me another hug, then walks out, shutting the door behind him. I quickly open my laptop and wait for the screen to come alive. I refresh my page, then go back to reading the posts up on that ho's page, then click back over to Sincere's. He has a new post up: WHY DO RELATION-

SHIPS HAVE TO BE SO MUCH DAMN WORK? WHY CAN'T YOU JUST LOVE SOMEONE AND THEY TRUST YOU TO LOVE THEM BACK?

He has over a hundred likes. And eighty-seven comments. I read them all. Then decide to add my two cents. IF YOU REALLY LOVE SOMEONE YOU'LL DO WHATEVER YOU HAVE TO TO MAKE IT WORK. YOU'LL ACCEPT THEIR FLAWS. AND LOVE THEM NO MATTER WHAT.

I wait for a response back from him. There is none. He simply clicks LIKE.

26

"Heeeeey, Boo-boo," Zahara says in her singsong voice, walking up to me at my locker. She's stylishly dressed in a brown and orange swirl-patterned dress with a banging pair of brown Gucci booties. She has her thick, woolly hair stuffed underneath a brown derby. No weave today. Even though I don't trust her, and I still think she's messy, she's still my girl. I just have to keep my eyes on her, very closely. Anywaaayz...I'm glad we've made up. Still, I'm not beat for a buncha chitchat this morning.

"Hey," I say nonchalantly. I still haven't spoken to Sincere since the incident that popped off at his house last Thursday. And now it's Tuesday. We had yesterday off and I was stuck in the house—okay, okay, I'm lying. I drove past Sincere's house twice. And even rang his doorbell. But his mother said he didn't wanna talk to me. I handed her a gift for him—a hundred-and-fifty-dollar pair of sneakers that I bought as a peace offering with money I saved up from my allowance. Okay, maybe as a bribe. Anywaaayz, his mom told me she'd give them to him, then slammed the door in my face. Can you believe that? Okay, well, maybe she didn't actually *slam* it in my face, but it felt like it.

Anywaaayz, I spent the rest of my day up on Sincere's Facebook page, watching and monitoring what he's up to. It's been FOUR whole miserable days!! I want my man back! I've called him and left him a buncha messages, apologizing. But he hasn't responded. Even though I'm still pissed at him for spitting in my damn face—so what if I spit in his face first—it doesn't make what he did right. That was a damn no-no! Two wrongs don't make a right. And what he did was dead wrong, and nasty. But I know we can work it all out and get through it. Okay, well...I guess I should mention I broke the screen on his phone when we got into it, then keyed up the side of his truck on my way out. *Punk!*

I bring my attention back to Zahara, who's staring me down. "What? Why you all up in mine like that?"

"Why you actin' all stank-a-dank this morning?"

"I don't know what you're talking about," I tell her, slamming my locker door, shifting my eyes away from her stare. She walks with me down the hall. I have my calculus class this period. "Oh, by the way, cute dress."

"Nope, not gonna work," she says, cutting her eye at me. "You should have said that when I first walked up on you instead of giving me that 'hey' like I'm some Penn Station hobo you was tryna shoo away."

In spite of being mad and sad and missing Sincere really, really bad, I laugh. "Zee, you crack me up, girl. What you doing after school tomorrow? I don't have dance, so I thought maybe we could hang out after school."

She stops in the middle of the hallway, raising a neatly waxed brow. "Wait, *you're* asking *me* what I'm doing after school? What, you and Sincere beefing or something?"

"No," I say, shifting my eyes. Because I know Zahara's jealous of my relationship with Sincere—even though she'd never admit it— there's no way I'm about to tell her much of anything. "Not really."

"Mmmph," she grunts, pulling out her iPhone. "Well, let me check my calendar and get back to you."

I laugh, shutting my locker. "Whatever. You do that."

"I'll let you know sixth period," she says, walking off.

Whatever, I think, walking into the bathroom. I go into one of the empty stalls and pull out my cell. I call Sincere again. It goes to voice mail. I leave him another message. Then I call, blocking my number; still no answer. I feel myself starting to hyperventilate. "Sincere, please call me. Please. I miss you. And I love you. I'm so sorry. Please, baby. Call me the minute you get this."

Two minutes later, I call his cell again. This time the recording tells me the mailbox is full. I have the urge to throw my phone up against the wall, but I don't. I send Sincere another text instead. He ignores this one as well.

When I get to class, I swing open the classroom door and hurriedly take my seat as Mr. Langston is passing out the graded tests from last week's calculus test.

"How special of you to make it to class after the bell, Miss Nichols," he says as I slip into my seat. "And I want to see you after class." There are a few "oohs" from the back of the room.

"Somebody's in trouble," Jarrell says, laughing.

I suck my teeth. Mr. Langston slides me my test. I flip it

over, glancing at it. I blink, blink again. I literally feel faint. *This can't be right!* Ohmygod. Am I in trouble!

The rest of my school day is ruined. I still can't believe I got a D on my exam! Although Mr. Langston tried to reassure me that this wouldn't affect my final grade, that I still have time to bring up my grade, I am sick over it. Getting a D is like getting an F. It's still failing. I never get anything less than an A-minus! Cs and Ds are not heard of from me. Never! And a B is rare. I never fail at anything!

Students here are expected to achieve and maintain high academic standings. If you get a grade less than a C, it has to be signed off on by a parent. I am sooo dead now! I feel like screaming. Mr. Langston offers me a buncha extra credit assignments to offset my grade. I don't need extra credit work. I need to talk to Sincere!

Mr. Langston tells me he needs the signed test back *tomorrow*. I'm not worried about the signature part. I'll do a little forgery. But I'm stressed about how it'll affect my final grade. I will have to ace everything in his class. I can't think any more about it. I sneak into the bathroom and try calling Sincere again. It goes straight to voice mail, but the mailbox is still full.

At the end of the day, I am at my locker getting my stuff. Ameerah is coming down the hall with Joe-Joe, laughing at something he's said. And Brittani is coming down the opposite side of the hall with Zahara. I lean up against my locker and wait. I watch Joe-Joe lean in and kiss Ameerah lightly on the lips and feel a pang of jealousy shoot through me.

"You getting ready to leave?" Brittani asks, walking up to me.

"Yeah, in a minute. I have to be at dance by three thirty."

"You still wanna hang tomorrow after school?" Zahara asks, squinting at me.

"Yeah."

"Umm, hold up," Brittani says, tilting her head. "All of a sudden you wanna hang out?" She eyes me. "What's that all about?"

I shrug. "Nothing. I miss chilling with my girls, that's all."

She twists her lips up. "Hmm...you and Sincere must be beefing or something."

"Why you say that?"

" 'Cause all of a sudden you wanna hang with your girls. Picture that."

"Yeah, Miyah, what's really good?" Zahara wants to know. "I wasn't gonna even call you out on it, but since Brittani did, then I wanna know, too. Are y'all?"

Careful what you tell them, I remind myself. *Never tell 'em everything*. "We're having some minor difficulties right now," I decide to say. "But it's nothing we can't work out."

Zahara raises her brow. "See. I told you. And the minute they're back all coochie-crunch, she'll be right back on her bull again."

"No, I won't."

Ameerah walks over to us. "Who's staying after school with me so I can watch Joe-Joe practice?"

"Don't look at me," Zahara says.

"Me either," Brittani says.

Ameerah looks at me. "What about you?"

"I can't," I tell her. "I gotta get to dance."

*   *   *

"No, Kamiyah," Miss Johvonna snaps, clapping her hands. "Stop the music. Look at you. You come down like big clunky elephant. Not light and airy like butterfly. What is the matter with you? Concentrate. You are all over the place like wild mongoose. You're wearing your troubles on your shoulders and it's showing in your movements— heavy and clumsy, like fat old walrus. Twelve years of training and you dance like newborn klutz. I do not like."

"I'm sorry, Miss Johvanna," I say, hanging my head, embarrassed by her tone and her disapproval. This whole mess with Sincere has me on edge. It's bad enough I can't eat, think, or sleep. But now it's affecting my dance. Everyone in class is staring at me, smirking. They are enjoying the fact that her most talented dancer is not so perfect after all. I try to catch my breath. My muscles ache. She has been making me stop and redo my steps for the last forty minutes. I try to forget the blisters sticking to my toe shoes. "I have a lot on my mind."

"I see. And none of it on ballet. Again, on *pointe*."

I do as I am told. Go up on the point of my right foot, then go into a series of hops.

"If you wish to be ballerina, you will need to block out all outside forces. When you hit the stage and the curtain goes up and lights come on, ballet must be all you bring out there with you. You are changing, Kamiyah. Do you not wish to be ballerina?"

"Yes."

"Then dance like one, or leave!"

In all the years of working with Miss Johvonna, she has never spoken to me like this. But everything she's said to me is true so I can't be mad at her. She knows better than anyone how badly I want to be a professional dancer. Miss Johvonna's the one person I'd never, ever, give attitude to; no matter how hard she is on me.

And for the next thirty minutes she yells out combinations, making us stop and start over. This is my punishment for ducking out on all those dance classes to be with Sincere. And now it's showing. And she's making the whole class pay for it. I follow Miss Johvonna's commands, avoiding the piercing eyes of those in back of me. If their stares were bullets, I'd be dead.

27

When all else fails, break into his Facebook and e-mail accounts! Trust me. You'll find out all you need to know in one sitting. So, here it is Saturday afternoon. I'm parked across the street from Sincere's house, waiting for him to leave to meet his boys at the gym. You wanna know how I know that's where he's going? Uhhh, helloooo. How else? I figured out the password to his Facebook account. I stayed up all last night until I finally figured out how to get into his account. It took me almost six hours, but I did it! Then I went into his in-box and read all of his messages. Once I figured out his Facebook password, it was easy for me to go into his Yahoo! account.

I didn't get to sleep until three o'clock this morning. Oh well. He should have returned my calls. Then I wouldn't have had to resort to such drastic measures. It's times like these when I wish he had Twitter, too, so I could spy on him that way as well. I glance at the time. It's 12:57 P.M. He's supposed to be at the gym at one, so I know he's going to be walking out of his front door anytime. I pull out my binoculars, zooming in for close observation. Two minutes later, the front door opens and it's Sincere, heading to his truck.

I pull out my cell and call him. I watch as he pulls out his phone, glances at the screen, then sends me to his voice mail. I call back. He does it again. I wait until he starts driving down his driveway, then pop a U-turn and pull up at the end of his driveway, blocking his path. He's staring at me, burning a hole in my skin as if he hates me. I take a deep breath and get out of my car. He's shaking his head as I walk up to his truck.

"Yo, you need to move your car," he says, cracking his window.

OMG, I miss him sooooo much! And I feel so weak and pitiful, but I don't care. I want my man back and I ain't too proud to beg. "Why won't you return any of my calls?"

"'Cause I'm not beat for you like that," he says, acting like he's not happy to see me. But I can see it in his eyes that he is. Still, he's treating me like I'm some stranger on the street. "Now move your car so I can go."

"No, not until you talk to me."

"There's nothing to talk about. I'm not effen with you, Miyah." He rolls his window up on me. Right in my face!

I knock on the window. "Please, Sincere. I don't know what I'll do without you. Please, give me another chance. Just let me talk to you. I'll make it up to you, I promise." He tries not to look at me. I press my face up to his window, peering inside. "*Please,* Sincere. All I want is to talk, then I'll leave you alone," I say, fogging up his window. I take my hand and wipe it away. Sincere is staring at me now. I look at him with pleading eyes. "Please, Sincere..."

Okay, he still wants to ig me. Now it's time for Operation Tear Ducts. Yup, when all else fails, *cry*! Tears always work. Well, *almost* always. 'Cause let me tell you, right now they're not doing one damn thing to help my situation. Sincere just stares at me, then shifts his eyes, looking straight ahead.

Okay, now I have to step it up a notch. I go into Operation Turn It Up. It's when you fall down on your knees, rocking and screaming and crying at the top of your lungs. Trust me. This will definitely get me what I want 'cause Sincere, like most dudes, hates it when you make a scene.

"*Pleeeeeeeeeease*, Sincere...whyyyy won't you talk to me?...I'm sorry...I'm sorry...I'm so so soooorry...I was so wrong for what I did. Pleeeeeease, Sincere..."

He swings open his door, quickly hopping out of his truck. *See, I told you.* "Will you please get up. You're gonna have my neighbors thinking I'm out here beating you up."

I look up at him with snot running down my nose and spit and drool and tears everywhere. "All I"—hiccup—"wanna do"—hiccup—"is talk"—hiccup—"to you. I-I-I'm so sorry..." I cry louder. This time he leans down and helps me up.

"C'mon, Miyah, will you stop with all the noise? Pull yourself together."

I wipe my face with the back of my sleeve. "I know...I...I was wrong...for what I did," I say, trying to catch my breath. Whew, all this crying is a lot of work. But at least it got Sincere out of his truck and willing to talk—okay, okay, listen, since I'm doing all the talking. He's leaning up against his truck with his arms folded and his face twisted up, like he's not buying it.

"I can't keep going through this with you, Kamiyah. All this fighting and arguing. It's crazy."

"I know. I promise you. It won't happen again."

"That's what you said when you slapped me."

I think back to that day in the school parking lot, try to remember if I promised that I wouldn't hit him again. I can't remember. He doesn't give me a chance to say anything.

"What you did was real effed up, Kamiyah, for real. My parents taught me to never put my hands on a female. But I really wanted to take it to your dome for what you did, hitting me then *spitting* in my face. Do you know how nasty that is? To spit in someone's face?"

"But you spit in my face, too," I reason.

"Yeah, *after*," he says, raising his voice, "you spit in mine. That was real foul."

"I'm really sorry."

He stares at me, shaking his head. "You should be. I didn't have a phone for four days, messing around with you. You didn't have to smash my phone up."

"I'm sorry, Sincere. I know I was wrong for that. I'll give you the money for the phone."

"I don't need your money. It was insured. But that's beside the point. You be bugging, Kamiyah, for real. I can't deal with it. Then you got me lying to my parents. Why you key my door up like that?"

"I didn't mean to. I don't know what came over me. When I get angry I don't think."

He frowns. "Then you need to get some help for that. That ain't cool, you acting all crazy."

I start crying again. "Sincere, *please*, let's work this out, okay? Don't give up on us. You have to believe me. My life has been hell without you."

He glances at his watch. "Well, welcome to the club. Now you know how mine's been. Look, I got somewhere to be. You need to move your car."

"No. Where do you have to go that's more important than talking to me?"

"Don't worry about it."

"Who you going to see? One of your Facebook hoes?"

"See. This is why it's not gonna work between us. Why you always thinking I'm going off to meet some other girl?"

I shrug. "I don't know."

"That's the problem. Everything's 'I don't know.' I'm sick of hearing that. You don't trust me. That's it in a nut-shell. I don't wanna be with anybody who can't trust me. Damn. Every dude ain't out here cheating, Miyah. But it's chicks like you who make us wanna."

"So you're seeing someone else now? Is that what you're saying?"

He huffs. "Didn't you hear anything I said? *No.*"

"I love you so much, Sincere. I've never felt like this about anyone. You're all I think about. I don't want to be without you. I don't wanna break up with you."

"Then you shoulda thought about all that before you spit in my face and keyed up my truck. I don't wanna be with anyone who can't control their temper."

"I'll change. I promise. Just give us another chance. I'll do anything you want. *Pleeeeease*, Sincere. Don't do this to us."

"You did this to us. I told you I wasn't going anywhere. And that still wasn't good enough."

"I'm sorry. I was soooo wrong. I can change, Sincere. I will change. Can you please give me another chance?"

He looks at me. I know I'm a pitiful mess. But I'm losing my man. And if begging him back is what I gotta do, then dang it, that's what I'll do.

"I don't know. You got me going through it, girl. You got my moms asking me a buncha questions. You coming up over here ringing my doorbell." He shakes his head. "Miyah, you crazy. For real."

"I'm really not. I just never loved anyone the way I love you."

"If putting your hands on me is what you call love, then I don't want it. I don't know how your parents get down. But mine don't fight like that. They have disagreements and they talk it out. I didn't grow up in violence. Maybe you did."

I only saw...well, I didn't really see it, I heard it... when my mother threw a vase. It was the night my dad moved out. I heard her yelling and screaming at him. Calling him all kinds of names because he told her he was moving out; that they needed space. Then I heard the noise—the shattering of glass. She had snatched one of her favorite crystal vases and thrown it at the door. It scared me. When I ran to see what happened, all I saw were tiny pieces of glass everywhere. It was then that I realized my family was broken.

"I didn't," I say, shaking my head. I am feeling desperate. I am losing him right before my eyes. "My dad has never put his hands on my mom and he's never raised his voice to her."

"Then where'd you get it from?"

"Watching my sister and her boyfriend," I admit. He

asks me if I ever hit any other boyfriends. I tell him no. But it's a lie. I used to fight my other boyfriend, too. But I didn't love him. I love Sincere.

He looks at me in almost this sad, pitiful way. That's not the look I want. I wanna see his love for me in his eyes. "Then you need help," he says. "Now, move your car or I'm gonna call the police."

I am stunned as he hops up into his truck and slams the door. He starts the engine and waits. He keeps his stare on me. I can tell he's angry and hurt. And I have caused this.

I don't want the police called on me. It is bad enough I have to go to court soon for fighting that girl. I don't need any more problems than I already have. I walk over to his truck, place my hand on the window, and mouth the words, "I love you," then walk back to my car, feeling defeated and all alone.

28

Desperate times call for desperate measures! That's what I am thinking as I lie on my side, propped up on my elbow, staring at Sincere as he sleeps. I'm happy to be back in his arms, and now...back in his bed. Soooo, drum roll please...I am officially no longer a virgin. Not that I didn't wanna hold on to my V-card, but I felt like I was losing control over this situation with Sincere and I needed to rein him in. For me to be happy, I need to be with Sincere. And I needed to do whatever I needed to do to hold on to my man, because I felt like he was slipping right through my manicured fingers. So what better way than give him my most prized possession? The one thing I held on to up until three days ago when he called me.

"Why you leave me all those crazy messages on my phone like that?"

No hello. No how are you; nothing. Not that I was complaining. But after how he played me in his driveway last

Saturday, I wasn't expecting to hear from him, especially since he wouldn't take any of my calls or respond to any of my texts after I left his house that day. But he finally called. Three days later. But who's counting? I guess he figured he had made me suffer enough. Anywaaayz, I was real hyped to hear his voice, but I kept it cute, tryna front like I wasn't really pressed.

"What messages?" I asked, playing like I didn't know what he was talking about.

"You know what messages I'm talking about. C'mon, don't play dumb. Those messages about if you catch me with another chick you're gonna beat her up."

"And I meant it, Sincere."

"You be wildin'. You know that, right?"

"Only when it comes to you."

"You can't go around beating up chicks or calling them up and threatening and harassing them. It's not cool."

"What are you talking about? Who have I been harassing?"

"Me, for one," he said.

"Sincere, how am I harassing you? I only wanted to talk to you, to hear your voice."

"Miyah, c'mon, stop. You've been calling me around the clock and leaving all kinds of crazy messages and texts. That's harassment."

"Well, you wouldn't take my calls. How else was I supposed to get your attention?"

"You're crazy as hell. You know that, right?"

"Only for you," I told him.

"Did you call Miranda, disguising your voice? And don't lie."

"No," I told him. I know it was a lie. Whatever! She had

no business calling my man. And I'ma still beat her down for disrespecting me if I ever run into her.

"Well, she wasn't getting those kinds of calls until you and her got into it over the phone. Now all of a sudden she's getting calls from restricted numbers from some chick disguising her voice and threatening her."

"Well, it's not me. Maybe she should leave other people's men alone and she wouldn't have those issues. I'm not thinking about that girl. Are you back messing with her now?"

"Miyah, is that all you care about? Why is it you always gotta go there? No, I'm not messing with her, or anyone else. We're cool, that's it."

"Did you ever mess with her?"

He huffed. "Yeah. For a quick minute. But it didn't work out. And *no*, I don't want her back. Anything else?"

"Do you still love me?" I asked, clutching the phone tight with it pressed to my ear. I was in bed with the covers up over my head. I didn't even realize I was holding my breath until he answered.

He sighed. "Yeah...unfortunately, I still do."

Oooh, that "unfortunately" cut me deep. It felt like Sincere had slashed me with a jagged, rusty blade when he said that. But at least I knew he still loved me. And that's all I cared about. "I miss you, Sincere," I said, closing my eyes. "You're all I have in this world. Can you please give me another chance?"

"I don't know."

Out of nowhere, my mother started banging on the door about me not doing the dishes. Whatever. I ignored her. I'm glad I had the door locked.

"Who's that?"

"The Witch."

"You shouldn't call her that."

"She shouldn't treat me the way she does."

"She's still your mom, Miyah."

"I don't care."

He sighed. "Then what *do* you care about?"

"You. Us," I told him. "I just want things to be the way they used to be between us."

"Me too. But you gotta chill, Miyah. Stop bugging out all the time over nothing. I'm not gonna hurt you. Damn."

"I know."

"You got my head all jacked up."

"I love you so much, Sincere," I whispered into the phone.

"Then you need to show it some other way. I won't put up with you putting your hands on me."

"I promise. I won't do it again."

"I wanna see you," he said.

"I wanna see you, too, Sincere."

"I'm still mad as hell at you for what you did. But I need to see you."

I took a deep breath. "When?"

"Now."

I glanced at the clock on my nightstand. It was almost eleven o'clock, past my curfew, and a school night. But it didn't matter. My man said he wanted to see me, and that's all I cared about. "I'll have to sneak out. Can you come get me?"

"Yeah. I'm on my way."

"Okay. I'll be standing at the corner."

And that night Sincere picked me up, snuck me back into his house, and we made up in the best way I could have ever imagined. At exactly 12:37 A.M., Sincere no longer just had my mind and soul. He now had my body, too.

So here I am, two days later, back in his bed—instead of being at school—still floating on soft, fluffy clouds, remembering how Sincere was making me feel no less than an hour ago. And now all I wanna do is kiss his body, and let him fill my body with his love. I pull back the sheets and take in the view. *Oooh, my baby's body is sick!* I smile. It's really true what they say about guys falling asleep after good sex. I never believed it until now. Sincere lets out a light snore, then rolls over on his side with his back toward me and that's all I need to do what I came to do in the first place. Well, *one* of the things. I slowly ease out of his bed, then tiptoe over to where his phone is. I pick it up. *Damn it!* I need a password.

I remember eavesdropping on another one of Erika's many phone conversations with her girls. *Oh, please. Boys always use the same pass codes for everything. They're real stupid when it comes to stuff like that.* I smile, keying in the same password he has for his Facebook and Yahoo! accounts. *Boom, there it is!* I'm all in.

I glance back over toward the bed to make sure he's still sleeping. I just got my man back, and getting caught going through his phone would be it for me—for us. I quickly upload the tracking program I need. When it finishes loading, I put his phone back exactly the way I found it, then quietly slip back into bed.

Know your man's every move!

29

"Hey, boo-thang," I say into the phone the minute Brittani answers. "What are you doing tonight?"

She sighs. "Nothing. It's a Friday night and I'm stuck up in this house, mad bored."

"Well, fear not, sweetness. Ya girl's got the perfect remedy for that. You wanna go bowling tonight?"

"Ooooh, hell yeah. I was about to lose my mind up in here. What time you wanna go? You know I need to do my hair and get real fly, 'cause you know there's gonna be a buncha cuties up in there."

"I know, right." I glance over at the clock. It's eight thirty. "We should step up in there like around ten. I can't drive my car, so can you ask your dad to drop us off?"

She laughs. "Girl, trust me. He'll be happy to get me outta the house. I have been wearing his nerves down ever since he got home from work. Ten is good. It still gives me time to do my hair and get fly."

I laugh. "Now we'll have to see if Zee can get her brother to pick us up."

"Good luck with that, boo. You know his selfish butt gets real stank when she asks him for rides."

"Yeah, I know. Hold on. Let me call her." I place her on hold, call Zahara, then click back over. Zahara picks up on the fourth ring. "Hey, boo-thang, ask your brother if he can pick us up from the bowling alley tonight. Tell him I'll give him gas money."

"Okay, hold on." She yells for her brother, then asks him if he can pick us up. "Kamiyah's gonna fill your tank up."

I blink. "Hold up...Wait a minute. I didn't say nothing about *filling* his tank up. I said I was gonna give him gas money, like in cab money. You know, like ten dollars."

"Uh, hellooo," she says. "I know what you said. I got this, boo. He said he's gonna pick us up. So when he drops you off at your house, you just hand him the ten dollars and run outta the car before he tries to run you down." She cracks up laughing.

"Ohmygod," Brittani says. "He's gonna be pissed."

"I know," Zahara says. "He shouldn't be so damn stingy all the time."

"Okay, anywaaayz, y'all...let's synchronize our watches. I wanna be stepping up in the bowling alley at ten. One of y'all call Ameerah and tell her to be ready so we can go and turn the place out. We can all meet up over Brittani's at like nine thirty."

"Okay," they say at the same time. We hang up. I run downstairs.

"Daddy, can you drop me off over Brittani's like around nine thirty?" He's in the family room watching the sports channel.

He looks over at me. "Sure. Where are you girls going?" I tell him Brittani's dad is gonna drop us off at the bowling alley. "Okay. Who's bringing you home?"

"Zahara's brother."

"Okay. Just make sure you're home by curfew."

"I will, Daddy." I walk over and give him a kiss on the cheek. I'm so glad my mom isn't here to ruin it for me. I run back upstairs to get ready.

At exactly 10:18 P.M., we step up in Union Lanes looking fly as ever in black low-riders and black long-sleeved shirts with FLY FRIENDS FOREVER written across our chests. The place is packed tight. The music is loud. But we are loving the energy. And the cuties are out real heavy tonight. I scan the place to see if I can spot Sincere, but I don't see him. But I'm not worried about it 'cause the GPS tracking system I loaded on his phone said this is where he is.

"Ohmygod," Zahara says, all hyped. "There are some cuties up in here tonight." She starts dancing to the music, being the attention whore she is. She drops down, then brings it back up, popping her booty. "Heeeey."

I roll my eyes, shaking my head. "Girl, will you c'mon and give the man your shoes so we can get a damn lane."

She stops dancing, taking off her boots and handing them to me. "Here. Did you tell him my size?"

"Yeah," I say, scanning the area.

"Umm, who you looking for?" Ameerah wants to know.

"Girl, no one. There's so many heads up in here I'm just tryna see who's who."

"I know, right," Brittani agrees. "Y'all wanna do a quick walk-through?"

The attendant hands us our shoes. Tells us there's a

lane open all the way down on the other end. *Perfect!* A
Tyga song starts playing.

"C'mon, y'all," Zahara says, popping her fingers to the
beat. "Let's do our walk-through dance and turn heads."

I'm not really beat, but I need to act like I'm here to
have fun, not spy on my man. So I agree. The lineup is as
follows: Zahara is always in the front—'cause she has the
biggest chest. Ameerah's next, followed by Brittani, then
me. And I'm always last 'cause I have the biggest booty.
Left hand goes up first, and we step off on our right foot,
then left, then sway our hips just a taste; not all stank and
nasty—always sexy. Then take a step back. Fingers snap,
then we drop down, bring it back up, then toss the right
hand up and repeat. We dance-step and finger-pop our
way through the crowd until we get to lane two. I'm pissed
'cause I don't see Sincere anywhere. But I keep it fly.

Fifteen minutes into the game, we're all laughing and
bugging out and talking to a buncha different boys—some
waaaay too old to be tryna talk to us—when I see Sincere
looking over here in my direction. I smile to myself, acting
like I don't see him looking over at me. I start laughing it
up real extra now, with one of the guys standing here kicking it with us. But I'm silently rolling my eyes up in my
head at his lameness.

I pull my ringing cell from outta my pocket. It's Sincere.
"Yo, what you doing all up in that dude's face?"

"What you mean?" I yell into the phone. "I'm not up in
no dude's face."

"Miyah, I'm looking right at you."

"Ohmygod, you're *here* at the bowling alley?" I act like
I'm surprised. "Where are you?"

"Yeah. I'm standing over by the video games watching

you. One of my boys spotted you when y'all were doing that little dance step thingy y'all do."

I turn around as if I'm tryna look for him. He throws his hand up. "Oh, wow…I didn't know you were gonna be here. Who you here with?"

"My boys," he says, sounding like he has an attitude.

"You sure you not here with no chicks?" I ask.

"Miyah, don't start that. I told you I'm here with my boys. Now what are you doing here?"

"Chilling with my girls."

"I thought you said you were on punishment."

"I thought so, too," I lie. When I spoke to him earlier today, I told him I was on punishment. Shoot, I had to tell him that so he'd think I was gonna be holed up in the house all weekend, so I could catch him out doing whatever, with whomever. *Always keep your man on his toes!* "My dad had a change of heart."

"Oh, a'ight. That's wassup."

"How long you been here?"

"Kamiyah, will you get off the phone," Zahara yells. "You're up next."

"For about an hour."

"Y'all feel like getting whipped in a game?" I ask, staring at him and grinning. "Me and my girls against you and your boys?"

He laughs. "Y'all don't want it with us, baby."

"No, y'all don't want it with us. Put the phone down and come over here and try us."

"A'ight, bet. Let me round up my boys. We'll be over there in a minute."

"We'll be waiting." I disconnect, smiling.

"What you grinning about?" Brittani asks.

"Y'all are not gonna believe who's here. Sincere and his boys. They wanna play against us."

"Where they at?" Zahara asks, walking off from the convo she was having with some guy. "Shoot, I need me a sexy college man, too."

I see Sincere walking over toward us with three other guys. And they fine, too. "Here they come now," I tell her.

"Oh yes, boo...oh yes," she says, looking over in their direction. "Fine, fine, and double fine. We got this."

I laugh. *We sure do, boo. And I got my man right where I want him to be—with me!*

30

"Oooh, I can't wait for the Halloween party this weekend," Zahara says, all excited and whatnot. They're waiting on me to get my stuff so we can go to homeroom. "Do y'all know who you're going as, yet? I'm going as Nicki Minaj. I already got my pink wig to set it off. And don't none of you try 'n' bite, either."

I shut my locker. "Oh, please. No one's thinking about you *or* Nicki. Do you, boo. I don't know who I'm going as. But I'll whip something up before Saturday night gets here." I pull out my phone to text Sincere.

"Oh no. Not this texting crap again," Brittani snaps, snatching my phone outta my hand.

"Girl, stop playing. Give me my phone back."

"No. Not until we're done talking. It's rude to start texting someone when you're still talking to someone else. I really hate it."

"Well, geesh. Tell me how you really feel. Now give me my phone back."

"I told you no. We're not done talking. Stop sweating him all the time."

I frown. "I'm *not* sweating him. I'm *texting* him. Besides, he's my man." Zahara and Ameerah stare at me. "What? Don't look at me like that."

"Mmmph," Zahara grunts. "I'm keeping my mouth shut 'cause anytime I say anything about Sincere or about how thirsty you be acting, you start getting all defensive and wanna snap my head off. No, thank you. Keep on clucking, boo."

"*Clucking?* Ain't nobody clucking nothing."

"See. There you go with the attitude."

"I don't have an attitude."

"Ohhhkay, riddle us this," Ameerah says, eying me. "How many times this morning have you texted Sincere?"

"I don't know. A few, why?"

"Did you talk to him this morning?" Brittani wants to know.

"Yeah, for a few minutes."

Zahara glances at her watch, then glances over at Ameerah and Brittani. "Real thirsty," they say in unison, laughing.

"I am not."

"Oh yes, you are," they say.

"You don't even let that boy breathe," Zahara states. "I mean. Dang, we know you in love and all, but fall back some. Stop smothering him."

"I'm not thinking about y'all. I'm going to homeroom. Give me my phone back."

Brittani hands me my phone. I walk off.

"Cuckoo, cuckoo, cuckoo," Brittani says. Ameerah and Zahara are laughing. "You're starting to act real nutty over him, Miyah. Not a good look, boo-thang. You better check ya'self." They keep laughing.

"Whatever," I snap over my shoulder. "I'll get up with y'all haters later."

"Kamiyah, you're wanted down in the guidance department," Mr. Langston says, the minute I walk up in homeroom. "Take your things with you."

"Okay," I say, giving him a confused look as I walk over to get a hall pass. He shifts his eyes. Jarrell winks at me as I walk by. I roll my eyes. *I wonder what they want with me down at the guidance office?*

"Miss Nichols, aren't you going the wrong way, young lady?" Mr. Donaldson questions as I make my way down the hall.

Ohmygod, he makes me sick! With his yuck-mouth self. I flash him my pass. "I'm going to the guidance counselor's office." He says something else to me, but I keep stepping without giving him a second thought or glance.

"Kamiyah, have a seat," Mrs. Wilcox says as soon as she sees me walking through the door. She's the secretary for the guidance department. "Your counselor will be with you shortly."

"Okay." I take a seat, pulling out my phone. She eyes me. I slip it back in my bag. "I'm sorry. I forgot."

"You know the rules, Kamiyah. No cell phones during school hours." She shakes her head, mumbling something about kids these days not knowing how to follow rules. *Whatever.* I roll my eyes up in my head, glancing at the time. The first-period bell rings as Mrs. Saunders comes stepping out into the waiting area, fly as usual in a black pencil skirt and pink blouse. Her heels are sick!

"Oooh, I love your shoes," I say.

She smiles. "Thanks. C'mon back."

I stand up and follow her. "What's this meeting about?"

"I'll tell you all about it once we get to my office."

"Oh, okay. You never..." My eyes pop outta my head when we get to her office door. I stop in my tracks. My stomach churns. *Ohmygod, ohmygod, I am soooo dead right now!*

"Oh nooo. Don't stop," the Wicked Witch says. Daddy is sitting next to her and they both look like they're ready to set it off. "Bring your grown butt up in here."

There's an empty chair in between Daddy and her. *Ohmygod! They're gonna tag-team me up in here.* I'm not gonna even front. I'm scared shitless.

Mrs. Saunders takes her seat behind her desk, tells me to close the door. "Your parents and I were discussing your academic performance and attendance for the marking period."

My heart drops. "Oh?" I say, closing the door. My parents eye me. I stay close to the door in case I gotta run out screaming.

"Please sit," Mrs. Saunders says, eyeing the chair between my very pissed parents. My mother tilts her head, waiting.

"No, that's okay. I'll stand."

Daddy frowns at me. "No, you're going to get your butt over here and sit. That's what you're going to do."

I blink, walking over to the chair. I know Daddy won't turn it up too much, but the Witch will. I eye Mrs. Saunders. *How dare she set me up like this! Smiling all up in my face.*

"Kamiyah," she starts, "I called this meeting because I

have some concerns that I felt should be discussed with your parents, and you."

"Well, if you're so concerned, how come you didn't discuss them with me first, before calling them?" I question.

"Kamiyah—Shut. Up," Daddy warns. *Ohmygod, he's never told me to shut up. I am gonna get killed for real now.*

Mrs. Saunders looks at me. "We're only thirty-five days into the school year and your attendance is a major concern. You've never had more than six absences in the three years you've been here. And here we are in the earlier part of your senior year, and you've accumulated more than ten absences. And you've gotten two failing grades so far. That's not like you, Kamiyah. You are one of our most gifted and talented students."

My left leg bounces. My hands are getting sweaty.

"Well, what do you have to say for yourself?" my mother wants to know. I hang my head and shrug my shoulders. "Don't sit there and shrug like you don't know. I want an answer. *Where* the hell have you been during school hours?!"

I glance over at Daddy. "Answer your mother. And answer her now. Where were you and what the hell were you doing?"

"I was with Sincere." It comes out in almost a whisper.

"You were *where*?!" she snaps in my ear.

I repeat myself.

"Doing *what*?"

On cue, I start crying.

"Kamiyah, there's no need to start crying," Mrs. Saunders says, handing me tissues. I stare her down, then stare at her hand. I wipe my eyes on the back of my sleeve.

"Oh, she can sit there and cry all she wants," the Witch says. "But she better start talking before I forget we're out in public and tear her up." She jerks her chair back, turning it to face me. "Now, I wanna know what you were doing with Sincere that you couldn't do after school?"

"Nothing, really. We were hanging out."

Slap! I'm shocked that she's slapped me. Right here in front of my guidance counselor. "Oh, so you wanna hang out while I'm paying for your tuition every month, huh?" *Slap!* "Answer me!"

I grab my face.

"Kayla, stop," Daddy says.

"Oh, I don't think so. We send her here to learn, not cut school and get failing grades."

"Mrs. Nichols, please. I understand you're upset. But please refrain from hitting her."

"Excuse you," the Witch snaps. "I'm missing a day of work to be down here because *she* wants to hang out with her boyfriend. I don't think so. I *will* hit her."

"Kayla," Daddy says. "This is not the place. We'll deal with her when we get home."

She stares me down. "You can kiss any freedom you think you have good-bye. You understand me? And that little boyfriend of yours? You're not seeing him—period."

I am sobbing now. I start yelling at her. "You can't stop me from seeing him! I don't care what you say. I will run away and get pregnant if I have to. But *I am* going to see him. I hate—"

Before I can finish my sentence, she's up outta her seat hitting and punching me. "I am not about to let you throw away everything your father and I have worked hard for. You will get these grades up! And you will graduate with honors and go to college like you've planned! Do you hear me?!" I am balled up in my chair, trying to block her fists. Daddy has to pull her off of me. "I'm sick of you! I'm sick of your disrespect! You will not see him, and that's that! And if you even think about running off and getting pregnant, I will beat it out of you!"

I keep screaming at her. "I don't care what you say! You can beat me all day! I am still going to be with him and there's nothing you can do to stop me!"

"Both of you. Stop it!" Daddy yells. "Stop this right now!"

Security comes bursting through the door. "Is everything all right in here?"

Mrs. Saunders looks over at the evil Witch, then looks at me like she's feeling sorry for me. *Two-faced trick!* I roll my eyes at her.

"Missus Nichols, is everything fine?"

"Yes," the Witch says, pulling herself together, then sitting back in her seat. "Everything's fine."

"Umm, y'all can stand right here at the door," Mrs. Saunders says, glancing back at the two security officers. *Oh, now she wants to be all scared.* "Kamiyah, sweetheart..."

"Don't *sweetheart* me," I snap. "I can't stand you."

Daddy yanks my arm, clenches his teeth. I have never seen him like this. "Stop it."

"I'm sorry you feel that way. I'm very fond of you. Your parents are upset; rightfully so. And it saddens me to have to tell you this, but we're going to have to suspend you."

My eyes almost pop outta my head. "*Suspend* me?"

"*Suspend* her?" my parents say at the same time.

She nods.

Daddy sighs. "For what?"

"For forging your wife's signature on her two failed tests and on her absence notes."

The wicked Witch stands up. Smooths out her skirt and grabs her handbag. I instinctively jerk, thinking she's gonna attack me with it. "I'm done, Missus Saunders. Thanks for your time," she says real calmly. "Erik, you take her home with you because we'll be burying her if you don't."

She walks out. And just like that, my whole world comes crashing down around me.

31

I'm suspended for the rest of the week! NO Sincere! NO Halloween party! NO TV! NO computer! NO car! I have nothing! My whole life is ruined. Daddy has taken the rest of the week off from work to babysit me. I can tell he's hurt and pissed. I feel so bad. All I can do is cry. "I'm sorry, Daddy," I sob. "I just wanted..."

He shuts me down. "All that crying isn't going to change what you've done, Kamiyah. So stop with the tears. You made your choices and now you'll have to deal with the consequences. Do you understand me?"

I nod, wiping my eyes with the backs of my hands. "Yes."

"I'm really disappointed in you."

"I know you are, Daddy." I know all the other times when I was crying it was all an act, but this time my tears are real. And I am hurting. Not because I'm suspended or because I've failed two classes, but because I can't talk to Sincere. My cell phone has been disconnected. And I'm not allowed to use the house phone. I might as well find a bridge and toss myself over it. 'Cause my life is over! They don't understand. Sincere is everything to me. I can't stop crying. I start hyperventilating, clutching my chest.

"Daddy, you have to let me call Sincere, pleeeeeease. I beg you."

He shakes his head. "No, I'll call him for you. Give me his number."

I scream. "Pleeeease, Daddy! Let me talk to him for five seconds, *pleeeease!*" Right now I am a hot mess. And I know it. But I will lose my mind if I can't hear his voice. And I will keep screaming until I do.

"I'll call him for you."

"I wanna call him. Daddy, *pleeeeease!*"

"Look, Kamiyah. I'm not going back and forth with you. I understand you're upset. But this is part of your consequence. Now, I'm nice enough to call him for you. That's it."

"No!" I scream at him. "I don't want you to call him."

I scream at the top of my lungs like a wild animal for almost thirty minutes until I am throwing up. Until my throat burns and my chest aches. I cry until my eyes are practically swollen shut. I keeping screaming and crying until I fall asleep.

It's a little after 10:00 P.M., and I can't believe I have slept for eight hours. My stomach growls and it dawns on me that I haven't eaten anything since this morning. And I will not eat anything *until* I talk to Sincere. I am lying in my bed, staring up at the ceiling, thinking. Trying to figure out how everything got so out of control. Trying to understand how *I* lost control. How I let my life fall apart.

I sit up when I hear yelling. My parents are arguing. I open my door, then tiptoe to the top of the stairs. They are both yelling back and forth. I step back toward Daddy's bedroom, to the cordless phone on his nightstand. The one he keeps resting in its charger.

I hurriedly dial Sincere's number, thankful I know it by heart. *Please pick up.* I am relieved when he does. "Hello?"

"Sincere," I whisper into the phone. "It's me. I'm in big trouble."

"What happened? I've been tryna call you all day."

"My phone is shut off. My parents found out about me cutting school and they've grounded me, forever. I got suspended, too. And they're really pissed."

"Oh, damn. How'd you get suspended?"

I tell him.

"They must be really pissed at me, too."

"She's tryna stop me from seeing you."

"That's effed up."

"I know. I don't know what I'm gonna do not talking to you. I can't even use the Internet."

"How long are you gonna be on punishment?"

"I don't know. I think until the end of the marking period. I have to get all As."

The yelling downstairs is getting louder.

"Did you have to *slap* her, Kayla?" I hear Daddy ask.

I'm never speaking to her again!

"Excuse you? Since when do I have to answer to you about disciplining our daughter? The last time I checked, I am her mother."

"And I'm her father. And I don't appreciate you slapping

and punching up on her like that. She has bruises all on her face."

I try to block out their arguing and focus on Sincere's voice. But I wanna hear what they're saying, too.

"You can do it, baby," he says. "You just gotta stay focused."

"I know. But I'm not gonna be able to focus if I can't see you, or even talk to you. If I have to run away, I will. I'm not gonna let her stop me from seeing you."

"Miyah, baby, don't talk like that. Running away is only gonna make it worse for you, and for us. We'll figure something out, okay?"

I start crying, touching the necklace he gave me for my birthday. "Okay."

"You have to do what they say, Miyah. And stop always fighting with your mom."

"I hate her."

"Don't say that. She's your mom."

"She's a hater."

"She's your mom, Miyah. I don't like when you talk like that about her."

"...I'm sick of you always taking up for that girl, Erik!" I hear her screaming downstairs.

"Unless you've forgotten, *that* girl's our daughter," Daddy yells back.

"I've gotta get out of here before I go crazy. You gotta come get me, Sincere."

"That isn't smart, Miyah. It'll only make things worse."

"Pleeeeease."

"C'mon, Miyah, chill. You're in enough trouble. All that's gonna do is get you in more trouble."

"I don't care."

"Well, I do. I wanna see you, too. But I don't want your parents any more pissed at me than they already are. Do it for me, a'ight?"

I keep crying.

"Stop crying, Miyah. It's not gonna change anything. We'll work it out."

"You promise?"

"I got you, Miyah. I told you I'm not going anywhere."

"You better not cheat on me, either," I warn him, grabbing a tissue and wiping my face.

He sighs. "Don't start that, Miyah. I'm not gonna cheat on you."

"You better not." I hear something smash downstairs. "I gotta go. I'll try to call you again. Pick up when you see this number—it'll be me."

"A'ight."

"I love you."

"I love you, too. Don't do anything stupid, you hear?"

"Yes." He kisses me through the phone. I kiss him back, then hang up, putting the phone back where I found it. I tiptoe out of Daddy's room back over to the edge of the steps. I finish listening.

"...She's gotten away with murder. And I'm sick of it! I should have beaten her behind a long time ago."

"Well, it's a little too late to be putting your hands on her like that."

"Well, *maybe* if you had been more of a disciplinarian, we wouldn't be having all these problems."

"No, maybe if *you* tried cutting her some slack, she wouldn't be so rebellious. The two of you are constantly at each other's necks because you're too rigid. This has to stop."

"Oh, excuse me, Mister Father of the Year! Just because you'd rather bribe her with trinkets and run out and take her on shopping sprees to get her to listen, do *not* try to put all of her mess on me. News flash, Erik: cutting her slack has her skipping school and failing tests to be out with some boy. Cutting her slack has her forging my name to notes and doing God knows what else. So you tell me, how much more slack should I give her before she ends up failing and gets herself pregnant, huh? So don't you dare go there with me! Not tonight. Maybe if *you* started backing me up, *we* wouldn't be having all these problems with her. That child gets away with murder. And you know it."

"Look," he says, raising his voice. Daddy hardly ever goes there. "First it was you and Erika at each other's throats. And every time I turned around, I was playing referee."

"Oh, here we go with this 'referee' mess again! Spare me, Erik!"

"Yeah, exactly, Kayla, here we go again—and now it's you and Kamiyah. I'm sick of it!"

"So what exactly are you trying to say here?"

"I'm telling you that I'm sick of playing referee."

"You're sick of it?" she shouts back at him. "Are you serious? Well, guess what? I'm sick of it, too. And I'm sick of *you*. How about you start playing Kamiyah's father instead of trying to be her damn friend and personal banker all the damn time! And how about you start playing my husband for a change and support me—your wife. How about you do *that* for a change, huh, Erik? Or is that too much to ask?"

"What would you like me to do? Run upstairs, grab a belt, and beat her down with it?"

"That would be better than what you've been doing, which is nothing at all."

"I have never put my hands on our daughters and I am not about to start now. So get over it, Kayla."

"No, you get over it! All *you* ever do is put that child before *me*. And I'm sick of it!"

"Look, you need to leave," Daddy says.

"Oh, so now you're throwing me out? Is that it, Erik?"

"No, I'm trying to prevent this from turning into a bigger mess than what it already is."

"You don't tell me when to get out. I leave when I'm good and damn ready!"

"Not when this house is in my name, you won't. And not when I'm the one paying the bills up in here. Now get out!"

Okay, now I'm getting really nervous. Their arguing has gotten out of control. I hear something else smash. I wanna run down the stairs and tell them to stop, but if I do that, then she'll corner me and start in on me. I don't feel like dealing with that right now.

Daddy says something about not putting up with her mess anymore. She starts yelling and screaming and cursing at him, then I hear something I've never heard before. I cover my mouth with my hand in shock. *Ohmygod! Someone just got slapped!*

32

Daddy drops me off at school thirty minutes before the bell rings. I am sooo happy to be back in school. And outta that house! The last week has been severe torture. I'm not speaking to the Witch. She's not talking to my dad. And Dad's still pissed at both of us. This whole situation is crazy. And I've had to be locked in the house in misery. And you're not gonna believe this, either: Daddy took the door off my bedroom and removed the doorknob from my bathroom door, 'cause I barricaded myself in my room for three whole days and refused to eat or come out or even talk to him until he let me see Sincere. Daddy thought I was playing, but I wasn't. I screamed and yelled and cried. And I was going to starve myself and stay locked in my room if I had to. It took three whole days, but Daddy finally broke down. And as soon as I heard Sincere's voice on the other side of the door, I dragged my dresser away from my door and swung it open, leaping into his arms. I cried so hard. It took Sincere two hours to calm me down.

Anywaaaayz, the Witch has stripped me of all of my fancy gadgets, and all of my handbags. But guess what? I don't care. I still have Sincere and I still have dance. Daddy takes me. And Daddy sits and waits. Ohmygod, how embarrassing is that?! I'm seventeen, for Christ's sake! And he's treating me like I'm a baby.

"You brought this on yourself, young lady," Daddy said when I whined about him sitting there and waiting for me. "Until we can trust you to do what you're supposed to do when we're not around, this is how you'll get treated. Like a baby."

And to add salt to my already gaping wounds, he's been driving me around in *my* car! I can just die! Anywaaaayz, I still don't know who got slapped that night when Daddy and the Witch were arguing, and I don't wanna know. But what I do know is, it really scared me. My parents have had their fights before. And the Witch has thrown and broken things when they've gotten into it. But I have never heard anyone getting hit. I hope I never experience that again. I look over at Daddy. I can't imagine him ever hitting her. I don't even wanna think it!

"I'll be here at three o'clock to pick you up," Daddy says, pulling up in front of the school. In my car! "And don't have me waiting."

"Okay." I climb out of my car, slinging my bag onto my shoulder, and shut the door. Zahara, Ameerah, and Brittani see me and come running out of the school's glass doors. I smile, happy to see my three besties.

"Miiiiiyah!" Ameerah screams, running up to me. "Ohmygod, what happened to you? We've missed you. Ohmygod, ohmygod, we have sooo much catching up to do. Guess who asked Zahara out?" She gives me a hug.

"Oh, shut up," Zahara says, pushing her out of the way, "and get out of the way." She gives me a hug, too. "I heard your mom snapped out in the guidance office and beat you down. Please tell me you didn't get a beatdown in front of Missus Saunders. Did you?"

"Yeah, I did."

"Ohmygod," she continues, "I woulda been too through if my mother came up here and got it crunked like that. I bet you won't be cutting school no more, will you?"

I shake my head. "Oh helllll no. I'm gonna be here every single day."

They laugh at me. And I don't care. I'm just so happy to see them.

"Good," Ameerah says, looping her arm through mine as we walk inside the building. "Now guess who pressed up on Zahara and asked her out?"

Zahara sucks her teeth.

"Who?"

"Stix!" Ameerah and Brittani yell out in the stairwell as we're climbing the stairs to get to our lockers.

"Ohmygod, for real? When?"

"At the Halloween party," Ameerah says. "Ohmygod, you missed it. They were all up on each other."

I eye Zahara. "You and Stix, really?"

She shrugs. "It was the Nicki costume, girl. It turned 'im on. And now I'ma turn 'im out. You know how I do it, boo."

I laugh. Ameerah tells me she went as Beyoncé and Brittani dressed up as Rihanna.

"But she looked more like a straight-up crackhead than a singer," Zahara adds.

I crack up laughing.

"Welcome back, Kamiyah." It's Mrs. Saunders. I roll my eyes at her, turning my head. "Hopefully that won't last long. It's good to see you, too."

Whatever! I ignore her. But, keeping it real, I'm not really that mad at her. I mean, I was. But I know she was only doing her job. Still, she shoulda at least given me a heads-up before she threw me under the bus like that. That was real low-down and dirty how she did me. So she's gotta be put on ice until I feel like apologizing to her.

"Anywaaayz," I say, turning my attention back to my girls. "Somebody let me use their phone real quick."

"Mine doesn't have any more minutes left on it," Brittani says.

Ameerah shakes her head, handing me her BlackBerry. "Poor thing. Who you calling, your boo?"

"Who else," Zahara says.

"Oh, please. I'm in a crisis. Y'all know I'm on shutdown, so I gotta talk to my man however I can." He doesn't pick up. I leave him a message. "Hey. It's me. I was hoping you would answer. Anywaaayz, I'm calling you from Ameerah's phone. Don't call it back. I'll try to call you later. Make sure you pick up. And you better not be somewhere up in some chick's face, either. I love you."

They look at me like I'm crazy. Well, shoot. Maybe I am, just a little. "What?"

"That boy has you strung real bad," Brittani says, laughing.

I shut my locker. "Yup, he sure does. And I have him strung, too. Trust."

"All right, I'll see y'all fourth period," Zahara says, walking off. "I can't be late for homeroom anymore or Mister Jones says he's gonna give me a week in detention."

"Yeah, I gotta go, too," Ameerah says, walking off. She heads in the opposite direction.

Brittani and I keep walking.

"Listen, I need a favor."

"Sure," she says, eyeing me. "What is it?"

I stop in front of my homeroom door, then dig in my handbag, pulling out my wallet to make sure I have enough money on me. I count out five twenties and a fifty-dollar bill from money I took outta my hidden stash in the back of my closet. Daddy has shut down my allowance *and* he took his credit card away from me. Well, I can't blame him. He was real pissed when he went through his bill. Daddy *never* goes through his statements, but he did this time and flipped. I had charged up over six hundred dollars buying Sincere sneakers and stuff. He's not giving me any more money until I pay him back.

"I need you to text Briana and ask her if she can come to the school during lunch and run us over to the mall real quick. Tell her I'll give her gas money."

"The *mall*? Why?"

"I need to get me a cell phone, ASAP."

She laughs. "Okay. I got you. But, um, you might wanna stay on school grounds. I'll go for you."

"Yeah, you're right. Okay, thanks." I give her another hug, then walk into homeroom just as the bell rings, relieved that by the end of the day I'm gonna be able to talk to my man. *Yeah, she really thought she was doing something, shutting my phone down. Ha! The laugh's on her.*

33

It's Thanksgiving morning and I'm not feeling like I have anything to be that thankful for. Well, I do. I have Sincere. But still. I don't have my car or my iPhone or iPad, my Sony flatscreen, DVD player, stereo, or any of my Louis bags. And I don't even have a door for my room! What kinda BS is that?! I have to get dressed in my bathroom, but sleep out in the open. No privacy; nothing.

Then I'm stuck in this house for the next five days, since there's no school today or tomorrow. So what is there to be thankful for? I'm a prisoner. And I'm still not speaking to the Witch for slapping my face up. Okay, okay...maybe I deserved it. But still...she didn't have to do me like that. She did me real dirty. And I'm so over her, right now.

Anywaaayz, dinner's going to be at *her* house, like it is every year. But I'm not going. I'm not eating her food. And I'm not gonna sit around and be forced to be nice to her. I don't wanna look at her.

"And why aren't you going over to Mommy's with the

rest of us? Umm, wait. Where's your door?" It's Erika. I haven't seen her in so long. Not since my birthday. It seems like forever. I get up from off the bed and give her a hug. She hugs me back.

"Ugh, don't even ask. It's part of my punishment. No door; no privacy. The whole prison-camp thing. I'm not going because I don't wanna be anywhere near the warden."

She laughs. "You're a long way from prison camp."

I grunt.

"Anyway, please tell me how you're not gonna be there when I share my big news? I thought you wanted to see the look on Mom's face."

"I did," I say, flopping back on my bed. "But now I'm not beat to even look in her mean, ugly face."

She shakes her head, sitting next to me. "How long are you on punishment?"

"Until I die."

She laughs. "Girl, stop. You created this mess. You do realize that, right?"

I shrug.

"I can't believe little Miss Perfect isn't so perfect anymore. You always did everything right. You were Mommy and Daddy's favorite."

"Ugh. I was never *her* favorite."

"Yes, you were."

"Please."

"Kamiyah, Mommy and Daddy spoiled you rotten because you were the baby. And you were their sweet, precious little angel. And I was their wild child. Now look at you. You've been cutting school, getting arrested, and failing classes. *That* is not the sister I know." I shrug. "Sounds like maybe this Sincere guy you're so into might be a bad influence on you."

I frown. "Are you serious? Sincere is *not* a bad influence on me. He goes to school and does what he's supposed to. He doesn't encourage me or entice me or try to twist my arm to do anything. Heck, he doesn't even suggest it. It's all me. I cut school to spend time with Sincere on the days he doesn't have classes."

"Okay, maybe he doesn't influence you or your decisions directly. But still, your involvement with him seems to be a bad thing."

I start counting backward in my head before I go off on her. Ten…nine…eight…seven…six…five…I take a deep breath. "I love him."

"Sounds like you're obsessed with him."

"I'm *not* obsessed with him."

"Okay, if you say so. But I've been there. And trust me, I know obsession when I see it. You say you love him, but, sweetie, he's become an unhealthy distraction for you. *Love* can sometimes be a distraction. And love sometimes makes us do some crazy things, like throw away all of our dreams. You used to dream of going to Juilliard and becoming a professional dancer. Now all you seem to dream about is being with this Sincere guy. What happened? Did you give up on that for love?"

I look at her. "Nothing happened. I mean, love happened. But I still wanna go to Juilliard, and I still wanna dance. That hasn't changed."

"Yeah, but you have. And not for the good. Have you even submitted your application yet? Daddy says you haven't said anything about it."

"I have one week to get everything in," I tell her. "All I

have to do is the essay portion of the application, then I'm done."

She rubs my hair. "Good. Don't let what might feel like love ruin everything you've worked so hard for."

"It *is* love," I tell her. "Sincere means everything to me."

"Sweetheart, that's the problem. He's become *everything* to you. You know I've been there. You know when I was your age me and my girls used to have a whole bunch of crazy rules that we lived by, and we used to call that kind of love 'crazy love'—becoming *obsessed* with a relationship. Being so consumed and so caught up in everything he does that you can't see anything else. Your whole world becomes about him, and only him. Girl, back then every last one of us was crazy for love. And we did and said some crazy things all in the name of love. Now here you are; just as crazy and obsessed as we were."

I stare at her. Tell her, again, that I'm *not* obsessed with my relationship with Sincere.

She tilts her head, raising her eyebrow.

I roll my eyes. "Okay, okay, maybe a little."

"Girl, there's no such thing as a *little* nothing. Crazy is crazy. No matter how you try to minimize it. If love has you coming out of character, becoming something or someone you never were before, it's crazy. Not love. Well, not a healthy love. It's a crazy love. I've had to learn that the hard way. And I finally know the difference. It took me falling in love with Winston to realize what real love is. It's not fighting some girl over a man, or constantly keeping tabs on him."

Ohmygod, she's gonna beat me in my head with this crap! "Thanks, Oprah," I say sarcastically.

She sucks her teeth, laughing. "Whatever, smart aleck." She stares at me, smiling.

"What?"

"My little sis is growing up. I still remember the day Mom brought you home from the hospital. God, I hated you. But I loved you more. You were this beautiful little baby that everyone wanted to hold and love. And all you did was smile and laugh at everything. Everyone still wants to love you, if you just let 'em."

I roll my eyes. "Besides *you* and Daddy and Sincere, who else?"

"Mom," she says, touching the side of my face.

"Please. That woman hates me."

"No, she loves you; probably more than she loves me. She hates the fact that you're so much like her."

I frown. "I am *nothing* like that woman."

"Yes, you are. And so am I. Why you think we don't get along?"

I suck my teeth. "Please. We don't get along 'cause she's always tryna be in control of somebody else's life."

She laughs. "Oh, and you don't?"

"Nope." She keeps laughing and I have to laugh, too. "Okay, maybe a little. But still."

"Face it, Kamiyah. You're a control freak, just like Mom. And just like me."

I crack up laughing. And it feels good to laugh with my sister. I miss her so much. I sit up and give her a big hug. And tell her how much I love her.

"I love you, too. I'm gonna tell you something I never told anyone—not even Mom or Dad know this." I look in her eyes, give her my undivided attention. "Remember when Leon and I used to have all those nasty fights and I'd be all beat up?" I nod. "Well, the only thing *anyone* ever saw were the bruises and black eyes Leon used to give me. That's *all* I wanted anyone to see. But what they didn't know is that *I* was the one who initiated those fights. *I* was the one slapping him up, and cutting up his stuff, and going through his things. *I* provoked him and pushed him until he couldn't take it anymore and he'd beat me. I'm not saying what he did was right. He should have walked away from me, but he didn't. He couldn't..."

I stare at Erika, shocked!

"And get this. The worse part of it all is this. When he'd beat up on me, that was the only time I felt like he really loved me."

"Now *that's* crazy," I say. "Sincere has *never* put his hands on me."

"That's great. And hopefully he never does. And hopefully *you've* never put your hands on him."

I shift my eyes. She stares at me. OMG, the way she's looking at me makes me feel so ashamed.

"You've hit him?"

I close my eyes and nod.

"Why?"

"Because sometimes he lets chicks disrespect our relationship and I have to check him."

"So you think it's okay to put your hands on him?"

I shrug. "Well, yeah." She frowns. "I mean, no. Well, if he didn't do stupid stuff to piss me off."

"Now, *that's* crazy," she says. "Maybe he's not who you should be with, then."

I frown. "Why you say that? I love him."

"Putting your hands on someone isn't what love is or what it does."

"Have you ever hit Winston?"

She smiles, shaking her head. "No. And I never will. That man downstairs loves me and he allows *me* to love *me*. And that makes it easier for me to allow him to love me. Winston is a good man. I'm not going to do anything to ruin that. I'm going to spend the rest of my life loving every moment of him, and me, and the life we build together."

I smile. She looks and sounds so happy. "I'm happy for you."

"Thanks. Now come on and get your funky butt up and showered and dressed so you can watch me crack Mom's face with my news. You know it won't be the same without you there. Besides, Thanksgiving is about family and the blessings that we have to be thankful for. It's about being thankful that you are surrounded by love, even when you're mad at the ones you love, or when your parents have put you on punishment until you're old and wrinkled."

I laugh. "Whatever." She stands up, pulling me up from the bed. We hug. "Thanks for the talk. It really means a lot."

"That's what big sisters are for. Now, are you coming to dinner with us or not?"

"Yeah, I guess."

She smiles. "Good. Hurry up and get ready. I'll go tell Daddy you're coming with us. He'll be happy. And, believe it or not, so will Mom."

I roll my eyes up in my head. "Okay, give me a sec." I

watch as she walks out, wait a few minutes until I know she's downstairs, then pull my TracFone from out of its hiding place. I call Sincere, smiling when I hear his voice.

"Hey…"

"Sincere, I love you."

"I love you, too."

"I know you do. You're my everything, Sincere."

"And you're mine, Miyah."

"I know I am. That's why I wanted to call you and tell you how sorry I am for hitting you and spitting on you, and for keying up your truck and going through your phone, and anything else I've ever done. I am so, so sorry." I feel myself getting really emotional. I try to stop myself, but the tears fall. "I hope one day you can forgive me for everything that I've ever done."

"I already have," he whispers. "Miyah, you drive me effen crazy, girl, literally. But I'm not going anywhere. As long as you keep your hands to yourself, I'ma always be your man."

I smile. "I promise you, Sincere. You don't ever have to worry about me putting my hands on you, ever again. But don't get too excited."

He laughs. "Uh-oh. What now?"

"Like I said, I promise you I will never hit you or break up anything that belongs to you. But I can't promise you that I won't go off, or get real nutty, if I find out you got another chick all up in your face, 'cause I'll probably still beat the ho down…."

He laughs. "You crazy, Miyah."

"I know I am; only for you, though."

"That's wassup."

"Still…you better not be up in no chicks' faces while

I'm doing this bid. And I don't want you Facebooking it up, poking it up, or tagging it up with none of them hoes either."

He keeps laughing. "I got you, Miyah. Chill."

"You doing this bid with me, or what?"

"Yo, you funny as hell."

"I'm not laughing. I don't know when this punishment thing is gonna be over. I need to know my man's gonna ride it out with me."

"So, I'm ya man," he teases.

"Boy, don't play. You always gonna be my man."

"That's wassup."

"Look, I gotta go," I whisper into the phone. "I think I hear someone coming. I don't want anyone catching me with this phone."

"A'ight, go on before you get yourself in more trouble."

"I love you."

"I love you, too," he says all sweet and sexy. "Hey?"

"Yeah?"

"I miss you like crazy, girl."

"I miss you, too."

He hangs up and I toss my phone back in its hiding place, then race around the room to get ready to spend Thanksgiving with my family. Okay, maybe I do have a whole lot more to be thankful for. Okay, okay...I *do* have a lot to be thankful for. Maybe I'll apologize to my parents today, before Erika drops the bomb on them at the dinner table. Then again, maybe I won't. Anywaaayz, I know I can't pick my parents; that I'm kinda stuck with them. But I can definitely pick and choose how I wanna deal with them. Daddy is always gonna be my favorite 'cause I know I have him wrapped around my finger. OMG!! Speaking of fingers, my fingernails are a hot mess! How in da heck am I gonna leave this house with my nails all raggedy?! Oh no, this is not it! I gotta get these raggedy claws handled before I go anywhere. Anywaaayz, let me go get fly. I need to let all know, and *see*, that the diva is baaaaack, okay?! I'll holla!

34

Three months later

OMG, guess what? I am *finally* off punishment! And I get my car back tomorrow! And I'm living with Daddy full-time. The Wicked—oops, I promised Sincere and my therapist—yes, I'm in counseling—can you believe that ish?! *Me* in counseling, like I'm crazy or something! Mmmph, What. Ever! Anywaaayz, I promised them that I would work on not calling her that anymore. I'll let you know how that works out. Anywaaayz, my mom agreed to not try to force me to live with her if I didn't wanna be there. And I didn't. And I still don't. Ohmygod, it's so much better at Daddy's! I mean, he's stricter than before—well, *his* version of being strict 'cause he still gives in to me, but not as much. I know just how far to push it with him. Still, Daddy lets me make mistakes and doesn't make me feel judged, like the Witch—I mean, my mom—does. And guess what? She and I are talking now. Well, thanks to my therapist, who, okay...I really, really like.

Okay, anywaaayz...get this. She and Daddy are in counseling, too. Can you believe it? Yup, they both realized that they have their own stuff to work on, which is fine by me. Shoot, fix your own stuff before you try to fix mine. Any-waaaayz, I heard—okay, okay, I was eavesdropping. You know how I do. So, I heard Daddy tell my mom how much he has resented her for shutting him out emotionally and how angry he's been at her for being so controlling. And she told him how she resents him for moving out. That she felt abandoned by him. OMG, and then I heard her crying. I have never, *ever* heard—or seen—her cry about anything, not even when my nana died. I almost started crying, too. I felt so bad. And I felt so guilty overhearing—okay, okay, eavesdropping—on all of that. That was simply TMI, for me!

Anywaaaayz, my grades are back on point. That one bad marking period was all it took for me to pull it together. Okay, okay...and that whooping and being put on punishment for like *forever*. Still, that was not cute, okay. Kamiyah Mychele Nichols is a straight-A student, boo-thang! And I ain't gonna be getting Bs, Cs, or Ds on nothing else, ever again.

Hold up, hold up...wait, wait, wait a minute! Guess what else? I got my audition letter for Juilliard. Yeeeeeeeah!!! My audition is next week. You have no idea how excited and nervous I am. Getting into Juilliard will be the greatest dream come true. Oh, besides having Sincere in my life, of course.

Speaking of my boo. He should be pulling up any minute. We're going roller-skating and out to eat. Then later on tonight, he's gonna hang out with his friends and I'm gonna hang out with my FFFF's (my Fly Fine Friends Forever—in case you forgot). Now, hold up...I have no idea where he's going and who he's gonna be with. And guess what? I didn't ask. Nope. I sure didn't. I have to trust him. Well, um, let's say I'm giving him the illusion that I trust him 'cause I still have my night-vision binoculars, and I still have that tracker on his phone. And I will use them if I have to. But so far I haven't had to pull out my binoculars in a minute. And I've only used the tracker system twice. And so far he's been on point.

Still, a girl's gotta keep her eyes on her man. That's why I'm still checking his Facebook and e-mail accounts—not every day like I used to, though. But every so often I do a run-through. I don't care what anyone says, I'ma keep my eyes on him 'cause I know how boys—okay, some boys—do. And I'm not the one! OMG, but wait! I can't believe I actually threatened my parents that I was gonna run away and get pregnant by Sincere if they tried to keep me from him. Now that was *craaazy* for sure! But I know some girls who do dumbness like that. Not me! Mmmph, dumbo.com! Shoot, I'm not tryna have no one's babies. Not even Sincere's. Well, not until he marries me. Okay, here he is now.

I grab my Louis—yes, I got all of my designer bags back—and my coat, then call out to Daddy. "Bye, Daddy. Sincere's here."

"Okay. Have fun."

"I will."

"Um, aren't you forgetting something?"

"Oh, I love you."

"I love you, too. But not that."

I hear her say, "Erik, I don't even know why you bother."

"Oh, bye, Mom. I love you, too." I shut the door before she can say anything. I love messing with her.

I open the passenger-side door of Sincere's truck and hop in. I lean over and give him a kiss on his soft lips. OMG, I love his sweet, dreamy, chocolate kisses. "You love me?" I ask him, buckling my seat belt.

He drives off. "You already know the answer to that."

"Well, I wanna hear it," I say, eyeing him.

He grins. "I love you. And only you."

I sit back in my seat. "Good. And you better not—"

"—have no other chicks up in your face. I know, I know. Yeah, yeah, yeah. You crazy, girl."

"I know I am. But you love me."

He reaches over and grabs my hand. "Yeah, I do."

I laugh. "That makes you crazy, too."

He laughs with me. "Yeah, only for you."

"And for love."

"Yeah, and for that, too."

I rest my head back on the headrest, smiling. I know what Sincere and I have might be what Erika calls a "crazy love." Maybe it is, sort of. But, shoot, I'm seventeen. I have my whole life ahead of me to try to figure out if it is or not. Who knows, with my parents in counseling and me in counseling—not that I think I need it, but *what*ever— maybe we'll get it right. Maybe we won't. Anywaaayz, I don't wanna think about all that. Right now, I'm living in the moment. This very moment, I'm loving my boo. And crazy or not, I am *never* letting him go.

CRAZY LOVE

Amir Abrams

ABOUT THIS GUIDE

The following questions are intended to
enhance your group's reading of
CRAZY LOVE.

Discussion Questions

Wassssup, my peeps, it's ya boy Amir coming at ya with some discussion questions for my joint, *Crazy Love*. Definitely hope you enjoyed the read as much as I enjoyed writing it. A'ight, with that being said, here goes:

1. What did you think of Kamiyah's character? Do you know anyone like her?

2. What did you think of Sincere's character? Do you know anyone like him? Do you think he should have broken up with Kamiyah for all the things she did in their relationship?

3. Are you, or someone you know, in a relationship like Kamiyah and Sincere's?

4. What is one of the craziest things you've ever done for love? Would you do it again?

5. When is it ever okay to hit someone? Do you think it's acceptable for chicks to hit dudes, why or why not?

6. Have you, or someone you know, ever been involved in an abusive relationship, where there's hitting, name-calling, or controlling behavior?

7. Is it ever okay to hack into someone's email, Facebook, or voicemail to check up on them? Have you, or someone you know, done any of these things?

8. Do you think being jealous lets someone know how much you love them?

9. Are you, or have you ever been, jealous in any of your relationships? If so, why? And how did you handle your jealousy?

10. Do you think Kamiyah will truly change her abusive and controlling behaviors?

1

London

Listen up and weep. Let me tell you what sets me apart from the rest of these wannabe-fabulous broads.

I *am* fabulous.

From the beauty mole on the upper-left side of my pouty, seductive lips to my high cheekbones and big, brown sultry eyes, I'm that milk-chocolate dipped beauty with the slim waist, long sculpted legs, and triple-stacked booty that had all the cuties wishing their girl could be me. And somewhere in this world, there was a nation of gorilla-faced hood rats paying the price for all of this gorgeousness. *Boom,* thought you knew! Born in London— hint, hint. Cultured in Paris, and molded in New York, the big city of dreams. And now living here in La-La Land—the capital of fakes, flakes, and multiple plastic surgeries. Oh… and a bunch of smog!

Pampered, honey-waxed, and glowing from the UMO 24-karat gold facial I just had an hour ago, it was only right that I did what a diva does best—be diva-licious, of course. So, I slowly pulled up to the entrance of Hollywood High, exactly three minutes and fifty-four seconds before the bell rang, in my brand-new customized chocolate brown Aston Martin Vantage Roadster with the hot pink interior. I had to have every upgrade possible to make sure I stayed two steps ahead of the rest of these West Coast hoes. By the time I was done, Daddy dropped a check for over a hundred-and-sixty grand. Please, that's how we do it. Write checks first, ask questions later. I had to bring it! Had to serve it! Especially since I heard that Rich—Hollywood High's princess of ghetto fabulousness— would be rolling up in the most expensive car on the planet.

Ghetto bird or not, I really couldn't hate on her. Three reasons: a) her father had the whole music industry on lock with his record label; b) she was West Coast royalty; and c) my daddy, Turner Phillips, Esquire, was her father's attorney. So there you have it. Oh, but don't get it twisted. From litigation to contract negotiations, with law offices in London, Beverly Hills, and New York, Daddy was the power-house go-to-attorney for all the entertainment elite across the globe. So my budding friendship with Rich was not just out of a long history of business dealings between my Daddy and hers, but out of necessity.

Image was everything here. Who you knew and what you owned and where you lived all defined you. So surrounding myself with the Who's Who of Hollywood was the only way to do it, boo. And right now, Rich, Spencer, and Heather—like it or not—were Hollywood's "It Girls." And the minute I stepped through those glass doors, I was about to become the newest member.

Heads turned as I rolled up to valet with the world in the palm of my paraffin-smooth hands, blaring Nicki Minaj's "Moment 4 Life" out of my Bang & Olufsen BeoSound stereo. I needed to make sure that everyone saw my personalized tags: LONDON. Yep, that's me! London Phillips—fine, fly and forever fabulous. Oh, and did I mention… drop dead gorgeous? That's right. My moment to shine happened the day I was born. And the limelight had shone on me ever since. From magazine ads and television commercials to the catwalks of Milan and Rome, I may have been new to Hollywood High, but I was *not* new to the world of glitz and glamour, or the clicking of flash bulbs in my face.

Grab a pad and pen. And take notes. I was taking the fashion world by storm and being groomed by the best in the industry long before any of these Hollywood hoes knew what Dior, Chanel, or Yves St. Laurent stood for: class, style, and sophistication. And none of these bitches could serve me, okay. Not when I had an international supermodel for a mother, who kept me laced in all of the hottest wears (or as they say in France, *haute couture*) from Paris and Milan.

For those who don't know: yes, supermodel Jade Phillips was my mother. With her jet black hair and exotic features, she'd graced the covers of *Vogue*, *Marie Claire*, *L'Officiel*—a high-end fashion magazine in France and seventy other countries across the world—and she was also featured in *TIME*'s fashion magazine section for being one of the most sought out models in the industry. And now she'd made it her life's mission to make sure I follow in her diamond-studded footsteps down the catwalk, no matter what. Hence the reason why I forced myself to drink down that god-awful seaweed smoothie, compliments of yet another one of her ridiculous diet plans to rid me of my dangerous curves so that I'd be runway ready, as she liked to call it.

Translation: a protruding collarbone, flat chest, narrow hips, and a pancake-flat behind—a walking campaign ad for Feed the Hungry. *Ugh!*

I flipped down my visor to check my face and hair to make sure everything was in place, then stepped out of my car, leaving the door open and the engine running for the valet attendant. I handed him my pink canister filled with my mother's green gook. "Here. Toss this mess, then clean out my cup." He gave me a shocked look, clearly not used to being given orders. But he would learn today. "Umm, did I stutter?"

"No, ma'am."

"Good. And I want my car washed and waxed by three."

"Yes, ma'am. Welcome to Hollywood High."

"Whatever." I shook my naturally thick and wavy hair from side to side, pulled my Chanels down over my eyes to block the sparkling sun and the ungodly sight of a group of Chia Pets standing around gawking. Yeah, I knew they saw my work. Two-carat pink diamond studs bling-blinging in my ears. Pink Hermès Birkin bag draped in the crook of my arm, six-inch Louis Vuitton stilettos on my feet, as I stood with poise. Back straight. Hip forward. One foot in front of the other. Always ready for a photo shoot. Lights! Camera! High Fashion! Should I give you my auto-graph now or later? *Click, click!*

2

Rich

The scarlet-red bottoms of my six-inch Louboutins gleamed as the butterfly doors of my hot pink Bugatti inched into the air and I stepped out and into the spot-light of the California sun. The heated rays washed over me as I sashayed down the red carpet and toward the all-glass student entrance. I was minutes shy of the morning bell, of course.

Voilá, grand entrance.

An all-eyes-on-the-princess type of thing. Rewind that. Now replace princess with sixteen-year-old queen.

Yes, I was doin' it. Poppin' it in the press, rockin' it on all the blogs, and my face alone—no matter the head-line—glamorized even the cheapest tabloid.

And yeah, I was an attention whore. And yeah, umm hmm, it was a dirty job. Scandalous. But somebody had to have it on lock.

Amen?

Amen.

Besides, starring in the media was an inherited jewel that came with being international royalty. Daughter of the legendary billionaire, hip-hop artist, and groundbreaking record executive, once known as M.C. Wickedness and now solely known as Richard G. Montgomery Sr., President and C.E.O. of the renowned Grand Records.

Think hotter than Jay-Z.

Signed more talent than Clive Davis.

More platinum records than Lady Gaga or her monsters could ever dream.

Think big, strong, strapping, chocolate, and handsome and you've got my daddy.

And yes, I'm a daddy's girl.

But bigger than that, I'm the exact design and manifestation of my mother's plan to get rich or die trying—hailing from the gutters of Watts, a cramped two-bedroom, concrete ranch, with black bars on the windows and a single palm tree in the front yard—to a sixty-two-thousand-square-foot, fully staffed, and electronically gated sixty-acre piece of 90210 paradise. Needless to say, my mother did the damn thing.

And yeah, once upon a time she was a groupie, but so what? We should all aspire to be upgraded. From dating the local hood rich thugs, to swooning her way into the hottest clubs, becoming a staple backstage at all the concerts, to finally clicking her Cinderella heels into the right place at the right time—my daddy's dressing room—and the rest is married-with-two-kids-and-smiling-all-the-way-to the-bank history.

And sure, there was a prenup, but again, so what? Like my mother, the one and only Logan Montgomery, said, giving birth to my brother and me let my daddy know it was cheaper to keep her.

Cha-ching!

So, with parents like mine my life added up to this: my social status was better and bigger than the porno-tape that made Kim Trick-dashian relevant and hotter than the ex-con Paris Hilton's jail scandal. I was flyer than Beyoncé and wealthier than Blue Ivy. From the moment I was born, I had fans, wannabes, and frenemies secretly praying to God that they'd wake up and be me. Because along with being royalty I was the epitome of beauty: radiant chestnut skin, sparkling marble brown eyes, lashes that extended and curled perfectly at the ends, and a 5'6", brick house thick body that every chick in L.A. would tango with death and sell their last breath to the plastic surgeon to get.

Yeah, it was like that. Trust. My voluptuous milkshake owned the yard.

And it's not that my shit didn't stink, it's just that my daddy had a PR team to ensure the scent faded away quickly.

Believe me, my biggest concern was my Parisian stylist making sure that I murdered the fashion scene.

I refreshed the pink gloss on my full lips and took a quick peek at my reflection in the mirrored entrance door. My blunt Chinese bob lay flush against my sharp jawline and swung with just the right bounce as I confirmed that my glowing eye shadow and blush was Barbie-doll perfect and complemented my catwalk-ready ensemble. Black diamond studded hoops, fitted red skinny leg jeans, a navy short-sleeve blazer with a Burberry crest on the right breast pocket, a blue and white striped camisole, four strands of sixty-inch pearls, and a signature Gucci tote dangled around my wrist.

A wide smile crept upon me.

Crèmedelacrème.com.

I stepped across the glass threshold and teens of all shapes and sizes lined the marble hallways and hung out in front of their mahogany lockers. There were a few new-bies—better known as new-money—who stared at me and were in straight fan mode. I blessed them with a small fan of the fingers and then I continued on my way. I had zero interest in newbies, especially since I knew that by this time next year, most of them would be broke and back in public school throwing up gang signs. Okay!

Soooo, moving right along.

I swayed my hips and worked the catwalk toward my locker, and just as I was about to break into a Naomi Campbell freeze, pose, and turn, for no other reason than being fabulous, the words, "Hi, Rich!" slapped me in the face and almost caused me to stumble.

What the...

I steadied my balance and blinked, not once but four times. It was Spencer, my ex-ex-ex-years ago-ex-bff, like first grade bff—who I only spoke to and continued to claim because she was good for my image and my mother made me do it.

And, yeah, I guess I'll admit I kind of liked her—some-times—like one or two days out of the year, maybe. But every other day this chick worked my nerves. Why? Be-cause she was el stupido, dumb, and loco all rolled up into one.

I lifted my eyes to the ceiling, slowly rolled them back down, and then hit her with a smile. "Hey, girlfriend."

"Hiiiiii." She gave me a tight smile and clenched her teeth.

Gag me.

I hit her with a Miss America wave and double-cheeked air kisses.

I guess that wasn't enough for her, because instead of rolling with the moment, this chick snatched a hug from me and I almost hurled. Ev'ver'ree. Where.

Spencer released me and I stood stunned. She carried on, "It's so great to see you! I just got back from the French Alps in Spain." She paused. Tapped her temple with her manicured index finger. "Or was that San Francisco? But anyway, I couldn't wait to get back to Hollywood High! I can't believe we're back in school already!"

I couldn't speak. I couldn't. And I didn't know what shocked me more: that she put her hands on me, or that she smelled like the perfume aisle at Walgreens.

OMG, my eyes are burning…

"Are you okay, Rich?"

Did she attack me?

I blinked.

Say something…

I blinked again.

Did I die…?

Say. Something.

"Umm, girl, yeah," I said, coming to and pinching myself to confirm that I was still alive. "What are you wearing? You smell—"

"Delish?" She completed my sentence. "It's La-Voom, Heather's mother's new scent. She asked me to try it and being that I'm nice like that, I did." She spun around as if she were modeling new clothes. "You like?" She batted her button eyes.

Hell no. "I think it's fantast!" I cleared my throat. "But do tell, is she still secretly selling her line out of a storage shed? Or did the courts settle that class action lawsuit against her for that terrible skin rash she caused people?"

Spencer hesitated. "Skin rash?"

"Skin to the rash. And I really hope she's seen the error of her…ways.…" My voice drifted. "Oh my…wow." I looked Spencer over, and my eyes blinked rapidly. "Dam'yum!" I said tight-lipped. "Have you been wandering Skid Row and doing homeless boys again—?"

"Homeless boys—?" She placed her hands on her hips.

"Don't act as if you've never been on the creep-creep with a busted boo and his cardboard box."

"How dare you!" Spencer's eyes narrowed.

"What did I do?!" I pointed at the bumpy alien on her neck. "I'm trying to help you and bring that nastiness to your attention. And if you haven't been entertaining busters, then Heather's mother did it to you!"

"Did it to me?" Spencer's eyes bugged and her neck swerved. "I don't go that way! And for your information, I have never wandered Skid Row. I knew exactly where I was going! And I didn't know Joey was homeless. He lied and told me that cardboard box was a science experiment. How dare you bring that up! I'm not some low-level hoochie. So get your zig-zag straight. Because I know you don't want me to talk about your secret visit in a blond wig to an STD clinic. Fire crotch. Queen of the itch, itch."

My chocolate skin turned flaming red, and the South Central in my genes was two seconds from waking up and doing a drive-by sling. I swallowed, drank in two deep

breaths, and reloaded with an exhale. "Listen here, Bub-
bles, do you have Botox leaking from your lips or something? Certainly you already know talking nasty to me is
not an option, because I will take my Gucci-covered wrist
and beat you into a smart moment. I'm sooo not the one!
So I advise you to back up." I pointed my finger into her
face and squinted. "All the way up."

"You better—"

"The only commitment I have to the word better, is that
I *better* stay rich and I *better* stay beautiful, anything other
than that is optional. Now you on the other hand—what
you *better* do is shut your mouth, take your compact out,
and look at the pimple face bearrilla growing on your
neck!"

She gasped.

And I waited for something else nasty to slip from her
lips. I'd had enough. Over. It. Besides, my mother taught
me that talking only went thus far, and when you tired of
the chatter, you were to slant your neck and click-click-
boom your hater with a threat that their dirtiest little secret was an e-mail away from being on tabloid blast. "Now,
Spencer," I batted my lashes and said with a tinge of concern, "I'm hoping your silence means you've discovered
that all of this ying-yang is not the move for you. So, may I
suggest that you shut the hell up? Unless, of course, you
want the world to uncover that freaky blue videotaped secret you and your mother hope like hell the Vatican will
pray away."

All the color left her face and her lips clapped shut.

I smiled and mouthed, "Pow! Now hit the floor with
that."

3

Spencer

I can't stand Rich! That bug-eyed beetle walked around here like she was Queen It when all she really was, was cheap and easy, ready to give it up at the first hello. Trampette should've been her first name, and ManEater her last. I should've pulled out my crystal nail file and slapped her big face with it. Who did she think she was?

I fanned my hand out over the front of my denim mini-dress, shifting the weight of my one-hundred-and-eighteen-pound frame from one six-inch, pink-heeled foot to the other. Unlike Rich, who was one beef patty short of a Whopper, I was dancer-toned and could wear anything and look fabulous in it. But I *chose* not to be over-the-top with it because unlike Rich and everyone else here at Hollywood High, *I* didn't have to impress anyone. I was naturally beautiful and knew it.

And yeah, she was cute and all. And, yeah, she dressed like no other. But Trampette forgot I knew who she was *before* Jenny Craig and *before* she had those bunched-up teeth shaved down and straightened out. I knew her when she was a chunky bucktooth Teletubby running around and losing her breath on the playground. So there was no way Miss Chipmunk wanted to roll down in the gutter with me 'cause I was the Ace of Spades when it came to messy!

I shook my shoulder-length curls out of my face, pulled out my compact, and then smacked my Chanel-glossed lips. I wanted to die but I couldn't let pie-face know that, so I said, "Umm, Rich, how about *you* shut *your* mouth. After all the morning-after pills you've popped in the last two years, I can't believe you'd stand here and wanna piss in my Crunch Berries. Oh, no Miss Plan B, *you* had better seal your own doors shut, *first*, before you start tryna walk through mine. You're the reason they invented Plan B in the first place."

I turned my neck from side to side and blinked my hazel eyes. *Sweet…merciful…kumquats!* Heather's mother's perfume had chewed my neck up. I wanted to scream!

Rich spat, "You wouldn't be trying to get anything crunked would you, Ditsy Doodle? You—"

"OhmyGod," London interrupted our argument. Her heels screeched against the floor as she said, "Here you are!" She air-kissed Rich, then eyed me, slowly.

Oh, no, this hot-buttered beeswax snooty-booty didn't!

London continued, "I've been wandering around this monstrous place all morning…" She paused and twisted her perfectly painted lips. "What's that smell?" London frowned and waved her hand under her nose, and sniffed. "Is that, is that you, Spencer?"

"Umm hmm," Rich said. "She's wearing La-Voom, from the freak-nasty-rash collection. Doesn't it smell delish?"

"No. That mess stinks. It smells like cat piss."

Rich laughed. "Girrrrl, I didn't wanna be the one to say it, since Ms. Thang wears her feelings like a diamond bangle, but since you took it there, *meeeeeeeeow!*"

The two of them cackled like two messy sea hens. Wait, hens aren't in the sea, right? No, of course not. Well, that's what they sounded like. So that's what they were.

"I can't believe you'd say that?!" I spat, snapping my compact shut, stuffing it back into my Louis Vuitton Tribute bag.

"Whaaaaatever," London said, waving me on like I was some second-class trash. "Do you, boo. And while you're at it. You might want to invest in some Valtrex for those nasty bumps around your neck."

I frowned. "*Valtrex?* Are you serious? For what?"

She snapped her fingers in my face. "Uh, helllllllo, Space Cadet. For that nastiness around your neck, what else? It looks like a bad case of herpes, boo."

Rich snickered.

I inhaled. Exhaled.

Batted my lashes.

Looks like I'm going to have to serve her, too.

I swept a curl away from my face and tucked it behind my ear.

Counted to ten in my head. 'Cause in five...four... three...two...one, I was about to set it up—wait, wait, I meant set it off—up in this mother suckey-duckey, okay? I mean. It was one thing for Rich to try it. After all, we've *known* each other since my mother—media giant and billionaire Kitty Ellington, the famed TV producer and host of her internationally popular talk show, *Dish the Dirt—*

along with Rich's dad, insisted we become friends for image's sake. And in the capital of plastics, appearance *was* everything. So I put up with Rich's foolery because I had to.

But, that chicken-foot broad London, who I only met over the summer through Rich, needed a reality check— and *quick*, before I brought the rain down on her. News-flash: I might not have been as braggadocious as the two of them phonies, but I came from just as much money as Rich's daddy and definitely more than London's family would ever have. So she had better back that thang-a-lang up on a grill 'cause I was seconds from frying her goose. "You know what, London, you better watch your panty liner!"

She wrinkled her nose and put a finger up. "Pause."

Did she just put her finger in my face?

"Pump, pump, pump it back," I snapped, shifting my handbag from one hand to the other, putting a hand up on my hip. My gold and diamond bangles clanked. "You don't *pause* me, Miss Snicker-Doodle-Doo. I'm no CD player! And before you start with your snot ball comments get your facts straight, Miss Know It All. I don't own a cat. I'm allergic to them. So why would I wear cat piss? And I don't have herpes. Besides, how would I get it around my neck? It's just a nasty rash from Mrs. Cummings' new per-fume. So that goes to show you how much you know. And they call me confused. Go figure."

"You wait one damn minute, Dumbo," London hissed.

"Dumbo?! I'll have you know I have the highest GPA in this whole entire school." I shot a look over at Rich, who was laughing hysterically. "Unlike some of *you* hyenas who

have to buy your grades, *I'm* not the one walking around here with the IQ of a Popsicle."

Rich raised her neatly arched brow.

London clapped her hands. "Good for you. Now...like I was saying, *Dumbo*, I don't know how you dizzy hoes do it here at Hollywood High, but I will floor you girlfriend, okay. Don't do it to yourself."

I frowned, slammed my locker shut. "Oh...my...God! You've gone too far now, London. That may be how *you* hoes in New York do it. But we don't do that kind of perverted nastiness over here on the West Coast."

She frowned. *"Excuse you?"*

I huffed. "I didn't stutter, Miss Nasty. I *said* you went too damn far telling me not to do it to myself, like I go around playing in my goodie box or something."

Rich and London stared at each other, then burst into laughter.

I stomped off just as the homeroom bell rang. My curls bounced wildly as my stilettos jabbed the marbled floor beneath me. *Welcome to Hollywood High,* trick! *The first chance I get, I'm gonna knock Miss London's playhouse down right from underneath her nose.*

But first, I had more pressing issues to think about. I needed to get an emergency dermatologist appointment to handle this itchy, burning rash. My heels scurried as I made a left into the girls' lounge instead of a right into homeroom. I locked myself into the powder room. I had to get out of here!

OMG, there was a wildfire burning around my neck. *Ooooh, when I get back from the doctor's office, I'm gonna jumpstart Heather's caboose for her mother trying to do me in like this.*

I dialed 9-1-1.

The operator answered on the first ring, "Operator, what's your emergency?"

Immediately, I screamed, "Camille Cummings, the washed-up drunk, has set my neck on fire!"

4

Heather

My eyes were heavy.
Sinking.

And the more I struggled to keep them open, the heavier they felt. I wasn't sure what time it was. I just knew that dull yellow rays had eased their way through the slits of my electronic blinds, so I guessed it was daylight.

Early morning, maybe?

Maybe...?

My head was splitting.

Pounding.

The room was spinning.

I tried to steady myself in bed, but I couldn't get my neck to hold up my head.

I needed to get it together.

I had something to do.

Think, think, think...what was it...

I don't know.

Damn.

I fell back against my pillow and a few small goose feathers floated into the air like dust mites.

I was messed up. Literally.

My mouth was dry. Chalky. And I could taste the stale Belvedere that had chased my way to space. No, no, it wasn't space. It was Heaven. It had chased my way to the side of Heaven that the crushed up street candy, Black Beauty, always took me to. A place where I loved to be...where I didn't need to snort Adderall to feel better, happier, alive. A place where I was always a star and never had to come off the set of my hit show, or step out of the character I played: Wu-Wu Tanner. The pop-lock-and-droppin'-it fun, loving, exciting, animal-print wearing, suburban teenager with a pain in the butt little sister, an old dog, and parents who loved Wu-Wu and her crazy antics.

A place where I was nothing like myself—Heather Cummings. I was better than Heather. I was Wu-Wu. A star. Every day. All day.

I lay back on my king-sized wrought iron bed and giggled at the thought that I was two crushed pills away from returning to Heaven.

I closed my eyes and just as I envisioned Wu-Wu throwing a wild and crazy neighborhood party, "You better get up!" sliced its way through my thoughts. "And I mean right now!"

I didn't have to open my eyes or turn toward the door to know that was Camille, my mother.

The official high blower.

"I don't know if you think you're Madame Butterfly, Raven-Symoné, or Halle Berry!" she announced as she moseyed her way into my room and her matted mink slippers slapped against the wood floor. "But I can tell you this, the cockamamie bull you're trying to pull this morning—"

So it was morning.

She continued, "Will not work. So if you know what's best for you, you'll get up and make your way to school!"

OMG! That's what I have to do! It's the first day of school.

My eyes popped open and immediately landed on my wall clock: 10:30 A.M. It was already third period.

I sat up and Camille stood at the foot of my bed with her daily uniform on: a long and silky white, spaghetti-strap, see-through nightgown, matted mink slippers, and a drink in her hand—judging from the color it was either brandy or Scotch. I looked into her glassy blue eyes. It was Scotch for sure. She shook her glass and the ice rattled. She flipped her honey blond hair over her blotchy red shoulders and peered at me.

I shook my head. God, I hated that we resembled. I had her thin upper lip, the same small mole on my left eyelid, her high cheekbones, her height: 5'6", her shape: busty: 34D, narrow hips and small butt.

Our differences: I looked Latin although I wasn't. I was somewhere in between my white mother and mysterious black father. My skin was Mexican bronze, or more like a white girl baked by the Caribbean sun. My hair was Sicilian thick and full of sandy brown coils. My chocolate eyes were shaped like an ancient Egyptian's. Slanted. Set in al-monds. I didn't really look white and I definitely didn't look black. I just looked...different. Biracial—whatever that was. All I knew is that I hated it.

Which is why, up until the age of ten, every year for my birthday I'd always blow out the candles with a wish that I could either look white like my mother or black like my father.

This in-between thing didn't work for me. I didn't want it. And I especially didn't like looking Spanish when I wasn't Spanish. And the worst was when people asked me what was I? Where did I come from? Or someone would instantly speak Spanish to me! WTF! How about I only spoke English! And what was I? I was an American mutt who just wanted to belong somewhere, anywhere other than the lonely and confused middle.

Damn.

"Heather Suzanne Cummings," Camille spat as she rattled her drink and caused some of it to spill over the rim. "I'm asking you not to try me this morning, because I am in no mood. Therefore, I advise you to get up and make your way to school—"

"What, are you running for PTA president or something?" I snapped as I tossed the covers off of me and stood to the floor. "Or is there a parent-teachers' meeting you're finally going to show up to?"

Camille let out a sarcastic laugh and then she stopped abruptly. "Don't be offensive. Now shut it." She sipped her drink and tapped her foot. Her voice slurred a little. "I don't give a damn about those teachers' meetings or PETA, or PTTA, PTA or whatever it is. I care about my career, a career that you owe me."

"I don't owe you anything!" I walked into my closet and she followed behind me.

"You owe me everything!" she screamed. "I know you don't think you're hot because you have your own show, do you?" She snorted. "Well, let me blow your high, missy—"

You already have…

She carried on. "You being the star of that show is only because of me. It's because of me and my career you were even offered the audition. I'm the star! Not you! Not Wu-Wu! But me, Camille Cummings, Oscar award–winning—"

"Drunk!" I spat. "You're the Oscar award–winning and washed-up drunk! Whose career died three failed rehabs and a million bottles ago—!"

WHAP!!!!

Camille's hand crashed against my right cheek and forced my neck to whip to the left and get stuck there.

She downed the rest of her drink and took a step back. For a moment I thought she was preparing to assume a boxer's position. Instead, she squinted her eyes and pointed at me. "If my career died, it's because I slept with the devil and gave birth to you! You ungrateful little witch. Now," she said through clenched teeth as she lowered her brow, "I suggest you get to school, be seen with that snotty nose clique. And if the paparazzi happens to show up, you better mention my name every chance you get!"

"I'm not—"

"You *will*. And *you will* like it. And *you will* be nice to those girls and act as if you like each and every one of them, and especially that fat, pissy, princess Rich!" She reached into her glass, popped a piece of ice into her mouth, and crunched on it. "The driver will be waiting. So hurry up!" She stormed out of my room and slammed the door behind her.

I stood frozen. I couldn't believe that she'd put her hands on me. I started to run out of the room after her, but quickly changed my mind. She wasn't worth chipping a nail, let alone attacking her and giving her the satisfaction of having me arrested again. The last time I did that it took forever for that story to die down and besides, the creators of my show told me that another arrest would surely get me fired and Wu-Wu Tanner would be no more.

That was not an option.

So, I held my back straight, proceeded to the shower, snorted two crushed Black Beauties, and once I made my way to Heaven and felt like a star, I dressed in a leopard catsuit, hot pink feather belt tied around my waist, chandelier earrings that rested on my shoulders, five-inch leopard wedged heels, and a chinchilla boa tossed loosely around my neck. I walked over to my full-length mirror and posed. "Mirror, mirror on the wall, who's the boom-boom-flyest of 'em all?" I did a Beyoncé booty bounce, swept the floor, and sprang back up.

The mirror didn't respond, but I knew for sure that if it had, it would've said, "You doin' it, Wu-Wu. You boom-bop-bustin'-it fly!"